The Robin's Nest

Whippoorwill Gap PWF Series
Book 1

L. C. MAXIE

SPOON CREEK PRESS

Contents

One

EVERYONE AROUND THE TABLE exclaimed as the perfectly cooked pot roast in a rich brown gravy was served with mashed potatoes and carrots. Jason Adler turned his handsome, wine-flushed face towards Harper Wood. "Every woman needs a man to look after her. Would you like to have dinner sometime?"

"Excuse me." She placed her napkin on the table and stood. Walking past the other four dinner guests, she made her way down the hall to the coat closet, where she picked up her wool coat and black leather handbag. Before heading out the front door, she glanced at herself in the entrance mirror and quickly turned away from her blanched reflection. Her makeup had done nothing to disguise the shadows beneath her puffy eyes. Stepping out into the cool night air, she quietly pulled the door closed behind her.

Back at her house, as she swallowed her migraine medicine, she promised herself: *Never again.* She closed her eyes to block out the luxurious guest suite's black, gold, and tan décor and buried herself under the bed's slick black comforter. Before the medicine carried her off to sleep, she promised herself once again that she was done with manipulation. Especially from men she'd just met.

After dozing fretfully in the tomb-like quiet for a few hours, Harper woke up and checked her phone. It was 5:00 am. Groaning, she rolled over, swallowing to quell her queasy stomach. Last night had been a train wreck, and she knew the reckoning was coming. To distract herself, she reviewed the day before, beginning with her chat with Susan, her housekeeper, at breakfast.

✦⋱✦

"HAVE YOU FINISHED WITH the Grands' Halloween costumes?" Harper asked as she poured a cup of coffee and looked in the fridge. She grabbed a mozzarella stick and a handful of blueberries. Then, reaching into the vitamin cabinet, she pulled out a bag of collagen and spooned some into her coffee.

Susan shook her head. "Surely you can eat more than that." She pulled a slice of toast from the toaster and spread it with butter before placing it in front of Harper. "The costumes are coming along. I'm struggling a little with Jacob's squirrel tail, but I think I've worked out a plan with stiff black wire. I just need to make sure I place it up high enough that he can sit down when he needs to. And I still need to attach the claws to Ava's pink monster costume."

Harper ignored the toast and continued picking at her bowl of fat, juicy blueberries. "Thanks, Susan, but bread has too many carbs. So, tomorrow's the big night, huh? It must be exciting. They're at the perfect age to enjoy Trick or Treating."

Susan wiped her hands on a pristinely white dish towel as she frowned at Harper's thin frame. The two women had been fighting this battle for years, and Harper knew Susan hated to admit defeat. "Yes, they are. Anything special you'd like me to do today?"

"Whatever's on your schedule is fine. I won't be home for dinner tonight because I've been invited to the Mulhennys' for a Halloween-themed dinner. So, you can skip that."

"That's fine, Mrs. Wood—I'm glad you're going out. If you don't mind my saying so, I think you need to go out more often. As for today, the gutter cleaners will be here, so it may be noisy outside. I'll plan to leave around four as usual, but I won't make dinner. I'll have a salad ready for your lunch. Is there anything else?" She stood still in the uniform Tim had insisted she wear for the past however many decades she'd worked for them. It was an outdated pair of straight khaki pants with a white button-up shirt covered with a thin, navy blue knit blazer. Once Tim was gone, Harper had asked her to wear whatever she wished to work, but Susan insisted on keeping to tradition.

Harper's brain crawled sluggishly, which was typical for mornings. But the talk of Halloween reminded her she'd meant to give Susan the afternoon off. "You've got a lot to do at home, getting those costumes ready. Why don't you take off at noon today? That will give you a little extra time."

Susan smiled with relief as she smoothed her graying hair. "Thank you! Yes, that would make everything run a bit smoother. Since the kids moved in with me, I sometimes struggle to get everything done."

Harper flipped up her laptop lid, hoping to fill a little time. Ever since Tim died, she had felt too tired to do much of anything, and she had no desire to go anywhere.

After his funeral, she had considered going back to work, but knew she'd be starting the same routine she had come to loathe at the community college where she'd been teaching over the last few decades. The students didn't seem to want to be in her English and creative writing classes any more than she did. Besides that, trying to please a demanding, implacable administration left her exhausted.

She looked around her cavernous kitchen. Despite the sun shining in the windows over the sleek white cabinets and basalt countertops, the whole scene seemed overlaid with dismal haze.

After briefly checking the dispiriting news, she took a walk around her neighborhood. Even with sunglasses, it was painfully bright in the late October sunshine, with the last of the leaves, still a mixture of green, red, yellow, and orange, clinging stubbornly to the few trees gracing her neighbors' massive yards. Fall had been her favorite season when she was younger, traipsing around the countryside with her Grandma Sophie. But now the bright weather only mocked her.

She wondered again if she should buy an old Victorian cottage in the historic Oakwood neighborhood. That's what she'd wanted to do when she and Tim first moved to Raleigh, North Carolina. Charming bay windows and a broad front porch on a leafy street had been her dream.

Her husband had vetoed her wish, and instead they bought this house in a newly built gated community next to a golf course and country club, where every home was obscenely large for the number of people it sheltered. And now that she was free to move wherever she wanted, she couldn't drum up the enthusiasm to do it. At fifty-seven, she felt her life was already over. What was the point of moving to another part of town? Only her surroundings would change, not her circumstances.

Deep in her reflections, at first she didn't notice the small person hunched under a bush by her front gate. As before, the visitor was dressed in green and brown, with long, silky black hair that fell to its knees. Any visible skin wasn't light, like in illustrations of mythical, human-like creatures in picture books from her childhood. Instead, this one looked more like a Native American. She'd seen the diminutive being twice since Tim died, each time regarding her the same way. It was a curious look, as if to say, "Can you see me?"

The first time it had happened, she'd been driving home after a trip to an attorney's office. It was a spring afternoon, and she had stopped the car and gotten out for a closer look at the diminutive person. A closer inspection revealed nothing there. She decided her eyes were playing tricks on her.

The second sighting had been in August. That time she'd been walking in the early evening. Expecting the image to prove itself a mirage like before, she stopped. But this time the little creature didn't move. Confronted with such an unexpected encounter, Harper had been so unnerved she'd half-jogged, half-walked back to her house as rapidly as she could. Though shaken, she'd since convinced herself it was only her imagination.

She'd been a child the last time she'd seen anything like that. Now in late middle age, the return of these sightings was anything but a welcome addition to her life. This time, instead of approaching the bush, she stayed to the other side of the blacktop before quickly making her way up the curving driveway to the house. She could feel its eyes on her as she passed. Not a good start to the day.

THAT EVENING AT 6:00 pm sharp, she pulled up in front of the Mulhennys' house. Even though they lived only a few miles from Harper in an adjoining, equally exclusive subdivision, she hadn't seen them since Tim's funeral. But when Nora Mulhenny, a community volunteer and socialite, had called with the invitation, she had politely insisted that Harper come.

Harper had never enjoyed the Mulhennys' company—they were friends of convenience. Tim had been the brains, while Bob Mulhenny had been the money behind Surgical Solutions, the lucrative software business for hospitals and surgeons that paid for Harper's discomfitingly comfortable lifestyle.

But her hosts weren't the only reason Harper hadn't wanted to come. She had always loathed dinner parties. When her parents held them long ago, she would beg to spend the night with her Grandma Sophie. The adults had always seemed tight and phony at first, then, after the drinks began to flow, too loud and boisterous. Dinner parties conjured woeful memories. But this time, she had been too weary to find an excuse not to go. At any rate, it was inevitable that she'd see them sometime. Bob had already had his lawyer contact her with an offer to buy out Tim's stocks in the company.

As she pulled her shiny black SUV into their wide driveway, Harper saw only two other cars. One, a gray Mercedes, belonged to the Smiths, which wasn't surprising: they were mutual friends, another couple connected to Bob and Tim's business. She didn't recognize the other, a more modest red Honda. Nora hadn't told her who would be there, but Harper had hoped there would be only a few other people. She'd always disliked crowds.

She flipped down her visor and checked her dusty rose lipstick in the mirror. Harper had forgotten to ask if costumes were expected at the Halloween-themed dinner. To be on the safe side, she wore a black dress, tights, and shoes. She could always say it was her version of a witch's costume. But, she thought uncomfortably, she hadn't visited a salon in so long that they might not take it as a joke. She'd combed her shoulder-length gray-blonde hair into what she hoped would pass for a sleek ponytail tied with a simple black band.

Looking toward the house, Harper saw Nora watching her from the doorway and groaned inwardly. It was too late to leave and send a text that she had a migraine. And by now she was positive she'd have one before the evening ended.

"Harper, it's so good to see you! You look great!" Nora headed down the sidewalk to give her a quick hug and an air kiss. As usual, Nora looked like she'd just completed a day at the spa followed by a makeover for glamour shots. She was wearing a small pumpkin tiara in her auburn hair, but was otherwise dressed in black from head to toe. Harper had no idea how she managed it: you'd never guess from looking at her that she was over sixty.

"Thanks, Nora. It was kind of you to invite me." Harper handed over the bay- and tobacco-scented candle she had purchased at a giftshop on the way as the obligatory gift.

"Oh, heavenly," Nora said with a slight frown as she sniffed the candle.

Nora stored her coat and bag in a walk-in closet near the door and led Harper to the spacious living room. "I think you know everybody, except Jason Adler. Bob will introduce you to him. He's the rector at St. John's Episcopal."

Harper cursed to herself. She should have seen this coming. *Why?* she asked herself yet again. *Why did I agree to come to this?*

On entering the room, Harper was greeted by polite hellos. Obviously they were all on their first drinks. She already knew the Smiths, an attractive couple near her age who had served as frequent companions for her and Tim. They sat around the coffee table with a man she didn't recognize. This must be Jason.

They all stood as Bob greeted her. "Well! Harper! It's so nice to see you. We've been worried about you. Good to see you're getting out again. You know Gary and Kelly."

Harper exchanged polite smiles with the couple. "And this is Jason Adler. He's the rector at St. John's Episcopal. Jason, this is Harper—she was married to my business partner, Tim Wood. We were all heartbroken when Tim passed away from pancreatic cancer in the spring."

"Hello." Jason reached for her hand with well-practiced sympathy. "It's nice to meet you. I was sorry to hear about your husband. I've heard a lot of wonderful things about you, though, from my church community." Jason's hand was warm, and he gave her a confident smile.

Harper nodded, her jaw stiffening. "Nice to meet you." She withdrew her hand and took a seat on the couch as heat erupted across her face and chest. *How dare they?* She thought. *How dare they set me up like this without a word of warning?*

Nora came back in and waved toward a woman in a black and white uniform who was wiping down the bar. "Tonight's signature cocktail is the Bloody Mary, of course. Would you like one of those or something else?"

"A glass of cabernet would be good, thank you." After Nora brought it over, Harper took a sip. It was good wine. She'd have to be careful not to drink it too quickly.

She sat back and glanced around the room, marveling once again at Nora's excellent taste. The decor, which ran to American traditional, didn't come across as stuffy at all. There were cozy alcoves and slanted ceilings; warm wool and cotton upholstery complemented the dark wood furniture. The effect was comfortable. But it wasn't stodgy, as Nora had honored the season with graceful displays of cream-colored pumpkins, dried hydrangea, and fairy lights around the room.

It contrasted starkly with Harper's home of high ceilings with sharp right angles made up of steel, glass, and stone, along with its uniformly dreary color scheme of black, gold, and white. Massive mirrors everywhere made the space seem even emptier. Better Homes and Gardens vs. Luxe, she thought to herself. Still, the effect was similar in that, while the Mulhennys' house was more home-like, it told a visitor no more about its inhabitants than Harper's did. No indications of hobbies or trips invited curiosity, and no family portraits, startling art, or surprising pops of color presented themselves.

The men sat down and picked up their conversation about the business market, while Nora excused herself and disappeared down the hallway. Harper was grateful that Kelly Smith, whose husband Gary worked for Bob at Surgical Solutions, had an open place beside her.

Kelly held out a well-manicured hand, with nails lacquered in black, to squeeze Harper's shoulder. The scent of Black Opium wafted toward her along with it. "It's great to see you again. How are things going? It was heartbreaking, what happened to Tim. He was much too young. We've all missed seeing you around! Is Olivia coping well? Have you gone back to work?"

Harper took a sip of her wine while considering her reply. She wanted to steer clear of personal matters, even with Kelly, the one person here she could possibly claim as a friend. "No, I haven't gone back to work. I can't seem to find the energy."

"I'm sure you miss Tim. We all do. But you can't stay in that big house all by yourself all the time."

Harper had always liked Kelly, but now she felt a surprising surge of irritation. "That's not why I'm not working. I'm not working because I don't know what I want to do. And as for Olivia ..." She shrugged. "It's hard to tell how she's doing when she's up in Toronto. I talk to her once or twice a month, but I haven't seen her since just after the funeral."

Kelly, whose daughter Jenny had been close friends with Olivia since they began kindergarten, showed a flash of surprise, but quickly covered her expression. She looked down to swipe an imaginary crumb from her immaculate burnt-orange sweater. "Well, Olivia has always been independent. Surely she'll be home for the holidays. But I thought you'd go back to work at the community college—why wouldn't you? You seemed to love your job there."

Harper studied the unmanicured nails wrapped around her own wineglass. "While I was home taking care of Tim, I realized that I don't like the job anymore. Maybe I'm just tired of it. I'm sick of grading papers and writing lesson plans. So, no, I don't want to go back to that."

Kelly nodded. "You need to try something different." She smiled. "I could give you a job in my shop if you'd like. No pressure, just part-time. It would get you out of the house and around other people."

Kelly's shop, a boutique called Celia's, was named after her now-deceased corgi. In it, she sold luxury clothing, perfumes, shoes, and accessories. Harper wanted to say I'd rather die, but managed to respond, "Wow. That's really sweet of you Kelly, I'll give it some thought."

"Being around people would do you good ..." Kelly began before Nora appeared in the doorway.

"Let's move into the dining room. Dinner is ready."

Naturally, Harper found herself seated beside Jason Adler at the intimate dining room table that boasted an appropriate centerpiece—a cauldron filled with dry ice that provided enough smoke to make the lit candles and grinning jack-o'-lanterns atmospheric. The dinner was uncomfortable from the start. She smiled uneasily as they made a toast—to her. They marveled at what good care she had given to Tim during his illness. They said she had held up well in its aftermath. And they all thought it was wonderful that she had taken the time to mourn properly. Then they agreed it was time for her to get on with her life. As they talked, Harper felt her head erupt with the arrival of a full-blown migraine.

"Thank you," she murmured when it was mercifully over. She was grateful when the caterers came in with small cauldrons of pumpkin soup. As the wine was poured, the conversation became freer and more jovial. The noise level climbed steadily. While the Mulhennys and the Smiths talked, Jason inevitably turned to her.

As she lay in bed the next morning, she thought wretchedly over the rest of the dinner, which threatened to bring back the just-easing migraine. She knew the pre-dinner glass of wine had been a bad idea, but she hadn't wanted to draw attention to herself by refusing it. The wine caused the headache to compound with every sip. Annoyingly, she hadn't been offered anything without alcohol, not even a glass of water.

And then there was Jason. Recalling his smug, handsome face made her stomach churn. The Polo Intense cologne that accosted her from somewhere behind his black button-up shirt clashed with Kelly's Black Opium, causing Harper's stomach to flip. The combination instantaneously produced the sensation of an icepick piercing her head just above her left eyebrow. He'd been pleasant enough. He hadn't preached at her or invited her to church, which was nice. Yet she couldn't remember what they talked about early on. As he'd later droned on about his weight-lifting routine, she'd politely feigned interest. This was a common role she played: the interested listener. It had been a frequent requirement before Tim died. But in the intervening months of solitude, faking had come to feel unnatural. She felt like a robot running an unwelcome but familiar program.

To be fair, the Mulhennys' choice of Jason for the dinner party had been well thought-out. Tim and Jason were equally attractive, except where Tim was dark, Jason was fair. Of course, that made no difference to Harper. What struck her was how equally matched the two men were in demeanor.

Leaving the dinner party behind in her thoughts, she recalled the night she and Tim became a couple. It was her first weekend back at Wake Forest University for her sophomore year. She had gotten a little wild at a frat party.

After spending her freshman year alone, with no friends, she had discovered during summer vacation that people were right: alcohol really did make social interactions easier. She'd begun hanging out with a crowd, back home in Winterfield, that taught her many things in addition to that fact. She'd returned to Wake Forest confident that she would now make friends and fit in. In one way it had worked: fitting in hadn't been a problem, but making *real* friends still eluded her.

She'd never used a beer bong before that night. After quickly forcing down a few glasses of cold keg beer, she decided to give it a go.

She remembered running outside to throw up on the bushes near the back door. Then, looking up, she saw Tim standing there with a beer in one hand and a concerned expression on his deeply tanned face. "Hey," he said, "I know you. We had math class with Finkle last semester."

Harper's eyes teared up from the embarrassment of getting sick in front of someone ... anyone. She stood up, planning to make her way back to her dorm, but the young man suddenly tilted sideways and she stumbled. "Are you okay? It's Harper, right? My name's Tim." He put his hand on the strap of her sundress. "Don't worry about a thing. I'll take care of you."

He was as good as his word. He took care of her from that point on. But did he love her? She considered the question before leaving her bed. Harper had her doubts. She'd come to believe love was possible for a few lucky people, but not for her.

Sighing heavily, she reached over to her nightstand for an intricate silver compact mirror with gold vines winding around its outer case, a childhood gift from her grandmother. It had come with a handwritten note that said, "Always remember how magical you are."

She opened it, despite the familiar brown and gray mottling on the mirror's surface that had long rendered it unusable. She squeezed it tight. "Grandma," she whispered, "what happened? How did things go so wrong?"

Two

ON A BLEAK, RAINY Sunday afternoon a few weeks later, Harper answered her phone, attempting to sound animated. "Gina! How nice to hear from you!" She had always thought fondly of this former coworker. Since her dinner at the Mulhennys', she had admitted to herself that she was depressed. Maybe a lively chat with lighthearted Gina Merriweather would lift her outlook.

As expected, Nora had called her—concerned, sure, but also angry—the day after the dinner party. "We were all so worried! How could you leave without saying goodbye? It ruined the party." Nora yammered on, giving her whiplash from the turns she took between caring and chastising. She even suggested Harper call Jason to apologize. Harper hadn't argued, but neither had she written down his phone number.

She knew she hadn't handled it well, but Harper was still angry at having been set up like a socially inept teenager. Getting up and walking out may have been rude, she told herself, but it was better than tossing her wine in his face. No, she didn't regret leaving like she did, and she no longer felt obligated to feign a close friendship with the Mulhennys.

She turned her attention to Gina. "It's been a while since we've talked, Harper. Everyone at work misses you. I've been hoping you'd call me. I wondered how you've been, but I didn't want to intrude. I figured you knew you could call me if you wanted to talk."

"I know, Gina. I'm holding up okay." Harper raised her eyes to gaze through the small study's doorway into the living room with its cathedral ceiling, home to a smattering of impersonal furniture. The massive black marble fireplace, as usual, stood cold and empty.

"Hum." Gina hesitated, sounding unconvinced. "Listen, I know this is out of the blue. You probably already have plans for Thanksgiving. But Jim and I planned to go to Whippoorwill Gap—you know, the mountain tourist town out near the Blue Ridge Parkway? We planned a trip out there for the holiday. Last summer, we reserved a room in a B&B downtown and have two tickets to see Johnny Goodfellow and the Plowshares at the Birdsong Theatre."

Harper opted for a safe response. "Sounds like fun."

"Yeah, but then one of Jim's cousins passed away unexpectedly from a heart attack yesterday. I didn't know this cousin well—Tanya was her name. But the two of them were close growing up. Jim's folks are pretty torn up about it. So he feels like he needs to go home to Wrightsville Beach and visit with his family over the holidays.

"I don't need to go with him. It's been a tough semester at the college, and I'd really like to go on the trip. But I'd rather not go alone. I know it's a long shot, but if you're available, I'd love to have you go along as a travel buddy. The whole trip will be on me! What do you say?"

Harper looked at the streaks of rain running down the windows and at the ashy gray sky behind. She had nowhere to go for Thanksgiving. In the years since Grandma Sophie had gone, her remaining grandparents and both her parents had passed away, too. She had given Susan the entire week off to enjoy a relaxed holiday with her own family. Harper wasn't close to any of her remaining cousins, and Olivia wasn't coming home until a few days before Christmas. And while Kelly Smith had invited her over to their house for Thanksgiving dinner, she was leery of accepting another dinner invitation after the disastrous evening at Halloween.

Harper thought of Gina's warm smile and infectious joy. "When are you leaving, Gina?"

"On Wednesday around noon. It's a four-hour drive, so that will put us there around four o'clock, just in time to settle in and freshen up for dinner. Please say yes. I need to vent with someone who knows what it's like at work!"

Harper hesitated for only a few seconds. They'd been comfortable coworkers for over a decade. And Gina was the perfect combination of fun and undemanding. "I don't mind staying here for the holiday. You know how I am—can't get enough alone time! But actually, a trip like that sounds good. And you're not treating me, I insist on paying my share." Harper suspected the income gap between them bothered her more than it did her friend.

"Wonderful! Can you drive over to my house on Wednesday? I'll do the driving from there."

Harper agreed and put down the phone, then sat still for a minute. She'd been futilely trying to concentrate on a new novel when the phone rang, and now found she had no desire to pick the book up again. From where she sat on a couch in her den, the house looked like a dark, cold cavern. It wasn't a home; it was a mausoleum of memories or a stage-set where her life had been frozen in time. And now movement, either forward or backward, seemed impossible.

Harper and Tim had spent most of their married life there. Just before they'd bought this house, and before Olivia was born, Harper had finished her Master of English degree, and Tim had gone into business.

Tim and Bob's idea for a communications and online advertising service for surgeons had sounded farfetched to her, but it had taken off like a turbojet. Even so, buying this massive house had struck her as an insane risk, but Tim's confidence carried the day. And he had been right—about the money, at any rate.

Harper climbed the stairs to the guest bedroom suite she had lived in since Olivia was a toddler. She'd been recuperating in the hospital after giving birth to Olivia when she'd discovered Tim's affair. It had been such a shock. When a dozen roses were delivered to her at the hospital, she'd been touched and pleased. But those feelings evaporated when she read the card written in Tim's careful script.

Melissa—

Our time in Cancun was amazing. I can't wait to see you again.

—Tim

Evidently the florist had mixed up the delivery addresses. Harper felt gutted. *Who was Melissa?* She and Tim had never had a passionate relationship, but it never occurred to her that he was unhappy, much less that he was seeing someone else. *How could he do this while we were expecting our first child?*

Back at home, when Harper confronted him with the note, he claimed that Melissa was merely a secretary who went on a business trip with him. He'd been trying to cheer her up, poor thing—she was going through a tough time. Harper had gaped at him in disbelief, a cold, quiet rage building inside that she would never get over.

"When did you have time to go to Cancun? The only trip you've told me about lately was a business trip to Chicago, and you told me it was miserable."

Tim had hung his head. "I'm sorry, Harper. I've just been so overwhelmed at work, and you've been so preoccupied with having this baby ... Look, I made a mistake. It will never happen again."

Harper had picked up the vase of wilting flowers and thrown it at his feet, where the vase shattered on the kitchen's stone floor. Then she withdrew to Olivia, who had slept peacefully through the whole confrontation in her second floor nursery.

She moved in with Olivia and had her clothes and other belongings relocated to one of the guest suites. Perhaps she should have left him, but she ultimately decided she and Olivia would be better off staying. How could she take care of a newborn baby on her own? She had no family to help. Even if he paid alimony and child support, she'd probably need to get a job. She had done nothing wrong. And he'd sworn it would never happen again. She didn't believe him, but it gave her some dignity. Yet from that time on, even though they were married and had a child, she'd felt like a kept woman. In some ways, she was ashamed of her cowardice.

From her perspective, their marriage had been an empty shell. Why else would he have done something like this? Later, she viewed their whole setup as a business arrangement. He took care of her and their daughter financially. And she served as a hostess and domestic manager for him. This was why she'd never tried to make the house suit her own preferences. It was Tim's house, after all, not hers.

She'd fulfilled her role perfectly, she thought now—she kept her weight under control and dyed her hair the pale honey color he liked best until he passed away. She'd attended the events he needed her to. She was faultlessly polite to him and all his associates, and she let him make most of the decisions about Olivia. In many ways, it had been a very easy, if emotionally empty life.

Harper often wondered how things would have turned out had she left. There was no way to know. She'd made her decision to stay with him and had made the best of it, telling herself it was better for Olivia. She never examined that assumption too closely.

When Tim contracted cancer, Harper began to rethink their life together. She knew in her heart that, while her husband had messed up in a big way, perhaps she could have been more forgiving. She didn't have the heart to leave his care entirely to paid nurses. So Harper took charge and made sure he was as comfortable as possible in the master bedroom suite. And Tim was grateful. Their relationship had ended as friends. She was glad for that.

Looking around, she realized her husband had never really inhabited this house either. It was a backdrop, not a home. It was tasteful, elegant, luxurious, and completely lacking in heart.

At the top of the stairs, she caught her reflection in one of the house's infinite mirrors and stopped. *That's what I've become: tasteful, elegant, and completely lacking in heart.* Well, at least she *had* been elegant. The Harper looking back at her now appeared gaunt, unkempt, and colorless.

This wouldn't do. She needed to get herself polished up for this trip, at least the parts that showed. She couldn't have Gina asking embarrassing questions. The last thing she wanted was pity. Tomorrow, she would call her salon to get her hair done. Gray was streaking the natural blonde hair that she had refused to dye since the funeral, and while she didn't mind the gray, the style needed to be trimmed and shaped. She'd see if they could work her in for a facial, too. And maybe she'd buy some new makeup. The dry, dull feelings she'd lived with for years were evident in her face.

She pulled her suitcase from the closet, laid it open on the bed, and sat down. Suddenly, she was hit by a sadness so profound her chest felt in danger of collapsing to its smoky core.

Friends and acquaintances seemed to agree that she and Tim had the perfect marriage. And if looked at from the outside, that made sense. But now Harper, with a dart of pain piercing her heart, confronted the fact that she'd never given Tim a chance to make up for his mistake, though she knew he'd tried. And now it was too late.

In some ways, Harper had been proud of Tim. He had worked hard. He was a good father to Olivia. He'd never put pressure on Harper to work, though goodness knows they didn't need extra income. But when Olivia started kindergarten, Harper had wanted to start her own career. She wanted an accomplishment that was hers alone, something to distract her from her mind-numbing homelife. So she accepted a full-time job as an English and creative writing instructor at the nearby community college. It seemed the perfect way to show off her skills and gain a bit of independence.

But between the job, keeping up with Olivia, and managing the house, she had been so busy that she hadn't realized how little she saw of Tim until Olivia left home. She thought of her parents' cold, lonely house in Winterfield, the year before her dad left her and her mother. Now it seemed her adult life with her own family had continued the tradition. This house was grander, but the relationships were just as distant. She agreed to marry Tim because he'd made her feel safe. Had it been worth it? It didn't really matter. It was too late to start over now.

Harper went to the closet and began to pull out perfectly tailored pants, sweaters, and jackets for the trip. As she examined each piece of clothing, she was confronted with the fact that she didn't even like her clothes. Now that Tim was gone and she no longer needed to impress his associates, it seemed everything she owned belonged to a well-polished mirage, not to her. *That's one thing I can work on*, she thought. *When I get back from this trip,*

I'm getting rid of these clothes and buying clothes I like ... clothes that make me happy.

+ˊ+

ON WEDNESDAY, HARPER ENJOYED the ride to Whippoorwill Gap in Gina's bright green compact SUV. The weather was cold and cloudy, but Gina cranked up a New Wave playlist that transported Harper back to happier times. And she found herself enjoying Gina's stories about their former coworkers. The same people that had annoyed Harper were still annoying Gina. But coming from her good-humored friend, it all sounded like an amusing sitcom instead of a tragedy.

As they left the Piedmont behind and began climbing the foothills to the Blue Ridge, Gina paused from talking, grinned mischievously, and glanced over at her friend. "Doesn't all this excitement and drama make you want to come back to work?"

Harper smiled and shook her head. No, it didn't, but it made her happy all the same.

That night, after a delicious dinner at an elegant winery on Main Street, of grilled pork chops with mashed potatoes and shiraz for Gina and mushroom risotto and chardonnay for Harper, they settled in for the evening at the Will O' the Wisp, the cozy little B&B Gina and Jim had chosen to stay in. Over a cup of decaf coffee in the B&B's lounge, Harper said, "I love this place, Gina. It's so cozy and cheerful! I wish I lived someplace like this instead of that warehouse I call home."

Gina gazed at the crackling fire in the room's fireplace. "You can't mean that. Your house is so nice. I'd give anything to have a full-time housekeeper."

"I agree. It's a nice house. And it's perfect—for someone else, not for me. I've never liked large spaces. My idea of the perfect home is small and sweet, a place where I'd feel cocooned and safe. The house I've got is so big it feels spooky. I've never liked it." She looked around. "But this place fits me exactly."

Gina pursed her lips. "I see what you mean. Now that you mention it, this place does suit you. It's quiet and, well, understated—like you. Have you ever been to Whippoorwill Gap before, Harper?"

Harper sighed. "Yes, a few times. My grandma died near here. We had to come out here a few times after that."

Gina choked on her chocolate chip cookie. She fixed her large, brown, sympathy-filled eyes on Harper. "I had no idea. I'm so sorry to hear about that, Harper! Do you feel like talking about it?"

Harper stirred her coffee and looked at the table. "No one knew she was planning a trip. My parents and I had gone to Myrtle Beach for a week in July, like we always did for my birthday. It was strange because Grandma had mailed an extra birthday present to me there. She had already sent a birthday present with us when we left. She'd never mailed me a second present like that before. Here"—she dug into her jacket pocket and pulled out her compact mirror—"this is what she mailed to me."

Gina studied it. "I've noticed that before. You used to pull it out whenever you were upset about something."

"I still do." Harper turned it over in her hand before moving on. "While we were at the beach, we got a phone call from one of Grandma's neighbors. Her car had plunged off one of the cliffs near here. They found the car, but they never found her body. She was my favorite person in the world. I guess I've never really gotten over it."

"Oh, Harper! That sounds horrible! I'm surprised you agreed to come here with me. Do you have any idea why she came here?"

"No, that was another puzzle. She never mentioned coming to Whippoorwill Gap. The last time we heard from her was in the note she attached to this mirror. The reason I carry it with me everywhere is because her note said I should always keep the mirror with me to remind me of how magical I am." She grimaced. "Magical ... I loved Grandma, but that always seemed ironic to me. And, as you can see, the mirror is completely useless now."

Gina leaned over and looked into the mirror, then frowned. "Well, it's tarnished, but you could have it refinished or replace the glass."

Harper glanced inside, then pulled it closer to her face. The upper right quarter of the mirror was no longer tarnished. "That's strange. For years, the surface has been completely covered. Now a chunk of it looks okay, only misted over. Maybe I'm losing it."

Gina finished her coffee. "You've just been through a rough time. Let's call it a night. Tomorrow is Thanksgiving and they're having dinner for us here in the dining room. What do you want to do until then?"

Harper opened the slick magazine lying on a side table filled with "Things to Do Around Whippoorwill Gap." There were suggestions for everything, from thrill rides and hang gliding to antique store shopping. "Could we ride around the area? I'd like to see where Grandma Sophie went off the road. I haven't been there since I was a kid."

"Sure, Harper, if you don't think it will make you too sad, we could do that. I'll bet the scenery around this town is stunning. Maybe we could ride to the top of Old Man Mountain while we're out." Harper agreed that would be fun; she'd never been to the top of the famed mountain, and she'd like to see it.

By the next day, the skies had cleared up. It was a sunny forty-five degrees when they left the town behind. But when they drove out to find the spot where her grandma's car had left the road, Harper was disappointed to discover the highway had completely changed. The site of the accident was only a little over a mile outside of town, but the entire area had been filled in and flattened to make way for more traffic. The section of rural road with the horrifying gap in the guardrail that Harper had been traumatized by as a child was obliterated.

That night, for Thanksgiving dinner, Harper and Gina dined with the other guests in the Will O' the Wisp's dining room. The owners, Terry and Shelly, had made a traditional Thanksgiving dinner with turkey, homemade stuffing with cranberries and chestnuts, glazed Brussels sprouts, mashed potatoes, and pumpkin pie with homemade whipped cream. They even had Tofurky for the vegetarians. They washed it all down with local wine. The eclectic group of guests, happy to be on holiday, kept the conversation flowing effortlessly while they enjoyed the tasty dishes.

After the dinner, Harper found herself feeling relaxed for the first time in years. That night, she dreamed she was flying through the sky in the company of a great horned owl. It was so vivid; she woke up exhilarated the next morning.

Each year, on the Friday after Thanksgiving, Whippoorwill Gap held its annual Christmas Parade which was scheduled to begin at two in the afternoon. Harper and Gina decided to skip the parade for a morning of hiking and a leisurely afternoon of naps and reading. After getting dressed, they grabbed breakfast in the dining room, then hiked the six-mile paved trail hugging the Ayotte River, which wound in and around the city. The route was known for its natural beauty, and for the shops and watering holes interspersed along the way. They began and ended on the trail's entrance in Puckett's Park, which was tucked into a corner of downtown, across the street from the Birdsong Theater's parking lot.

When they arrived at the park to begin their trek around 9:00 am, they were startled by a loud hooting down by the trailhead. Looking up, they saw a magnificent great horned owl in a tree near the river. It looked to be at least two feet in length, with fierce round eyes and enormous claws. Harper was disconcerted. After her dream the night before, this seemed too coincidental for comfort.

Gina tilted her head back in amazement. "Would you look at that? I didn't know owls come out during the day."

Harper looked at it nervously. It looked her straight in the eye as it ruffled its feathers. "They don't attack people, do they?"

Gina laughed. "I've never heard of that happening, but I guess there's a first time for everything." She stepped on the trail. "Let's just keep moving and hope for the best."

Their hike was gorgeous. The river was wide but shallow, and rolled over and around large rocks with a satisfying series of gurgles and roars. With the leaves gone from the trees, they had an excellent view of the water and its occasional falls. They made steady progress, but even without stopping at any shops, the hike took three hours. By the time they made it back to the park, both were hungry.

As they approached the trailhead, they were surprised to find the owl still sitting in the tree. They bid it a friendly, if tired, hello, then headed to Divine Coffee, the first shop on the street, for lunch. Since the afternoon parade was set to start in a couple of hours, the shop was busy. They ordered their lunch at the counter and took their cups of steaming chai to the only vacant table in the spacious shop.

Gina looked thoughtful. "I wonder if seeing an owl is an omen. We'll have to look that up."

Intrigued by the thought, Harper said, "Look up robins, too. Have you ever seen so many? I thought they had all flown south by this time of year."

"They don't migrate south, but they do change their behavior, so people don't see them as often in the fall and winter." Gina held her phone out so she could read about it.

Harper glanced at the screen and handed it back. "That explains why I've never noticed one this time of year before. But it doesn't explain why they're out today."

After they had rested their feet and finished their lunches of vegetable beef soup for Gina and corn chowder for Harper, with both enjoying pumpkin bread for dessert, the women decided they had enough energy to explore some of the town's shops before the parade.

As they left Divine Coffee and headed up the hill towards Main Street, the first storefront they passed was a forlorn shop with dark windows and a rusted metal sign above the door reading, "The Robin's Nest." A "For Sale" sign was posted on the door. Harper placed her hands around her face and peered inside.

Gina pointed at the robins still gathered around. "Well, the name's appropriate."

Harper inspected what she could of the shop's interior. It revealed a dark, abandoned space. But something about it caught her fancy. Inside she could make out shelves and stacks of what looked like old books. If someone wanted to sell it, she wondered, why hadn't they cleaned it out? She could sense that Gina was eager to move on, but Harper was mesmerized.

What sorts of books were they? Why were they still in the shop? She moved to different spots along the windows, straining to see inside. She could make out the doorway to an old staircase going to an upper floor. Something about this shop brought up feelings of ... what? Nostalgia? She thought back to the Saturdays she used to spend in libraries and bookstores with Grandma Sophie. She found herself pining to explore the inside.

Gina cleared her throat and Harper turned to the street. "I'm sorry, Gina. You know how I am about books. I'm just wondering why they're still in there and how much they want for the place."

Gina snorted. "Way too much, would be my guess."

Harper nodded. But there was something about this shop. She had an eerie feeling it needed her attention. Without thinking, she pulled her grandma's mirror from her pocket and glanced at it. She shook her head in wonder when she saw that an even greater portion of the surface was clearing of tarnish. After replacing the mirror and pulling out her phone, she took a picture of the realty sign. In the distance, she heard the owl hooting from the park.

Gina looked up from her phone. "There's an open bookstore up on Main Street—Whippoorwill Gap Books. Let's head up there."

Harper pocketed her phone and joined her friend. "That sounds good, Gina. But could we stop in some of these other stores? I'd like to look at the clothes."

Gina eyed her friend's expensive, impeccable hiking ensemble and bobbed her head. "Sounds good to me."

Harper's cheeks turned pink. "I know it sounds silly, but I hate my clothes. I'm in the market for a new look."

"Doesn't sound a bit silly to me. Everyone deserves to be comfortable, and what you wear matters."

They stopped in a couple of shops before arriving at Whippoorwill Gap books. Gina looked at souvenirs and bought a pouch of pipe tobacco for Jim. Harper bought herself a burgundy peasant blouse embroidered with tan and light blue flowers. In the same shop, she picked up a pair of low-heeled gray suede boots. She thought it would be perfect to wear to tomorrow night's concert featuring Johnny Goodfellow and the Plowshares, the up-and-coming Americana band.

The bookstore on Main Street was bustling with people waiting out of the cold for the parade to start. Everything here was new, yet like the rest of the town, it gave off a hip but cozy vibe. Both women bought novels to take back to the Will O' the Wisp to read that afternoon. Gina picked up a paranormal romance while Harper settled on a psychological thriller. The man with the curly black-hair and startling blue eyes who checked them out welcomed them to Whippoorwill Gap before complimenting their choice of reading material.

Harper asked him if he knew anything about the abandoned bookshop downtown. He looked at her intently.

"Yes. It belonged to a friend of mine, Frank Bailies. He passed away while working in the shop one day last fall. We were all sad to see him go. His shop's been empty for almost a year now. It was in rough shape before he passed away. I can't imagine why anyone would want to open it again. Why? Do you know someone who's interested?"

"No," Harper said, looking down at her book. "I just wondered."

As they left the shop, Gina said, "Maybe you should've asked Mr. Hunky back there for a date. He seemed friendly enough with you."

"Please, Gina. He's not my type. I'm surprised you'd even notice with Jazzy Jim to go home to."

"Jazzy Jim?! I'll have to tell him you called him that!" Gina laughed. "Being married doesn't mean my eyes don't work!"

Despite Gina's comments about his friendliness, Harper had instantly disliked the man in the bookstore. Nevertheless, she felt compelled to find out about the closed shop before she left town. Tomorrow was Saturday and they planned to explore antique shops before heading to the concert. Then they would be leaving for Raleigh early on Sunday morning. So she decided to call the realtor today. She waited until Gina became engrossed in her story of shape-shifting wolves to go outside with her phone. It was answered after one ring.

"Migration Realty."

"Hello. My name is Harper Wood. I'm here in town from Raleigh. I'd like to speak to someone about the property you have listed at 1230 Oak Street ... That's right, the shop that has a sign that says 'The Robin's Nest.'"

Three

"You'll get your keys when we get word that your loan has gone through."

Harper tapped the bank's app on her phone. "I'm paying cash."

"Oh." The peppy, efficient, and—Harper guessed—thirty-something real estate agent looked momentarily knocked off balance. Harper had arrived in town the night before. While spending the night at the Will O' the Wisp, she had mulled over the purchase. If she moved, Gina was the only thing she would miss from Raleigh, but they weren't best friends; they were occasional buddies. And Gina could always come to visit.

Hoping to glean more information, she discussed the neglected little shop with one of the Will O' the Wisp's owners. Shelly said the property had fallen on hard times, for sure, but Frank was elderly when he passed away. It had been hard for him to keep up with changing business trends. But she said that area of town had increased its foot traffic since the revitalization, starting with the Birdsong Theatre opening, around nine years ago. In her opinion, it wouldn't be a bad investment.

"And it would be good to give Bryan Greene a little competition," Susan said with an impish grin. Harper remembered her instant antipathy for Bryan Greene and decided her instincts had been on target.

Caution was one of Harper's defining traits. But when she remembered how optimistic she'd felt when peeking into the shop's windows, she decided it was time to take some risks. She couldn't really remember the last time she'd felt that way. And with the money Tim had left her, she could afford to make a few mistakes.

Within minutes of entering the store with the chirpy, well-dressed realtor, Monica Tolbert, Harper had made up her mind. The first thing she noticed was that the store, despite being closed for over a year, carried the refreshing scent of river water and pine trees. The aroma reminded her of her grandmother and their hikes in the summer. She took that as a positive sign. But there was also something undefinable in the shop's atmosphere that made Harper feel secure and peaceful. While she couldn't nail down the reason, she had an uncanny feeling that she belonged here. It made no sense, but there it was. Her hand reflexively reached into her pocket and closed around her mirror. "I'll take it."

Monica blinked and brushed the elegant silver reindeer pin on her lapel. "Do you want to make an offer first?"

Harper fixed her round eyes coolly on the agent. "No. I think what they're asking is reasonable."

Harper never haggled over money. She'd seen her parents do it in their real estate dealings, and she knew it was expected. But she'd made up her mind: she wanted to leave Raleigh. And now that she'd found something promising, she wanted to waste no time waiting on counteroffers.

After locking the shop's door behind them, the two women made their way up the street to Migration Realty, where Harper signed the paperwork. Her bank wired the money immediately. Within two hours, she had the keys in her hand. Tired but happy, she spent one last night at the Will O' the Wisp, where the hosts gave her and all the guests a free glass of champagne to celebrate. The next morning she left for Raleigh, eager to put her monstrous house on the market.

Her housekeeper Susan reacted to the news with dismay until she found herself presented with a severance package worth two-and-half years of salary, plus health insurance—enough to take care of her until she retired. As part of their agreement, Susan would continue to take care of the property until it was sold.

The easy part over, Harper debated how to tell Olivia. Her daughter could be temperamental, and Harper wasn't sure how she might react. And even though she knew Olivia probably wanted to spend a fair amount of her upcoming holiday visit with friends, she hoped to convince her to take a short trip to Whippoorwill Gap to see the shop.

Olivia favored her mother in appearance. She had Harper's blonde hair but had inherited Tim's blue eyes instead of her mother's hazel ones. At five foot, nine inches, she looked down her mother's five foot, six. Friends had often suggested that she should try her hand at modeling, but Olivia wasn't interested. Her daughter's personality and drive reminded Harper of Tim and her own parents. Olivia earned good grades, was a good athlete, and enjoyed being around people; she had always been popular with her classmates. She picked her close friends carefully and usually well. But while she clearly adored her father, she had always been impatient with her mother.

Harper first suspected she embarrassed Olivia when Olivia entered kindergarten. She never asked Harper to come eat with her for lunch. Her playmate Jennifer Smith had always begged Kelly to come. Naturally, as Olivia got older, she became increasingly mortified by her mother.

"Couldn't you at least have *tried* to get a job teaching at Duke or Chapel Hill?" she had asked her mom as an eighth grader.

Harper had explained that no, she couldn't, not unless she wanted to go back to school for a PhD. With only a master's degree, she wasn't eligible to teach at either one.

Olivia crossed her arms, a gesture she'd picked up from her dad. "Why don't you get a PhD then?"

"I could if I wanted to. But I'm happy where I am. Why add extra pressure when it won't make my life any better?"

Harper had been shocked when her thirteen-year-old had rolled her eyes. She'd seen her daughter demonstrate disrespect this way toward other people and had corrected her for it. But she'd never been so rude to Harper. Before she could speak, Olivia continued. "I plan to make a *name* for myself. When people hear the name Olivia Wood, they will stand up straight."

Harper, too stunned and hurt to reply, had gaped at her daughter. Olivia shook her head in disgust and stomped up the stairs to her bedroom, locking the door behind her. From that point on, Harper knew her daughter respected her as little as her parents and her husband did. But what was worse, Olivia also seemed contemptuous.

Harper was at a loss as to how to turn things around. She'd been tempted more than once to tell Olivia about her father's affair, but she always decided against it. Why disillusion her daughter about her dad? Chances were, Olivia wouldn't have believed it anyway. In her fury when she'd confronted him, Harper had thrown her only proof, the note he'd written to his "secretary," to the kitchen floor with the vase of roses and left it there. She'd never seen it since.

But things were different now. Olivia was older, and Harper hoped that by buying a business and taking control of her life she would build a bond between them. While opening a used bookshop couldn't compete in prestige with a grand academic title, it provided Harper with an opportunity to take the reins for her life. If all went well, Olivia would be proud and supportive of her decision.

+ +

On Christmas Eve, Harper picked Jeremy and Olivia up at the Raleigh airport, braving the crowds and the dicey weather. She'd made reservations at Olivia's favorite restaurant, Babette's Bites, where they chatted over Middle Eastern dishes and made their plans for the holiday. Jeremy, she discovered, would fly back to Toronto in three days, while Olivia planned to stay through January second.

Mother and daughter got along well while Jeremy was there. Harper liked her tall, quiet son-in-law. He worked hard as a biotechnology and pharmaceutical firm researcher, supporting Olivia while she worked on her Master of Business Administration. They complemented one another. With his laid-back and caring demeanor, Jeremy balanced out Olivia's feistiness and drive. But like Tim, he was also ambitious.

When Harper first announced over dinner that she'd purchased the shop and planned an imminent move, Olivia seemed surprised but not upset. She appeared amused by it until Jeremy left. Then, when Harper suggested they take a trip out to see her new hometown, Olivia balked.

Pouring herself a mug of English breakfast tea after Jeremy caught an Uber for the airport, Olivia said, "Mom. You know I want to spend time with Jenny and Cassidy. I'm only here for a short visit and I don't want to spend part of it in a little town in the middle of nowhere."

Harper stirred cream into a cup of decaf. "We'll only be gone for one night, Olivia. I thought we would head out day after tomorrow and come back the next day. That gives you several nights to do something with your friends."

Olivia sat quietly for a minute, frowning at the ceiling. "I guess you're right. I should see where you'll be living. But please don't expect me to visit a lot there. *This* is my home." She looked at her mom as her voice grew tighter. "*Raleigh* is my home. My friends are here. My memories of Dad are here."

Harper was surprised to see tears in her eyes. Olivia had never been prone to crying. But then, she'd never gotten a chance to say goodbye to her dad, either. She reached over to hug her, but her daughter pulled away. "It's bad enough that he's gone. Now you want to take away all my connections to him, too."

"Olivia, you know that's not why I want to sell this place! I've never been happy here. It's not fair to ask me to stay just so you can visit occasionally. And this house is huge! It's much too big for one person to live in." She took a deep breath. "Look, I know this is hard for you. And I know how much you loved your dad. But I don't think he would want me to hang on to this place unless I wanted to. It's just a house."

The younger woman gave an exasperated sigh. "In case you've forgotten, Mom, it's also where I grew up. You don't have to hang on to this house. But couldn't you at least find a condo or a small house in Raleigh to keep? All my friends are *here*. Where am I going to stay when I visit them?"

"You could get a hotel room ..."

Olivia shook her head and looked away. "You could afford to keep a small house here."

Harper's throat constricted in frustration. "That's not reasonable, Olivia. Even a small house would cost more than it's worth." She looked at Olivia's pretty profile and decided to change the subject. "Let's not argue. I've saved some of your dad's things for you to keep if you'd like. Why don't we go upstairs and look through them?"

Olivia rolled her eyes, pulled her phone from her navy blue Adidas jacket's pocket, and got to her feet. Harper bit her tongue. She had hoped Olivia had outgrown the eye-rolling, but evidently not.

While her mother waited, Olivia made plans to meet her friends at a winery that night. Then the two women made their way upstairs to the master bedroom suite. Harper told her to claim any furnishings she wanted, as most would be donated to charity. But Olivia wanted remarkably few of the items Harper had collected for her there.

Olivia claimed Tim's watch and his Wake Forest class ring, but she declined his Eagle Scout memorabilia. She wanted a picture of him that had hung in his office, taken when Surgical Solutions went public. But Harper was disappointed that she rejected family pictures of the three of them or any of Harper and Tim together. She also declined all pictures of her grandparents. Since Olivia had never been close to any of her grandparents, that made more sense. Both Harper's parents were dead by the time Olivia was six, and Tim's parents lived in Alabama. They'd only seen the two of them once or twice a year and now they, too, were gone. Perhaps one day Olivia would be more interested. In the meantime, Harper planned to keep all family photos Olivia declined for herself.

Next they went to Olivia's childhood bedroom and began going through her things. Harper asked if Olivia wanted any of the furniture in the room, since she picked it out herself. When they last decorated it, they had closely matched everything in the room to the bedroom of a *Gossip Girl* character. Black, white, and pink were the predominant shades. Olivia snorted. "No, Mom. My tastes have changed since I was fourteen."

Harper stopped short. "Do you realize that was only thirteen years ago, Olivia? It just hit me—that hasn't been all that long ago. It's strange how time seems to speed up with the years."

"Seems like forever to me. But I guess that makes sense, with me being so much younger and all." Olivia pulled out her phone and glanced at it, then put it away.

Then she walked over to the small trophy case her dad had given her for Christmas one year. Olivia had been an excellent basketball player, and had also excelled at swimming and equestrian events. Both her parents had been proud of her achievements.

She ran a hand over one of its black lacquered sides. "I'd like to keep this. I think I could make room for it."

Harper nodded. "You've got it, Sweetheart. I'll have it all packed and shipped to you sometime in January." She hesitated, then added, "Olivia, I'd be happy to give you any of my jewelry if you'd like ..."

"*No*, Mom." Olivia was beginning to sound irritated. Then she paused and softened her tone. "Our tastes aren't the same."

"Okay. Would you like some of the books I read to you when you were small?" Harper had saved *Little House in the Big Woods*, *Anne of Green Gables*, and picture books, in case Olivia wanted them.

Olivia grimaced. "Do what you like with those. Children's books aren't my thing."

Harper felt desperate to connect with her only child. She hesitated for only a moment before holding out her precious, intricately decorated mirror. "Would you like the 'fairy mirror' Grandma gave me when I was a kid? You used to play with it when you were little."

Olivia barely glanced at the mirror in her mother's hand. "I remember wondering why you seemed to like that mirror so much, since it was all tarnished and no one could see themselves in it."

Then she looked at her mother's downcast face and relaxed her features. She smiled for the first time that day. "No, Mom. Your grandma gave that to *you*. I wouldn't dream of taking it."

Disappointed, but also relieved, Harper put the mirror back in her pocket. "Don't want anything of mine?"

"If you're going to insist I take something, I guess I'd like the pearl earrings that Dad gave you when I was born. I know you wouldn't mind giving those up."

This was unfair. Harper wanted to say, *I'd give anything for you to know how much I love you*, but she couldn't force the words out. Instead, in a strained voice she said, "Of course, Olivia. Of the two, you were the best gift."

At that, Olivia smiled again. They retrieved the earrings from Harper's bedroom, then went downstairs to a small dinner of leftover ham, with its Christmas fixings, before Olivia changed out of her activewear and her friends picked her up.

The Will O' the Wisp was closed when Harper called the next day to reserve a room, but their voice message recommended an inn on the outskirts of town called The Bird in Hand. Harper made a reservation for a room that promised a spectacular view of the mountains, with two double beds. She and Olivia headed out after breakfast the next morning.

The inn was lovely, perched on a mountainside with wide lawns, porches, and forest trails threading the property. The room was done up in mountain cottage style, in shades of evergreen and sumac red with accents of ochre. It provided a stunning view of the surrounding countryside. Olivia, despite her misgivings, was impressed by Whippoorwill Gap's quaint business district and surrounding neighborhoods, still decorated to celebrate the Christmas season. Afraid to risk a bad dinner, Harper had reserved a table for two at the winery where she and Gina had eaten dinner their first night in town. It was good choice; Olivia was pleased with the food and the warm, elegant atmosphere.

The next morning, after eggs Benedict at the inn, they made their way to the Robin's Nest. Olivia, who clearly enjoyed the trip so far, had little to say as they entered the bookshop. She took in its subdued, shabby blue interior without comment.

But Harper, once again, had a palpable sensation of home-coming. Her heart rate slowed as her spirits rose. She delighted in the running water and pine smells that permeated the shop, despite the late December chill. Owning it felt miraculous.

But Olivia proved oblivious to its charms. "I wonder why were you so quick to buy this? This doesn't seem like something you would do. Couldn't you have rented it for a while to see if you would like it?"

Harper, engrossed in looking at the shelves, answered absently, "No, renting wasn't an option. It was a 'buy as is' offer."

"Did you come down and look at the inside before you bought it? Geeze, what are you going to do with all these old books? Nobody's going to buy these," Olivia shouted from the back of the shop.

"Of course I came back and toured the shop before I bought it, Olivia. I didn't want to be stuck with black mold. And I also wanted to be sure I would feel comfortable living here."

Olivia turned around and looked at her mother, her mouth hanging open. "You mean you plan to *live* here? Mom, you can't be serious."

Harper stiffened. "Yes, I'll have the upstairs remodeled. I plan to live there and run the shop from this floor and the basement. Would you like to look upstairs? There's a beautiful view of the park and the river from up there."

Annoyance wafted from her daughter like a cloud of pollen. "Okay. But I'll be honest, from what I see now, I think this is the craziest idea you've ever had. Why don't you just buy a small house near here to live in? And I don't understand why you want to *work* anyway. Why don't you get a small house in Raleigh and travel like a sensible person?" She shuddered. "This place gives me the creeps!"

Once they were upstairs, looking at the promised view, Harper tried to explain. "I like the idea of living and working in the same building. Think of the time I would save every day on the commute! And besides, if I decide I don't like living here, I can always rent this floor out to someone else."

"I guess." Olivia bounced up and down on her toes. "It's freezing in here. Let's go downstairs, look at the basement, and then go get something to eat. The quicker we get back to Raleigh, the happier I'll be."

The basement held tables and stacks of boxes. Most of the visible books had titles like Ghost Tales from the Lower Appalachians and Native Folk Remedies. Harper couldn't wait to get back here to start digging through these boxes. Who knew what delights might be within? It was thrilling to feel enthusiasm for the first time in years.

Without thinking, she opened one of the boxes and began flipping through its contents. Olivia walked around looking at the shelves for a few minutes before announcing, "You can stay in here if you want. I'm getting hungry, so I'm going to the coffee shop next door. I'll wait for you there. Want me to order something for you?"

Harper reluctantly closed The Olive Fairy Book by Andrew Lang. "Okay, Olivia. I guess you've seen all you need to see. I'll lock up and join you there." Harper placed the book back on the table and frowned. There was a small, perfectly dried daisy on the table where the book had been lying. She hadn't noticed it before. Where had it come from?

Maybe it fell out of the book. She placed the daisy inside the worn green cover and carried it out with her. *After all*, she thought with a fresh jolt of adrenaline, *everything in the shop belongs to me now*. She locked the door behind her and made her way to next door.

Harper entered the warm, bustling coffee shop, where she was immersed in the cheerful sounds of clinking cutlery and conversation, and joined Olivia at the counter. She recognized the plump, middle-aged woman behind it, who gave her a big, warm smile. "Hello, there! I've been seeing you a lot lately. Welcome back. Are you new to the area?"

Her sunny smile demanded a wide one in return. "Yes! I'm happy to say I am. I bought the bookshop next door."

"Really?" The woman's black eyebrows shot up. "We knew it had sold. Then I guess we'll be neighbors. I'm Deanna Chandler. I run this little joint." She proudly waved a hand around the large room. "Your order's on me as a welcome gift. What will you have?"

"American, black, with a cup of vegetable beef soup for me, please," Olivia said without hesitation. Deanna nodded and looked at Harper. "And what would you like ...?"

"Harper. My name is Harper Wood. And this is my daughter, Olivia Howard." Deanna smiled and nodded at Olivia.

"I'll have a coffee with cream and a cinnamon bun. Thanks so much, Deanna. Once I get the shop running, I'll treat *you* to a free book."

Deanna expanded to her full five foot three inches. "Great! We were all hoping it would still be a bookstore, weren't we, Walt?" She turned to a fit-looking man, roughly Harper's age, sitting at the counter. He sported a startling head of brown, black, and gray locks which escaped the red Whippoorwill Gap ball cap on his head. She'd never seen anything quite like it.

When he looked at Harper, she was as amazed at his large brown eyes, streaked with flecks of gold, as she was with his hair.

"Welcome to Whippoorwill Gap." His resonant voice struck her as musical, somehow familiar, and haunting.

"All right, get yourselves a table and I'll be over with your order in a wink." Deanna bustled back toward the kitchen.

After settling at a table near the window, Olivia asked, "When did you start drinking cream and eating cinnamon buns? Come to think of it, you've been eating all kinds of stuff you never used to eat. Don't you care if you gain weight?"

Harper stopped smiling and looked at her daughter. "I hadn't thought about it. But it is the holiday season and I feel like celebrating. And honestly, Olivia, I've always been a bit too thin. Would it be terrible if I put on a few pounds?"

Olivia looked at her phone. "I guess not. It's your health. You're the one who always drilled into me that your health is everything."

"Well, now I think maybe it's unhealthy to be too strict with yourself. This is just lunch. I'll make up for it with a healthy dinner when we get home. How about that?" Olivia raised her shoulders and lowered them quickly as Deanna brought their lunch.

Olivia eyed Harper's plate. "That *does* smell good."

Harper cut off a chunk and scooted it to the edge of her plate. "You can have some."

"Don't tempt me." Olivia chuckled and blew on a spoonful of steaming soup.

Harper reached absentmindedly into her pocket and pulled out her mirror. On opening it, she gasped in surprise. Olivia glanced over. "That's probably not the most hygienic thing to be handling while you eat."

"It's strange. The mirror seems to be clearing up." She held it up for Olivia to see. "It's mostly only misted over now. How is that possible?" She returned the mirror to its place in her pocket. "Did you know your Great-Grandmother Sophie died near here?"

Olivia blanched, her eyes wide. "No! I didn't know that!" She looked at her mother with renewed horror. "Don't tell me you bought that place because you wanted to be near where your grandma died!"

Harper considered this seriously. "No. I didn't buy the place to be near where Grandma died. I wasn't thinking of that at all when I decided to buy the shop. I know it sounds crazy, but I bought the shop because it felt like I was meant to own it. But the fact that Grandma died near here doesn't bother me at all. I hadn't thought about it, but I guess it does make me feel closer to her somehow. Is that bad?"

"I've just never understood you, Mom. It's not bad, it's just, well, weird. That's the thing about you ... you've always been different. Different from my friends' moms, different from my teachers, different from all the other adults I've ever known. When I was growing up, I never could understand why you were so quiet. You'd just stare at everyone else with those great big eyes, saying nothing. It was embarrassing."

Harper stirred her coffee. She watched as Walt paid his bill and walked to the door. He nodded to them on the way out. Harper felt something deep pull in her abdomen as his eyes looked into hers.

The shop was warm and cheerfully noisy. But her patience with her daughter was running low, and she worked to keep her voice level. "Olivia. I'm sorry if I embarrassed you while you were growing up. But you're old enough to understand that I couldn't help, and I still can't help, being the way I am. I wasn't put on this earth to please other people, not even you. If I were meant to be like everyone in Raleigh, I would have been. And the fact is, you were never around a lot of the people in Raleigh.

How do you know there isn't a whole herd of people there who are just like me?"

"I'm sure there are people like you there, Mom. They probably all hang around libraries and museums. They aren't the kind of people I hang around with."

Harper glanced around the room, anywhere other than at her daughter. "That's fair enough, I guess."

Harper reflected that even though Olivia's comments stung, they had done one good thing: they had convinced Harper that she was making the right move. If she was too weird for Raleigh, Whippoorwill Gap might be a better fit. Time would tell.

After they finished their lunches, she walked to the counter and thanked Deanna again, adding that she would soon be back for good. As they left the coffee shop, hugging their coats close against a blitz of cold wind hurtling down the street, she noticed another sizable group of robins huddled on the sidewalk in front of the bookshop. And now that the temperatures were even colder, it seemed especially odd to see them out here.

As she and Olivia dashed across the street to Harper's SUV, she heard an owl hoot. Glancing back at the park, she saw a lone great horned owl in a huge tree by the river, silhouetted against the blue sky.

Four

HARPER WALKED PAST THE group of robins gathered by the basement's back door entrance, and for the first time, entered her building alone. From now on, she would park in the lot behind the building and enter through this door. Once she climbed the stairs to the main floor, she walked to the threshold, turned around to look at her shop anew, and took a deep breath. The fresh, invigorating aroma she remembered still permeated the air. She noted with renewed satisfaction the surprisingly neat books, some on shelves, others stacked behind the checkout counter, still more arranged on tables. It was as though they were waiting on her. Then she flipped on the overhead lights to augment the pale, cold January sunlight filtering through the windows.

Amazingly, all of this was hers and hers alone. It felt as though her deepest wish, long hidden, had been granted. But mixed with her elation was a tinge of fear. *Okay, now that you own it, what are you going to do with it?*

She intended to open a used bookshop under the same charming name, the Robin's Nest. Her own nest would be upstairs. The bird references struck her as ironic: Harper had feared birds since she was a small child. One lonely afternoon, with her parents gone for a few hours and Grandma Sophie unable to keep her, she had turned on the television and, in rapt horror, watched the Alfred Hitchcock movie The Birds. She'd had an unreasonable fear of the winged creatures ever since.

Upstairs, she examined her future living space. She walked around, envisioning different floor plans and imagining how it might be furnished. Right around the corner on Main Street was a highly rated vintage shop, the Bric 'a' Brac, where she hoped to buy necessities.

For the time being, she was settled into a darling small rental cottage with a golden stone exterior on Poplar Street, on the other side of town. Since it was fully furnished, she'd gotten rid of most of the contents of her house in Raleigh. And she had traded her SUV for her first pickup truck, a mid-sized red Ford with a covered bed, to haul whatever needed hauling.

Exploring the building thoroughly without the constant chattering of Monica, the perky agent, helped ease her anxieties. Now she could focus and develop a clearer sense of the place.

Harper ambled down to the basement, where the walls were painted a darker shade of blue that she had never liked. The color reminded her of her freshman year dorm, bringing back all the loneliness of that miserable time. The paint peeling away in spots revealed the basement's previous shade of yellow. *That's what this floor needs—bright, sunny yellow.*

This is where she'd start her work on the shop. While carpenters got her apartment ready to live in, she'd be far from the noise down here. She decided one of the first things to do was to have a small elevator installed. That would save her a lot of backbreaking labor. Then she'd move everything she could to the main floor and clean this room out from top to bottom.

She looked up at the four basement windows facing Oak Street in the front of the shop. They were high and small, roughly two feet wide and one foot tall, and level with the sidewalk. Through them, she could see more robins out front, so she stopped to watch them for a minute. They seemed to be peeking in the windows. *What is going on with those birds?* But she found herself smiling at them—they looked so comical. If she didn't know better, she'd think they were watching her.

Once again, she marveled at the condition of the property. For a building that was constructed over a century ago, it was surprisingly clean and solid. She detected no mold, by sight or smell. It wasn't even dusty. Maybe someone had cleaned it when she called to say she wanted to look at it.

The basement only needed bright lighting and color to make it more inviting. She began making notes to discuss with the contractor.

Looking over the boxes, she wondered about Frank Bailies, the previous owner. Monica told her he had owned and managed the store since 1970. The Robin's Nest had been marginally profitable until the early 1990s. That was when he'd stopped selling new merchandise altogether to focus on used books. At first, he concentrated on pulp fiction and comic books. He held comic book and games club events on the building's top floor until demand for that waned, too. Since then, he'd only resold donations. Frank was in his late seventies when he had a heart attack in this basement only a year before. Since then, the shop had sat unused.

Harper wondered with a shiver if the shop could be haunted. The thought didn't really disturb her, because she doubted, from what she'd heard and seen, that Frank Bailies would make a threatening ghost.

With her early plans decided, Harper headed back upstairs, where she admitted to herself that she didn't yet have a complete vision for the shop. She wanted it to be successful, but maybe not too successful. She didn't want to work too hard or too many hours per week. Perhaps three full days, she thought vaguely, with two additional afternoons per week, would be plenty of time to devote to the shop once it opened. What kinds of books and where to place them had yet to be determined. But she suspected figuring everything out as she went along would be part of the fun.

She walked around, examining the shelves that lined the walls almost floor to ceiling. Frank's niece and nephew had decided to sell the building as it stood, thinking the seemingly worthless inventory not worth dealing with. Harper felt grateful for their lack of imagination.

But, looking at the books, she could understand why they decided to leave them there. The inventory was out of date. Table displays held paperbacks propped spine-side up, but all of them were worn and spotted.

She saw science fiction, fantasy, Harlequin romances, westerns, and horror titles aplenty. Most of those she'd get rid of. She decided to research the rest before donating any that weren't too brittle to charities.

She stopped when she came to a small section of children's books. Beautiful old hardbacks were interspersed with paperbacks and poetry volumes. Harper adored vintage children's books.

At the rear of the main floor, she was surprised to see that a folklore section took up the entire rear wall. Above and underneath the large windows, it claimed a surprising amount of the shelving along the right wall, as well. She hadn't noticed these books before. Maybe folklore was a hot topic of study at Sequoyah, a small liberal arts college on the outskirts of town.

As she thoughtfully examined these shelves, she came across a few books lying face down, open on the floor. As she bent down to pick up the copy of Celtic Twilight by W.B. Yeats, she was interrupted by a knock on the door. Quickly propping the book against the shelf, she went to see who was there.

Through the glass, she saw Monica Tolbert, the chatty realtor, standing outside. Even the woman's perfect, pale blue suit and styled dark hair annoyed her. She reminded Harper of the world she had escaped. An angry little knot forming below her throat, Harper wondered what she could want now.

"Hello there, I saw the lights on and thought I'd stop by to see how you're getting along. Is there anything I can do to help you out? Any questions you'd like answered?" Monica's smile faded as she looked at Harper's face.

Smile! Harper prompted herself right before plastering a pleasant expression on her face.

"No, Monica, I don't think there's anything you can do. I'm just taking a closer look at the inventory before deciding what my next steps should be." Then a thought occurred to her. "But maybe you could email me the list of contractors we talked about?"

"Sure, Harper. I won't keep you. But I did want to tell you to expect a visit from the Whippoorwill Gap Chamber of Commerce Welcome Wagon. They'll have goodies and information for you, too. Of course, they'll want you to join the Chamber of Commerce." She paused and looked at her. "It would be a good thing to do."

Harper nodded silently and fixed her large hazel eyes on the agent.

"Well. Call us if you need us. We're always happy to help our new residents. Remember, we're right up the street. Have you found a place to stay yet?"

"Yes. I'm renting a two-bedroom cottage on Poplar Street until I get settled here." Harper's eyes strayed longingly to the doorway.

"That's nice. Beautiful old houses in that part of town." Monica glanced at her phone. "Well, I need to run. I'll get the list of contractors to you. Oh, and I would imagine you'll want to get acquainted with Bryan Greene. He owns and operates the bookstore on Main Street. They don't sell used books, so you won't be competitors—unless you decide to sell new books too, of course. He'd be a good source of information. Have a good day!" And with that, Monica swept out into the crisp, cold, windy morning.

Harper locked the door behind her and noticed there was a shade above the door. She pulled it down, but brittle with age and sun exposure, it broke apart in her hand. She whipped out her list and added "Get a shade for the door" and "Cover the windows with paper." Until she was ready to open the shop to the public, she didn't want people looking inside.

A short while later, her growling stomach prompted a trip to the health food store a few doors up the street, the Great Green Grocer's. She decided to pick up lunch along with a hot pot and some tea. While there, she met the owner, Evie Adams, who, dressed in the most voluminous black skirt Harper had ever seen, seemed friendly enough. As Evie checked her out, her bronze bracelets jangled merrily. She decided she and Evie would get along just fine.

Back in the Robin's Nest, she used the hot pot to make a cup of jasmine tea to accompany the clam chowder she'd bought. After munching on a Honeycrisp apple for dessert, she headed to the park for a quick walk.

Puckett's Park was deserted on this bracing, blustery January day. Harper, happy to have the place to herself, scrutinized the park's trail map on the welcome display. While the park connected with the River Walk she had hiked with Gina, it also had its own half-mile walking trail that meandered through the park's five acres.

She intended to walk the shorter park trail today. But then she noticed a small, unmarked and unpaved path past the sign that appeared to head down toward the river. With the afternoon sun shining brightly overhead, she decided to take the path to see where it led. Once she got to the river and looked around a bit, she'd walk the park trail before heading back to the shop.

As she started down the path, she heard an owl hooting. *What is it with the birds around here?* Looking up behind her, she saw the large owl in a tree, which unnervingly, once again, seemed to be looking directly at her.

She plucked up her courage. "Hello, how are you this afternoon?" She waited. The owl blinked at her. She was still uneasy at the thought of turning her back to it; she could imagine its talons closing on the crown of her head and pulling out her hair. She backed down the path a few steps. To her relief, the owl spread its wings and flew away, towards the park.

Harper turned and made her way down the bank. But even though she was heading straight towards the river, she somehow missed it. That was perplexing because she could hear it running. It must be close by. The path became narrower, and it twisted, turned, and even forked a few times. The thickening trees seemed to be closing ranks about it, giving her a sense of claustrophobia. Twice, she tripped over unexpected tree roots which jutted from the ground. She continued taking the downhill path and became increasingly frustrated when the river never came into view. After tripping yet again, she forced herself to stop and listen. She could no longer hear the river, the birds, or even the wind sighing through the branches above. All was completely silent.

Then she began to hear low music. It sounded like a bell choir was practicing around the next bend in the path. Rustling sounds and muffled laughter led her to believe that perhaps a group of people were enjoying an afternoon of play in these woods. Curious, she made her way toward the source, but after following the sounds for what felt like twenty minutes or so, she never found where they came from. Instead, the noises unaccountably changed directions.

Bewildered, she gave up and in irritation, turned back, but was alarmed to see that the sun was sinking rapidly behind the hill. She guessed from its angle that she had only an hour or so of daylight left. Worse, the sound of the river had returned, but seemed far away. Finally, the path abruptly ended at a bright tangle of greenbriers. She turned around again to find there was no path behind her either. In terror, she realized she was completely lost.

She stood quietly, willing her heart to slow, and listened for sounds of the music, the river, or traffic. Except for the wind blowing through the pines, all was silent. Harper felt in her pocket for her phone and cursed to herself—since she'd only intended to take a short walk, she had left it in the shop. The idea of spending the night out here alone terrified her. And as cold as it was, she would likely freeze. Not knowing what else to do, she did what she always did when upset: she pulled out Grandma's mirror.

As soon as the mirror left her pocket, she heard fluttering up ahead. Looking up, she saw robins hopping about on the path, which had miraculously reappeared. Before that could register, she heard an owl's hoot and looked up. Once again, the owl was looking directly at her. "What do I do?" she whispered to it.

The great bird spread its wings once again and flew away. Then she looked toward the robins, who were chirping excitedly; they, too, followed the owl. But they flew ahead only by a few trees and stopped.

With nothing to lose, Harper walked to the tree where they perched. As soon as she reached the tree, they flew off to land in another about ten feet away. Harper followed them until she once again heard the river and found the footpath. She almost cried with relief. From there, it was a short walk uphill back to the park.

By now it was almost completely dark. The robins vanished, but she heard the owl and looked up at it.

"Thank you?" She wasn't sure if it had saved her or gotten her into the predicament in the first place. But she was so overjoyed to see her truck and the shop that it didn't really matter.

She picked up her phone and purse from the shop's checkout counter, where she'd left them. Looking at the phone, she saw four hours had passed since she'd left for her short walk. Outside, the streetlamps were already on. How was that possible? If forced to guess, she'd only been lost in the park for an hour at most.

As she started for the basement, she remembered the Yeats book she had propped on the floor when Monica stopped by that morning. She had always wanted to read that book and decided to take it home to enjoy tonight after dinner. Maybe it would help her relax.

But when she reached the bookshelf where she'd left it, it wasn't there. She looked around the floor where she had first seen it, but it was gone. Shaking her head in perplexity over the entire baffling afternoon, she suddenly spotted the book, one shelf up from the floor, between Katherine Briggs's encyclopedia of fairies and Yeats's Irish Folk and Fairytales. She pulled the book off the shelf and placed it in her bag.

As Harper made her way to the basement stairs, eager to get back to her cottage for dinner and a warm bath, she failed to see two small, round black eyes that watched her from the top of the bookshelf.

Five

HARPER CLUTCHED THE BRIGHT red gift bag filled with nail files, stickers, calendars of various sizes, screen wipes, other assorted doodads, numerous business cards, a mug, and a package of local fudge. The Chamber of Commerce Welcome Committee representative, Gracie Mitchell, sat across from her wearing a fluffy orange sweater. Her natural hair, wrapped in a green silk scarf, set off her bright eyes and gold hoop earrings. Harper guessed she was in her early forties.

"It's great to have you here, Harper. I'm a native—I've lived here all my life. I went to Sequoyah College back in the early aughts— 'Go Cardinals!'—and I run a tutoring service uptown called Rocket to the Top. I think you'll find this a great town for a business. We support each other. You're never alone in Whippoorwill Gap!"

After chatting for a few minutes more, Gracie swept out the door upon securing Harper's promise to come to the Chamber of Commerce meeting at 7:00 next Tuesday night at the Whippoorwill Gap Community Building. Harper had been so overcome by Gracie's forceful personality and distracted by her upcoming afternoon meeting with the contractor, she failed to come up with a good excuse not to go.

Her afternoon meeting went smoothly. She'd already had an architect draft her apartment's design along with the basement blueprints. The contractor immediately understood what was needed and agreed to speed up the process for an extra payment. He promised to have her apartment ready by July. She had decided to hold off on plans for the main floor until she knew what she wanted to do there.

With the contractor secured, Harper felt free to look at the shop's inventory with a critical eye. She had joined the American Booksellers Association back in December. They helped her find a market for the paperbacks. A local vendor was interested in the comics, and she sold them at a satisfactory price. She had introduced herself to all the used book dealers she'd found in the area. But she'd avoided the new bookstore uptown. She had no wish to see Bryan Greene again.

She wanted her shop's aesthetic to be bright and light. In her opinion, Frank had been a little too heavy on the shabby and too light on the chic. The windows must sparkle, and the décor be cheerful and cozy. She kept Olivia updated through their twice-monthly phone calls. To her surprise and delight, Olivia encouraged her to make over the shop to suit herself.

"If you're going to do it at all, Mom, do it right. And send pictures!"

Regret plagued Harper the next Tuesday, the day of the Chamber meeting. All day she ricocheted between nervousness and anger with herself. Suddenly, she yearned for the luxury of a bowl of canned soup and a night on the couch. After berating herself all morning for agreeing to go, she changed direction in the afternoon, berating herself instead for dreading it so much. What did she have to lose besides a few hours?

Gracie's dark eyes had twinkled as she extended the invitation to the meeting. In addition to the goodie bag, she'd given Harper a copy of the slick, twenty-four-page magazine outlining all the businesses in town that Harper had looked through during her November visit with Gina. Local restaurants and hotels stocked these for tourists. A quarter-page spread was free to Chamber members, who got discounts on larger spreads as well. Gracie told Harper that a full-page spread was provided to all new business owners for free for the first year.

It all sounded good, and Harper knew *she* was the problem. For her entire life, she had never joined anything if she could avoid it. Past experiences had proved that, without fail, she always resented any organization's demands on her time. The very idea of this meeting rankled her. It was likely she'd betray herself further by agreeing to join the organization simply to get home more quickly.

Through force of habit, she pushed through her misgivings. She prided herself on keeping her word: a promise made was a promise kept. Always. So, on that cold February evening, she kicked herself out the door and into the night.

Carefully dodging patches of ice here and there along the road, she showed up precisely five minutes before start time. She hoped to bypass awkward small talk by not allowing time for it. She'd dressed carefully, in a nice pair of black pants and a red sweater—a power color, her mother had told her. With any luck, the sweater would convey confidence and convince the others that she was not a person to be messed with.

When she walked into the community building's meeting room, around thirty people were already standing around or sitting at tables, cups in hand. Harper glanced around nervously for a couple of seconds before Gracie walked over. "Harper! I'm so glad you could make it! Let me introduce you to a few people before we get started."

They made their way over to a man who Gracie introduced as the president of one bank, and a woman who owned one of the town's gas and oil businesses. Harper shook hands with both. They asked her where she was from and how long she had been in town while Gracie fetched her a cup of tea.

As soon as the cup was in her hand, a tall man in blue jeans and a flannel shirt took the stage, and everyone found a seat. At that point, Harper realized she was probably overdressed. Some people wore workout clothes, but most were clad in jeans or hiking pants with sweatshirts. Her parents had stressed to her, once she was old enough for preschool, that clothes made the man, woman, or child. But she'd never felt comfortable in her clothes, and looking around, it occurred to her that maybe, like these people, she wasn't the "dress up" sort. Right then, she decided she'd stop wearing clothes she didn't like. Whippoorwill Gap didn't seem like the sort of place where she would need them. This weekend, she would gather up most of her hated wardrobe items, starting with these snug black slacks, and donate them to a thrift shop.

She recognized Willie Spears, the Chamber president. He owned the winery Harper had gone to with Gina and Olivia. Willie welcomed them all to the bi-monthly meeting and called on Monica Tolbert to read the minutes from their last gathering. Harper looked down at the agenda and realized with horror that "Welcome Guests" was near the top. She'd deliberately sat in the back and had to force herself to stay in her seat instead of slipping out the door.

He called Gracie up to the stage and handed her the mic.

"Whippoorwill Gap has had a quiet couple of months as far as new businesses are concerned, but that's not unusual for winter. We have two new businesses. The first, which opened earlier this month, is Tim's Tacks, a clothier who also does alterations. Most of you know Tim Elliott. He's lived in town all his life. He couldn't be here tonight because his mother is ill. We wish the family well. I'll send out an email with their addresses if any of you would like to send Tim or his mother Karen a card.

"But I'm happy to say the other business owner *is* with us tonight. Harper Wood has bought the Robin's Nest, the old bookshop near the park on Oak Street. It's the one that dear old Frank Bailies ran for years. Harper is a North Carolina native who moved here from Raleigh last month. Let's all give Harper a warm Whippoorwill Gap welcome!"

Harper's swelling anxiety turned to shock when they all stood up and looked at her, saying, "Hi, Harper!" at the same time. Then they all sat down. Harper thought of those addictions anonymous meetings and hoped this wasn't a sign of something ominous.

But before she had time to react, Gracie looked her way and said, "Harper, would you like to come up and tell us about yourself and your business plans?"

No! Harper thought, her heart and temples pounding. But she forced herself to join Gracie at the front of the room despite her blood feeling as though it had turned to half-frozen sludge.

She took the mic. "Hi, everyone. Like Gracie said, I'm Harper Wood. I bought the Robin's Nest in December and plan to turn it into a more traditional used book shop, selling mostly hardback books. I want to offer quality vintage books at an affordable price. I'm happy to be in Whippoorwill Gap and I thank you for your warm welcome."

As she sat down, her face hot and her hands shaking, she noticed Bryan Greene looking at her from one of the back corner tables, his dark curly hair set off against a Carolina Blue sweatshirt. When she looked back around, everyone's attention was on the stage, where the discussion had moved to "Old Business."

For the rest of the meeting, while the members argued over town ordinances that she knew nothing about, Harper concentrated on regaining her composure. After the meeting, several people came over offering handshakes or cheery "Welcomes." Several invited her to join the Chamber. One woman in a pink hoodie, whom Harper guessed was near her own age, patted her shoulder. "Lots to be done and we're always happy to have more help." Harper nodded without comment.

And then she found herself looking into Bryan Greene's bright blue eyes. "I don't know if you remember me. I'm Bryan Greene. I own Whippoorwill Gap Books. If I'm remembering correctly, you were in my shop a while back. I remember you because you asked me about the Robin's Nest. You may not be aware of the business agreement that Frank and I had. He purchased some of my leftover books to sell at his shop occasionally."

"Yes. Nice to see you again, Bryan. As of now, I haven't decided exactly how I want to run the shop, so I don't want to agree to any arrangements with anyone yet."

He tilted his head toward the ceiling, his face impassive. Looking at him closely, she guessed he was middle-aged, perhaps in his mid-forties.

"Are you planning to sell any new merchandise?"

"I'm not planning to right now, but that may change with time. Why do you ask?" She kept her eyes trained on his face.

"It worked out well for both of us, Frank and I, for me to sell strictly new books and him to sell used. No cross competition." He glanced up at Gracie, who had walked over with a clipboard and a pen in her hand.

"I'm sure we'll be seeing more of each other. Let me know if I can help you with anything." He nodded at Gracie and left.

"Well Harper, what did you think of our little group? A lot of us weren't here tonight and a lot of us never come. Do you think you would be interested in joining?"

Harper took a deep breath. "I most likely will, Gracie, but I'd like to get the business open first. I'm feeling a little overwhelmed tonight."

Gracie gave her a warm smile. "Of course. Take your time. But just so you know, we don't *expect* members to volunteer at all. There's no pressure, and you only volunteer for things that interest you." She lowered her voice. "Don't let Bryan bother you. I know he's a bit intense. You run your shop however you see fit."

Harper nodded gratefully, then made her way to the door. She was surprised to see a little group of robins out by her truck in the frigid February evening.

Back in her cottage on Poplar Street, she put on a new pair of Stuart plaid flannel pajamas, a Valentine's Day present she'd bought for herself, and curled up on the couch with a cup of passionflower tea and an orange to peel. The meeting wasn't bad, but it had been nerve-wracking for her all the same. Just like last fall, Bryan Greene made her uneasy. His manner reminded her of the same pressures she had hoped to leave behind in Raleigh. Why couldn't people let her run her life and business the way she wanted to? All these folks had made it without her in the past. Surely they could make it without her now.

She sighed and pulled out her mirror. Looking into it, she was astonished: the tarnish was gone, and even the mist was clearing. For the first time in decades, she could see her outline in the glass. She examined it closely, then laid it aside. Heading to the bathroom, she looked at her reflection in the mirror. Her hair was starting to develop dark streaks. How was that even possible? It should be getting grayer, not darker.

Back in bed, she opened her copy of The Secret Garden that Grandma Sophie had read to her when she was in third grade. Before slipping into its soothing, familiar story, she promised herself that Bryan Greene was not going to tell her what to do—not about the bookshop or anything else.

Six

THE NEXT MORNING, WHEN she arrived at the Robin's Nest, several carpenters were at the door waiting to begin work on her apartment. As they carried in their tools and equipment, she readied the brand-new coffee urn she'd just purchased for the shop. She wanted to keep everyone working caffeinated and happy until the building was finished.

While it brewed, Harper packed a few boxes of old books to ship off to charity. As she pushed a cartload of them toward the front, she saw a woman dressed in an unseasonably lightweight jacket peering through a very narrow section of the front window where the paper didn't quite meet. The woman motioned to her. Harper sighed, feeling her typical reflexive irritation at the interruption.

But on opening the door, Harper forgot her annoyance.

"Hi! Do you remember me? I'm Deanna Chandler from Divine Coffee next door. We met when you came to town with your daughter, back around New Years. I hope it's okay to stop in like this. I've been wanting to come over and welcome you since you got here! I just wanted to give you a chance to settle in first. Someone told me you went to the Chamber meeting last night, so today seemed like a good time to stop by."

She glanced at the coffee pot on the counter and smiled broadly. Then Deanna handed over a paper bag. "I see you've got coffee taken care of! I brought you some fresh cinnamon streusel muffins."

Harper felt a rush of affection for this woman she barely knew. She smiled at Deanna's plump face with its warm smile. "Nice to see you, Deanna! I'm the one who should be apologizing. I should have stopped in to say hi to *you* before now. My only excuse it that I've been so busy." She opened the bag and looked inside. "Oh, gosh! Those muffins look and smell fantastic!"

Deanna put a hand on the empty checkout counter. "Oh, I know there's a lot to do. The last owner, Frank, had a tough time the last few years. He was elderly and moved slowly. Business wasn't great, but he just kept plugging away. He was such a fixture in the community for decades—we were all shocked when he passed away. But I guess you've heard all about that."

Harper nodded. "Yes, Monica Tolbert, the realtor, told me about it during closing. He had a heart attack and a neighbor found him in the basement and called 911, but it was too late to save him. It's a sad story."

"Yeah, it *was* sad. He had a niece and nephew in Georgia. They inherited the place. But when they came up to look it over, they decided to just sell it and split the money. Everyone was surprised they weren't willing to clean it out or fix it up to make it more attractive. It had been for sale for over a year. I can tell you it hasn't helped the neighborhood, especially my shop, for it to be closed for so long—that's for sure."

She glanced around the open room. "Anyway, I think I can speak for everyone around here when I say, we're glad to have you here. I won't keep you; I need to get back to the coffee shop before the lunchtime rush begins. Good luck with your work here. Stop by and let me know if you need anything, anytime."

Harper promised she would. As she was closing the door, she was surprised to hear Deanna say, "Good morning! How's everybody doing today?" She peeked out to see only robins on the sidewalk. Smiling to herself, she placed the muffins on the counter beside the coffee pot. Taking out a piece of paper, she wrote "Muffins from Divine Coffee—help yourself" beside the bag. Then she pulled one out, enjoying tasty bites between taping boxes.

With that chore finished, she descended the stairs, flipping on the basement lights at the bottom. She paused to breathe in the pleasant smell of running water and pine that always seemed more prominent down there. Then she blinked in confusion. One of the tables was piled high with books, the emptied boxes lined up neatly under the table. That was strange because when she'd left the shop the day before, it was reversed—the tabletop had been completely empty, and the boxes on the floor were still full of books.

Harper turned on her heel and headed up the stairs to the top floor, where workers were busy tearing out old bathroom fixtures. They paused to look up at her. "Help yourself to the cinnamon muffins and coffee on the counter downstairs. And thank you to whoever unpacked the boxes for me in the basement."

They looked at one another, then shook their heads. One of them answered, "Ma'am, this is our first day here and none of us has been in the basement."

Harper frowned. "But, when I left yesterday, the boxes were all full and sitting on the floor. Today, I found three of them unpacked. The books are stacked on a table. I planned to unpack them this morning. I know I didn't do it."

She detected unease in their glances at each other. One of them muttered to the others, loud enough for her to hear, "I've always heard off the wall stuff about this place."

Seeing her alarm, one of them smiled at her and said, "Well, however it happened, it's good it's done." Harper nodded slowly and backed out of the room with a frown.

Great, now everyone in town will think I'm crazy. She went back down to the basement and began sorting through the books. Finding it hard to concentrate, she stopped every now and then to glance around nervously. Finally, she stopped working and closed her eyes to get a sense of her surroundings. How did things feel in here? Not threatening. Not dark. And there was that ever pleasant scent. No, she admitted, the only feeling she got was one of peace.

She tried to be as open minded as possible and wondered who had helped her. Could it be angels? Ghosts? A person who somehow had access to the building? The latter was most likely, though not as romantic. But why were there no signs of another person there? If someone were coming in, wouldn't they track in leaves or leave some other sign? She had found nothing of the sort, only completed chores.

Once again, she closed her eyes, and this time whispered, "Thank you, whoever you are, for the help." Somehow, that small action helped her feel more in control and set her a bit more at ease. So with that, she finished sorting the books on the table.

Over the coming weeks, Harper adjusted to her invisible helper. Messes she left were cleaned up overnight. The building never seemed to need dusting. The windows always sparkled, even the top panes near the nine-foot ceilings.

But then one windy March morning, Harper walked in to find the coffee already brewing. By now she knew better than to ask the workers. Whether they were behind it or not, they always denied involvement. But to find the coffee brewing felt like a challenge, like a line had been crossed.

She waited until 2:00 that afternoon, when the lunch rush usually ended, to head over to Divine Coffee to eat her lunch. On entering the shop, she received a quick smile from the tall, freckled young man standing behind the counter. His name tag read "Travis."

"Welcome to Divine Coffee! What will you have?"

"I'd like a raspberry smoothie, please." She looked over the menu, which had changed since her trip here with Olivia. "And a small grilled chicken salad."

"Sure thing. Grab a seat and we'll bring it out when it's ready." He rang her order up.

"Thanks. Is Deanna in?"

"She's in the back." His smile faltered a little. "Do you need to speak with her?"

"Just for a second." She smiled as sweetly as she could to reassure him.

"Gotcha." He headed back to the kitchen and raised his voice. "Deanna, someone would like to speak with you."

Harper stood back to let the next customer approach the counter. When Deanna came out, she grinned. "Back for more muffins?"

"Hi, Deanna! No, but thanks again, they were delicious! I was wondering if you would be free sometime today or tomorrow to have a chat about the bookshop."

Deanna nodded. "Yes, of course, things should slow down here around two-thirty. Is it okay if we talk then?"

Harper nodded and sat down at a small back table with one of the books she had brought with her, then glanced around at the half-empty dining area before she opened it. Walt, the man with unruly hair and large tawny eyes, was sitting in a corner, watching her. She gave him a small smile and a nod. He nodded back and looked down at his cup. Harper opened her book of Italian folktales and began to read.

Within twenty minutes, Deanna had joined her with a chicken salad sandwich and cup of coffee for herself. They exchanged pleasantries for a few minutes. As the conversation lagged, Harper said, "Mind if I ask you a few questions about the bookshop?"

"Ask away," Deanna said before taking a bite of her sandwich.

Harper shifted in her seat. "Tell me what you know."

"Well, Frank bought the shop sometime in the late 1960s, I think. Before that, it had been a new bookstore. I think it was founded in the 1920s. At least, I know that's when this row of buildings went up.

"Anyway, in the 1970s, downtown Whippoorwill Gap, like most cities and towns, was somewhat derelict and unappreciated. Most of the businesses either closed or moved out closer to the interstate. People didn't come around here like they had in the past. And almost no one lived here." She took a sip of her coffee.

"Frank bought the place for a song and converted it into a used bookstore. He didn't need to make money. His father was a successful lawyer, and his mother came from a wealthy family who owned a textile mill, so Frank was set for life if he didn't spend too much. Most of his business was from paperback book exchanges and comics. Customers got discounts if they brought him more books to sell. He also sold magazines and newspapers. Comic books were probably his biggest turnover. You know, Dungeons and Dragons—that sort of thing. Some of those Japanese games, like, what do they call it?"

"Pokémon?"

"Yeah, that kind of thing. He started having competitions with those games." She stared out the window thoughtfully.

"But by the time I opened this coffee shop, around fifteen years ago, he was doing very little business. I used to go in to see him every so often. He was a quiet fellow. Some of the professors at Sequoyah College would come in and look at his books, especially his hardbacks. One of them told me it was a great place to find treasures. For years, people sent Frank books whenever their relatives passed away. Often they had no idea that some of those books were valuable. Is that what you were wanting to know?" Deanna's black eyes felt incisive as they inspected Harper's.

"Partly. But I'm puzzled." Harper hesitated, wondering how to voice her concerns without sounding insane. "You said he sold mostly paperbacks and comics and that he was getting lots of books from estates towards the end. I expect the shop was a bit messy if he was elderly."

"Messy? My goodness, yes! Books were stacked everywhere. He had piles and piles of books all over the place. Old magazines, too. When he passed away, they had to clear a path to get down to the basement to bring him out."

Harper's forehead wrinkled in confusion. "But when I bought the place, it was neat as a pin! Books were stacked on tables, lined up on the shelves, or in boxes. Did his niece and nephew hire someone to clean it?"

"Maybe his niece and nephew hired someone to come in and clean the place up. I don't remember that happening, but I guess it's possible."

Harper took a deep breath before plowing ahead with another question. "Have you ever heard rumors of unusual things happening in the shop?"

Deanna looked amused. "Well, yes. There were rumors that the shop was haunted when Frank bought it. But he never said anything about it, that I know of. Frank was a good man. If you ever hear anybody say anything negative about him, I'd say the person you hear it from is the one with the problem. Frank was a little eccentric, but that just made most of us love him even more. Why? Is anything strange going on?"

Harper wondered a bit at Deanna's defensiveness about Frank, but she decided to plow on with her main concern. "I've got to admit, funny things do happen in there. I've found books moved around. The shop seems to stay dusted and swept and I'm not doing it myself. Maybe I'm only imagining some of this."

Deanna sat quietly for a minute. "Maybe, but you don't strike me as the type that would hallucinate. Unless you have hobbies I don't know about, that is." She chuckled, then got serious. "I have an idea! Why don't you run to the public library and see what you can find about the history of the shop? They have a good local history collection. I've done some research there myself. Ask for Greta Smith. She'll get you started."

Harper considered this. Why hadn't she thought to do that before? "That's a good idea. I'll do that tomorrow afternoon."

"You're not afraid to be in that shop, are you? My husband Dashawn and I live right upstairs here. If anyone were to break into your shop, I feel sure we would hear it. We would call the police. I don't think you have anything to worry about, but we're here if you need us."

Harper thanked Deanna as she picked up her bag and sweater and headed back to the Robin's Nest. Once there, she called a locksmith.

The next afternoon, Harper went to the Whippoorwill Gap Public Library at the upper end of the street. As Deanna advised, she asked for Greta Smith and was directed to the art deco reading room, in the local history wing of the original section of the building. Harper looked around at the beautiful crown molding and the heavy wooden tables, and thought back to her childhood going to Winterfield's public library with her Grandma Sophie on Saturday mornings.

She reached into her pocket, rubbed her thumb over Grandma's mirror, and sighed happily.

After she and the librarian established that they would be on a first name basis, she began with a local history book Greta had handed over, *Hooting in the Holler: A History of Whippoorwill Gap*. At close to five-hundred pages, the volume covered the history of Whippoorwill Gap and the surrounding county from 1709, when the first settlers arrived in the area. The book had been published in 1985 and was written by Walter Howell, a local historian.

Looking in the book's index, Harper was surprised to find several entries under "Robin's Nest, The." According to one of its articles, the bookshop opened in December 1923 to a couple named Byrd. Harper made a note that perhaps the shop was named the Robin's Nest because of the founder's name—not, as she had suspected, because it seemed to be such an odd magnet for robins.

Martin Byrd had been a librarian at Sequoyah College from 1919 through 1923. When he bought the shop in 1923, he moved his wife Chloe and their daughter Daisy into the building's basement apartment. The daughter passed away from polio complications at age five, in November 1923, right before the shop opened. After that, the couple ran the shop together until their second child was born. At that point, they moved out of the basement apartment into a house on Poplar Street. Harper looked out the window and wondered briefly if she could be renting that very house now. From then on, the basement was used for storage. The article didn't mention the upper floor.

Martin Byrd ran the shop for a total of twenty-six years. It was the first bookshop in town and sold new books, magazines, and newspapers. When Martin passed away in 1950, his children sold the shop to a bookseller from Atlanta named Donald "Don" Givens. He was forty-two when he moved to town. In 1955, he married a widow from Whippoorwill Gap named Frances Perkins, who was older than Givens, with grown children of her own.

Harper paused to wonder why Don Givens didn't change the name of the bookshop. Were robins hanging about the shop that far back?

The Givens ran the shop for twelve more years before selling it to a local lawyer's son named Frank Bailies, in 1970.

From this point on, Harper was already familiar with most of the information. At the time, Frank was twenty-eight years old. He had turned the upstairs apartment, which had been rented out by both the previous owners, into a community meeting space.

For the first decade or so, the shop thrived. But as the economy changed and people stopped shopping downtown, his business began to dry up. In 1980, Whippoorwill Gap Books opened uptown and took away even more of Frank's business. Shortly after that, he turned to exclusively selling used books, paperbacks, and comics.

The article mentioned that around that time, Frank began to extensively collect used folklore books in collaboration with a professor, Max Carmichael, the head of the new Folklore Studies program at Sequoyah College. So that explained the folklore books. As she was finishing the articles on the shop, Greta walked over and promised to have a list of newspaper articles related to the history of the bookshop ready for Harper by the following week.

Harper then checked the book's index for Grandma's name, Sophia Hanover, and the accident. She couldn't find references to either one, so she found Greta Smith and asked if she could look at newspaper indexes from 1976 and 1977. The newspapers were in a small room in the back, roughly the size of a walk-in closet. The newspapers before 1996 had been filmed and placed in metal filing cabinets with a sign above them reading "Microfiche and Microfilm." Harper was surprised the collection hadn't yet been digitalized. Greta told her they had just received the funding to convert them, and that this room's contents were scheduled to be shipped out in two weeks. At which time, she added wryly, the worn, though charming orange carpeting would also become a library memory.

Harper spent the rest of the afternoon at the antiquated machines, engrossed in articles pertaining to her grandmother's accident.

She already knew Grandma Sophie's body had never been found. According to the Whippoorwill Gap Gazette, no one in the area knew her or why she was in town. She hadn't checked into any local hotels. No one remembered seeing her in any of the restaurants or at service stations. And she had no relatives, friends, or business contacts in the area.

Her car had been totaled. A search was conducted that covered the entire county to find her, but no traces were ever found. Only her purse and wallet were still in the car. They held her driver's license and a ten-dollar bill. No clothing, suitcases, or signs of a struggle provided clues to the mystery. Harper's mind drifted back to the old brown Buick that Grandma called Sadie.

Later articles spoke of legends and stories that sprang up around "Grandmother Sophia," the Ghost of Old Granville Road. People claimed to have seen her at night along the stretch of road where her car went over the cliff, attempting to wave down travelers for help.

An October 1986 newspaper article said local children were dressing up as "the ghost of Grandmother Sophia" that year. The costume trend was as popular as the Smurfs and Darth Vader. Reading about it made Harper feel melancholy.

She opened her mirror and looked inside. More puzzled than ever, she wondered again why Grandma had sent her the mirror.

It was obviously old, so why had Harper never seen it before? But more disturbing, why had her body never been found?

Seven

"Blast it!" Harper heard a loud, firm knock on the front door on a damp, chilly April afternoon. It was a few minutes past four o'clock, and she'd planned to run over to Puckett's Park for a quick couple of laps around the park's paved walking trail. After that, she looked forward to picking up takeout scallop hibachi from the Japanese restaurant on the highway. She'd been thinking about it all day.

Sighing to herself, she looked through a crack in the paper covering the display windows and saw a man she didn't recognize, with short-cropped dark brown hair, wearing a light blue polo shirt and a stone-colored windbreaker. The robins, bless them, were standing behind him in a rough semicircle, all of them looking up at the unwelcome visitor. If she hadn't been so annoyed, the sight would have struck her as funny.

Hoping to go undetected, she slowly backed away from the window. Perhaps she could hide until he left. But the man must have sensed movement at the edge of the paper; he suddenly swung his head around and their eyes met through the gap. He smiled and waved. His pleasant but serious face looked just worn enough that Harper reckoned him in his late thirties.

She extended a wooden stare. "Hi. Can I help you?" as she opened a two-inch wide crack in the door.

He held out an ID badge from the college. "Harper Wood? I'm Quinn Ellis from the Sequoyah College Folklore Department. Could I come in for a few minutes?"

"Could we just talk right here? I was on my way out and I have plans for this evening." Harper stood immobile in the doorway, blocking his entrance to the shop.

"Of course. Sorry for coming unannounced like this. I only found out yesterday that you'd stopped by our office to introduce yourself."

She and Jerome Willoughby, department head at the college, had agreed that she would send pictures of books she had questions about to the department's administrative assistant, who would forward them to the proper staff member. If something looked like it needed close investigation, they would let her know who to expect to drop by for a look. But she hadn't sent any pictures at all yet.

Harper allowed her lips to curve upward a razor-blade width. "Oh yes. I was interested in working with your department concerning the folklore items I found when I started going through the shop ..."

"Yes," Quinn cut in. "I worked with Frank before he passed away. Anyone who's familiar with the shop can tell you that I was here a lot. Frank consulted me about any folklore book he planned to purchase. Not being in the field, of course, he didn't know which books were valuable and which ones weren't." Harper got the impression this man assumed she was as ignorant about the collection as Frank had been. And it was true, she was, but something about him made her hesitate to admit it aloud.

Nettled, she looked him right in the eye. "I suppose the department sent you here, Mr. Ellis?"

He blinked. "Quinn. Please call me Quinn. They didn't officially send me. Lisa, our department secretary, told me that

Jerome is helping you out. I just wanted to offer you the same services I provided Frank. Before you open the shop, I'd be happy to go through all the folklore books. It would save you a lot of time because I'm familiar with them already. All I ask in return is that you allow me to pick a few books to keep for myself."

"Hum." Harper looked at his intense face and backed up a step while maintaining a firm grip on the door. There was something she didn't trust about him. Already irked that he had showed up unannounced, she said, "I think I'll wait until I hear from Dr. Willoughby. If he tells me you're assigned to help me, we can discuss the terms. My understanding was that your department's help would be a considered community service and I wouldn't be expected to pay for the advice. Of course, once the shop opens, you're welcome to come by and give me your opinion on anything I have. I'll look forward to seeing you then. But right now, I really must be going."

She placed her hand on the doorknob. "Have a good evening, Mr. ... Quinn."

He drew himself up straight. "It's *Dr.* Ellis. I *do* have a PhD. Do you know much about Frank?"

Harper blinked. "I know he single-handedly owned and ran the shop for years. He had a tough time with his business the last few decades. The neighbors were fond of him. Why? Is there anything else I should know?"

"Oh, yeah, Frank was a *nice* guy. Everyone liked him." He paused as if considering whether to let her in on a big secret. "Frank had some close friends. *Really* special friends, from our department. Max Carmichael was the first department head we had. He and Frank were, I guess you could say, *extraordinarily close.*" He looked at her, awaiting her reaction. She returned his gaze with a blank one of her own.

After seeing she wouldn't bite, he plowed on. "Anyway, Max helped him start the folklore collection. They were *very* good friends. Without our department's help, it's unlikely that Frank would have collected all those books. Most of them are worthless, of course." His volume ratcheted and his speech accelerated. "And I could save you a lot of time ..."

Now Harper interrupted, enunciated each word clearly, "I'll wait to hear from Dr. Willoughby, since I've already spoken with him. I need to leave now. Have a good evening, Dr. ... Quinn." At that, she stepped back inside, closing and locking the door behind her.

Harper gathered her things and went downstairs to watch him through the basement windows. After he crossed to the parking lot across the street, Harper looked with vexation at the robins clustered there. Then she shook her head in wonder. Every one of them was turned toward Quinn as if they, too, were watching him walk away.

From the basement, she heard the entrance bell jingle at Divine Coffee as its front door opened. Deanna walked out dressed in a heavy sweatshirt, accompanied by a matching hat and scarf. Harper threw on her brown sweater jacket and ran outside to catch her.

"Hi, Deanna!"

"Harper! I just closed for the day and thought I'd go take a walk at the park. Would you like to join me?"

"Yes. I would. Let me grab my bag." Harper went back inside the shop and gathered her things; she'd lock them up in her truck before heading to the park.

As the women walked into the park, the apple and dogwood trees made beautiful pictures in full bloom against a rapidly setting sun. The tops of the trees were highlighted with the pink and purple of the sky behind them. The chilly April wind seemed to blow Harper's anger away. She felt comforted to see the great horned owl stationed at his usual spot in the sycamore, watching as they walked underneath. She pretended not to notice when Deanna nodded to it respectfully.

Deanna spoke first. "Maybe it's my imagination, but you seem a little tense."

Until she said that, Harper had forgotten about her irksome guest. "Do you know Quinn Ellis?"

"Yes, Lordy. I do know Quinn Ellis. You've met him? He's a trip, isn't he?" She chuckled and shook her head.

The flames in Harper's chest began to smolder afresh. "He stopped by my shop this afternoon and left just before you opened your door. I'm surprised you didn't see him."

"Well, I wasn't looking for him." Deanna smiled. "What did Dr. Quinn want?"

"Is he trustworthy? He wanted to serve as a consultant for my folklore collection in exchange for some of my books. But when I asked, he admitted the department hadn't sent him. I went by to visit with the department head, Jerome Willoughby, last week. He agreed to help, but he didn't say anything about sending anyone out to work with me yet."

Deanna clipped down the trailway for a few minutes before responding. "Harper, do you know a lot about used books? I mean, I know you're a smart person and all, but have you done a lot of research into the rare folklore book market?"

Focusing her eyes on the path ahead, Harper prepared herself for an attack. But she had asked for this, so she answered honestly. "No, I haven't. That's why I went to the college and introduced myself to the folks at the Folklore Studies Department. I did the same at the college library to see if someone could advise me. Apparently, Quinn found out about my visit and took it upon himself to come see me. I don't trust him. My BS detector started ringing while he talked."

Deanna looked up at the budding branches ahead. "Quinn's all right. He's over eager and, no doubt his social skills could use some work. But he wouldn't hurt you, I'm sure of that. On the other hand, it wouldn't be a bad idea to be a little suspicious of his real motives. Frank was getting old when Quinn joined the department. For the last few years, he did 'help' in the bookshop a lot. But some of us suspected he might also be taking advantage of Frank. Around two years ago, one of my customers told me Frank had acquired a valuable folklore book. But when the man went to look at it, it wasn't on the shelf. When he asked if the book had sold, Frank said he had given it to Quinn for helping him out."

That caught Harper's attention. "Hum. When you said he was all right, I was starting to feel guilty for giving him the boot. I wasn't mean, but I was assertive. Now I think I did the right thing."

Deanna laughed. "Assertive is good."

They rounded the loop where the path ran along Oak Street and headed back to their row of buildings. "Another thing that bothered me was that he kept talking about Frank's *close* friends in the Folklore Department, with an emphasis on *close*. Do you know what that was all about?"

"Frank was gay, Harper. Everybody in town knew about it and no one cared. I think it's strange that Quinn would even bring that up. I'm not sure what was his motivation for that. But you don't need to be afraid of Quinn. He's harmless—just self-absorbed and intense at times."

Harper stopped when a golden retriever on a leash paused to sniff her hand. She leaned down and patted its head while the woman walking him watched without speaking. After a few seconds, she straightened up and continued walking. "Thanks. It's hard when you're new in town and don't know people. I'll send Dr. Willoughby an email about his thoughts on the best way to work together. Do you know him?"

"Dr. Jerome? Oh, yeah. He's been with the department, let me see, about ten years now. He comes in for coffee sometimes. He used to go visit Frank, too. I think working with him would be smart. Meanwhile, it's okay to be nice to Quinn. If you're firm about keeping things strictly above board with the department and in the shop, I don't think he'll give you any problems. It may be hard to imagine, but despite his quirks, Quinn has a way of growing on people after a while."

"Maybe. But I don't think I'll need to worry about Quinn coming back by before the shop opens. I made my wishes *very* clear."

They were approaching the shops, their red brick bathed in the saffron light of the setting sun. "Yeah, well, we'll see how that turns out. I need to head inside and start supper. Dashawn will be home soon. Goodnight, Harper."

Harper turned to the robins beside her truck. She closed her fist around the mirror in her pocket and looked toward the owl's dark outline against the western sky. Wishing all her feathered friends a silent *goodnight,* she opened her truck door and slipped inside.

Later that evening, she talked with Olivia about Quinn. Her daughter had strong opinions about him, though she'd never met him. "I don't like the sound of this guy, Mom. If he comes back around, I think I'd call the police."

"I think that would be a little extreme, Olivia. I have no proof he's up to anything illegal. And my next-door neighbor told me he's harmless." She picked up the fuzzy green and white throw on the sofa and rubbed between her finger and thumb.

Olivia's uncompromising voice came through the speaker. "Well, I'd be careful if I were you. A single older woman living and working alone is vulnerable, you know."

Harper had always felt Olivia was a better judge of character than she was herself. She hung up more uneasy than before and grappled with her daughter's comments for a while. She finally allowed herself to relax. If Quinn was somehow "helping" around the shop, wouldn't that be easier to deal with than a ghost?

As the days grew longer, Harper found herself engrossed in the shop's organizational structure and the apartment that was taking shape upstairs. Most days, she found herself lingering at the shop until just before dark, which came later and later every evening.

Since she was a young child, the ghost stories told by an older cousin had caused her to avoid the dark. Movies her parents allowed her to watch had cemented her fear. So now she tried to leave the shop at least thirty minutes before sunset.

One evening, engrossed in shelving the science books, she became distracted by a noise coming from the basement. A soft, enchanting melody, seemingly played with only bells for instruments, accompanied whispery voices drifting up the stairs.

Then she noticed with a cold stab of fear that no daylight filtered in through the paper-covered storefront windows. It was already dark outside. She left the books and grabbed her bag, stopping at the top of the basement stairs, where she stood listening before taking a few steps down to make her way to her truck in the back. The basement's lights were off, and, except for the music, all was still. After listening for another minute or two, she flipped on the lights above the downstairs staircase. The music stopped immediately. Her heart began to race. Up from the basement came a strong, pronounced smell of mud and riverside vegetation. Without thinking, she pulled her mirror from her pocket and held it tight.

"Hello? Is anyone down there?" She held her breath and listened intently. All was quiet. Why haven't I asked for Deanna's number to put in my phone? she asked herself. Listening again, she was met only with silence.

She slowly took another step down, ready to throw her bag at anything threatening. Suddenly the bells began to ring again, slightly louder. Harper yelped before turning to flee through the front door, which she locked frantically behind her. Then she made her way as quickly as possible around Divine Coffee's exterior, to the rear of the building, where she climbed into her truck and locked the door, breathing heavily.

After a miserable night mulling over the situation, she walked around the buildings the next morning and entered through the front door instead of through the basement. Next, she headed upstairs to get one of the workers to go to the basement with her. After last night, she didn't care what they thought of her. Cab, the easy-going, but reassuringly solid plumber, went to the basement with her, checking every foot of it before testing the locks on the doors and windows. In his opinion, unless someone had gotten keys to the new locks Harper had placed on the doors last month, there was no way someone had entered that basement.

Harper told him about the bells she had heard the evening before. To her surprise, he had an explanation.

He straightened himself and looked down at her, hooking a thumb to his right. "Robert Kirk at the jewelry store next door ... have you met him?"

"Not really," Harper confessed with embarrassment. Why hadn't she been over to talk to a next-door neighbor?

"Robert volunteers as the choir director at the Maple Street Presbyterian Church. He inherited the jewelry shop, but his first love is music. If I had to guess, I'd say he was working late in his basement last night and playing music to keep himself company."

Harper thanked Cab and reminded him she'd have coffee available all day. Then she sat down in a chair, taking in the basement's distinctive outdoorsy smell. Through the windows, she saw the robins in front of the shop. As usual, several of them seemed to be watching her. Everything was calm here. She pulled out her mirror and gazed into it. The mist that had shrouded its surface since she was in high school was almost gone.

She decided to relax. Cab was probably right: the music must be coming from next door. Her imagination was getting away with her. Thinking again of Robert Kirk, she decided it was time to visit all her neighbors whether she wanted to or not. If nothing else, it was the right thing to do.

With that decision made, she went back upstairs, where she worked for most of the day packing books in boxes. She'd move these to the basement until the construction on the main part of the shop was complete. The bells forgotten, she worked happily for the rest of the day.

Later that evening, before heading to the basement exit, she heard the bells again. But this time, after taking a deep breath, she flipped on the downstairs lights and boldly walked down the stairs with her bag in her hand. By the time she reached the bottom step, the music had stopped.

She looked around. Nothing seemed amiss: no monsters, no ghosts, no strange people with bells in their hands. But the smell reminded her so much of her grandmother, it was eerie. Once outside, she was greeted by the now reassuring sound of the owl's call. Breathing a sigh of relief, she locked the door behind her and drove to the cottage. But on the drive there, she swallowed as she realized something. No basement lights had been burning in either of the shops next to hers.

84

Eight

ON THE FIRST OF May, Harper arrived early at the shop, eager to tackle three remaining boxes of books she'd yet to open. It was a beautiful morning. Wildflowers were waving their colors in the breeze. The ground outside her rental displayed sprays of violet from the periwinkle vines underneath the oak and maple trees. Nature seemed to be celebrating Harper's new life with her.

By now used to the mysterious help, she wasn't terribly surprised to find the boxes she planned to open that day lined up on the worktable in the storage room, waiting for her. But on opening the first box, she yipped in surprise. Inside, on top of the books, lay a large, fresh daisy. Harper picked it up and examined it closely in the sunlight streaming through the back window. How had it gotten there? But the more disturbing question was how could it be *fresh*?

Picking up her mirror and purse as a modicum of protection, she walked into the section of the basement that would be open to browsing customers, where she investigated every corner. She peeked into the closet she'd had installed underneath the staircase and looked inside the new elevator. Everything seemed normal—nothing out of place. Then she froze as she heard light footsteps and whispering, along with childlike giggles coming from only a few shelves over. But when she stopped moving, the noises stopped with her.

Really, this was too much. Either she was going mad, or someone was in here with her. "Hello? Who's there? Please come out. I promise not to hurt you!"

Silence. It smelled as though she were down beside the river, dipping her toes in the sandy soil at its edge. What was going on?

Her heart beating fast, Harper rushed back to the storage room. She looked out the window to see if children were playing outside. All was quiet and empty. *I'm letting my imagination get the best of me.* She put a hand to her heart and concentrated on the slow inhales and exhales she practiced in tai chi. Once she felt steady, she gamely opened the other two boxes. The second box contained two daisies, while the third box had three. Then Harper spied more daisies, crisp and unwilted, scattered about the shelves. *Were they there when I came in?* She hadn't noticed. Following their trail, she found a beautiful blue vase, the perfect size to hold the daisies waiting at the end of the line.

As the hammering in her chest returned in force, Harper ran to the main floor. It was empty now, but the contractor had promised to begin construction within a week. Nothing there was out of place. Everything was reassuringly empty and still.

Harper heard the painters talking to one another upstairs. Even though she was tempted, she decided against asking the workers for assistance. And why should she need to? Angry now, she hauled her mirror from her pocket, pressed it briefly to her chest, and went staunchly back downstairs. There she gathered all the daisies and placed them in the vase. Then she stood still, listening closely, but she no longer heard whispering or footsteps. The view from the back window revealed only robins in the parking lot outside.

Sitting down in the office chair, she contemplated this gift from unseen hands. Daisies were her favorite flower. But who in Whippoorwill Gap knew that? No one. She had told no one. She might suspect Quinn, the folklore professor, but there were no signs of forced entry, and Quinn didn't strike her as fanciful enough to strew flowers about a woman's workspace. What kind of person *would* do something like that?

She breathed deeply and thought. It *must* be Frank. He had a heart attack and died down here alone. Though she'd never seen one, Harper had always believed in ghosts, so that wasn't an outrageous possibility. But something else played around the edges of her mind. If it were Frank, he wouldn't likely sound childlike. Her eyes grew wide as it hit her. What if Frank had a heart attack because he had seen something upsetting?

Suddenly she jumped up. "What was that child's name?" She ran out the back door and grabbed her book bag from the truck. Seated again at the table, she pulled out the research she had done at the library weeks ago and found the notes taken that first day. Martin and Chloe Byrd bought the shop in 1923. They had one daughter, Daisy, who passed away from polio complications before the shop was opened. According to her notes, the couple and their daughter had lived in the shop's basement apartment before the little girl died. She felt a chill go up her spine. Was it possible Daisy, too, had died in this very shop?

Harper stared at the flowers, too stunned to see them. Could this be the answer to all the mysteries in the shop? Could a little girl, dead for more than a century, be who was helping Harper out? But how could a ghost, especially the ghost of a five-year-old child, lift heavy boxes?

She gave her head a shake. The only logical explanation was that a live human was coming into the shop at night to help her. But even if that were the case—and there had been no signs of that—it wouldn't explain this. How long had the daisies been there? And how could they remain unwilted? She'd picked daisies often as a child. She was always disappointed when they lost their starch within hours, even in water. Yet every single one of these looked as though it were still planted in the ground. Something supernatural must be responsible.

Now thinking it would be prudent to make a friendly gesture, Harper walked to the doorway into the shop and cleared her throat. "Daisy? Frank?" she said in the steadiest tone she could manage. "If you're here, you're welcome to stay as long as you'd like. Please let me know if there is anything I could do for you. Thank you for the flowers."

Then, she went to the basement's small public restroom and filled the vase with water. When she returned, her breath halted. Another daisy, larger than the others, was waiting for her on the table, exactly where she had been sitting only a minute before. The bright yellow center surrounded by paper-white petals beamed up at her. There was no way she had missed it.

Swallowing her nerves, Harper added the newest daisy to the vase and began to dig through the boxes.

Later that day, during her lunch break, Harper trekked to the local sporting goods shop and bought herself a wooden bat. It wouldn't harm a ghost, but if she was being haunted by an unstable and possibly violent human, she wanted to be ready to defend herself.

In the late afternoon, Harper left the shop, still bewildered by the morning's events. On the way out, she had checked the vase of daisies and found all the flowers within still unsettlingly perky. Finding Quinn waiting by her truck out back stretched her nerves to the snapping point. He had an old book stamped with the college's library emblem called The Secret Commonwealth of Elves, Fauns, and Fairies, by Robert Kirk, in his hands. The author's name rang a bell for Harper, but she was too aggravated at seeing Quinn to think about that.

She didn't bother with a greeting. "What ... Why are you here, Quinn?"

Quinn returned the favor, thrusting the trade paperback at her. "I wanted to show you this book. If you ever come across an old copy of this, that's well, like a hundred years old or more, could you let me know? This is something I'm interested in collecting. I know you're still buying books in the field."

As with the first time Quinn had stopped by, she hadn't yet sent any questions about her books to the department, and they hadn't notified her of any staff members being sent around.

Harper bit back a retort that he was being a pain. Even though nothing about him felt aggressive, Olivia's earlier warning about vulnerable older women went through her head, and she felt the reassuring weight of the bat in her hand. "Quinn, I'm going to ask you something and I want an honest answer."

Quinn appeared surprised at her tone and nodded without moving.

She fortified her tone with indignation. "Have you been coming by here when I'm not around? And specifically, were you here last night or this morning?"

Quinn's brow furrowed in confusion. "No. Why would I be coming by here if no one's here? That's a strange question. Why do you ask? Did you see something unusual?" His eyes widened as he noticed the bat she was holding. "Look, if you think someone's messing about your property, you should go talk to the police ..."

She glanced at the park over his shoulder and saw Deanna give her a wave. Beside her was a tall man whom Harper took to be her husband, Dashawn. Seeing them gave her confidence and reminded her of Deanna's certainty that Quinn wasn't a danger. But if she was wrong about that, they would hear her if she yelled.

She turned her focus back to Quinn and forced herself to give a minuscule smile. Her shoulders relaxed. She believed him. Why would he suggest she call the police if he were up to no good? There were no signs of forced entry. And what were the chances he'd gotten a copy of her new key? Her heartbeat slowed further as it occurred to her Quinn was unlikely to have the power to enchant daisies into an unnatural freshness.

She attempted to bring the intensity down a notch. "I was just asking, Quinn. I noticed a few things had been moved around in the shop. It was probably the construction workers. I'm sorry if I came across as harsh." She opened her truck door and climbed inside. "I've been a little tired lately," she finished.

Quinn came around to the driver's side and began talking once again, but the sound was muffled by the closed window between them. Harper's heart burned with frustration and her desire to get on the road, but she rolled down her window and asked, her voice sharper than she intended, "What?!"

The sound of the owl softly hooting drifted across the parking lot. It was still daylight, and the spring afternoon was warm. The aroma of apple blossoms and river water danced her way on a breeze swept in by the clean May leaves. All combined to soften her attitude a bit. She inhaled deeply to steady her nerves, while waiting as patiently as she could for his answer.

He cleared his throat. "I said you can always call me if anything is bothering you. I'd be happy to come check it out. Here's my phone number." He handed over a business card.

She reached out and took it. "Thanks, Quinn. I appreciate your offer to help. Really."

"The books you have probably mean more to me than anyone else in the department. I'm really hoping you and I can be friends."

Despite her earlier misgivings, Harper found herself smiling into his earnest face. He suddenly struck her as one of the most wholehearted people she had ever met. Maybe Deanna was right—he would grow on her with time. "I'm sure we can be friends, Quinn. I will look forward to talking with you when the shop opens in October. But now, I really must be going."

He nodded and backed away from the door. As Harper left the parking lot, she looked in the rearview mirror. He stood there, still as a post, watching her. She felt uneasy leaving him there. His vehicle wasn't parked behind the building. She circled the block, then went back to check. Quinn was gone. She stopped the truck and got out to make sure the doors and windows of the Robin's Nest were locked up tight.

Satisfied that the shop was secure, she turned back to her truck. She yelped in surprise when she saw seven or eight robins gathered at her feet. How had they landed there without her sensing them?

"Well, hello! Where did you all come from?" Suddenly, they all began chirping. She watched them for a minute, completely baffled. They stopped chirping as she spoke to them again. "I'm going home now. Keep an eye on the shop for me?"

She shook her head in wonder as they moved toward the door like a well-trained military unit and stayed there, watching as she drove away. Really, it was almost like they could understand her.

Later that evening she pondered her move into the building next month. Still feeling a bit uneasy about living there alone, she decided it was time to meet the neighbors. Should an emergency arise, it would be good to know their names and have their phone numbers, especially Deanna's.

After flipping through an old cookbook she'd taken from the shop, Harper decided to make lavender Danish wedding cookies. They would be a perfect springtime treat and convey a subtle message of connection. She would place these in small, robin's egg blue bags and staple gift certificates for a free book to the outside. Armed with these, she would introduce herself to her neighbors.

She felt pleased with herself and excited at the plan. If all went well, she would create good will with everyone in the neighborhood. She called Olivia to share the idea. Her daughter sounded uncharacteristically sad, and Harper's stomach knotted up as it always did when Olivia was upset. When asked what was wrong, Olivia said she had a lot going on, but she was confident she would get everything worked out.

"I think meeting the neighbors is a great idea, Mom. I know it would make me feel better about your situation."

Harper reminded herself that Olivia was halfway through her work on her MBA. She was likely overworked and stressed. She would be glad when Olivia completed the program the coming spring.

Opening Grandma Sophie's mirror as she slipped into bed that night, Harper noticed with surprise that its surface was entirely clear. She could see herself in it for the first time since it had been given to her. "I almost feel you can hear me, Grandma."

She felt awash with melancholy as she remembered the spotty information she'd uncovered at the library about Grandma's mysterious accident. Harper had never gotten closure. With this loss, the loneliest, most miserable years of her life had begun. The authorities had declared her dead when she had been gone for a year. But really, there was no proof of that. What if she'd simply grown tired of them and walked away from them all?

As Harper peered into the mirror again, a new thought occurred to her. Could it be?

Suddenly, everything coalesced into a new theory. The outdoorsy smell in the shop that reminded her of Grandma ... the mirror clearing up ... her compulsion to buy the shop, in Whippoorwill Gap, of all places.

Looking into the mirror, she gasped. "Grandma, is it you? Are you the one in the bookshop?"

Nine

On her way to Divine Coffee's service counter, Harper smiled and nodded at Walt, then delighted in the warm and fuzzy feeling in her belly when he smiled back. As usual, his tanned, lined face gave no hint as to his thoughts, but his amber eyes held her fascinated.

Deanna greeted her cheerfully. "Hello, Harper! So good to see you! What are you having today?" Harper tore her eyes from Walt's and looked at the neatly chalked menu behind her. Looking at the options reminded her of her empty stomach and aching feet.

"Hi Deanna. I'm bushed! I've been handing out bags of cookies and gift cards to the shopkeepers and apartment dwellers up and down our street. Here's a bag for you and Dashawn. I hope you like them!"

"Oh, thank you Harper! Man, those cookies look *good!* I just love it when someone else cooks for me. Did you make these yourself?"

Harper felt proud. "Yes. I did. Something about Whip-poorwill Gap's brought out the baker in me. But don't expect too much. I doubt they are as good as anything you make. And speaking of things you make, could I have a grilled chicken salad with the lime vinaigrette and a large glass of unsweetened tea?"

"Sure thing! Since things are clearing out now, I think Abby can handle it. I'll bring my lunch over and join you while you eat if that's okay."

At this, the pretty, brown-eyed young woman sporting a dark ponytail and a Divine Coffee t-shirt smiled over her shoulder at Deanna. "I absolutely can! Take a break."

Harper gratefully made her way to her favorite corner table by the window, one of many that were empty of customers that afternoon.

When she brought Harper's salad, Deanna sat down with a Reuben and chips for herself. Despite a busy morning of work, she looked as cool as her salads. "It's nice to have a little break in the action. April and May make up the off season around here. When the college lets out for the summer, things slow down a little, but then come summer, tourists make up the difference. Once the public-schools let out next week, business will start picking up again." She took a sip of her tea. "It was nice of you to get out and introduce yourself to the neighbors. I'll bet they were all tickled to meet you."

Harper smiled and took another bite of her salad, swallowing appreciatively before answering. "My gosh, this is good! What do you put in that dressing to give that zing? To answer your question, I wanted to get everyone's phone number and to give them mine. You'll find my number inside, on your gift card. Would you be okay with giving me yours?"

Deanna pulled her phone from her apron pocket. "Absolutely! How about exchanging them now? I'll put you in my phone and then shoot you a message. And it's probably the cilantro you're liking in the dressing. So, how did it go? What did you think of the neighbors?"

Harper recounted her morning, beginning at the law offices on the corner of Oak and Main Streets where she left a bag of cookies with gift certificates at the front desk. Making her way down the street, her next stop was the CPA's office. There she met Ida Barker, who lived in the top-floor apartment. "She seems nice enough. Her apartment is full of antiques and expensive decorations." She paused thinking of Ida, a woman she'd guessed was in her early seventies, with a no-nonsense, short silver haircut, who wore a form-fitting jogging suit.

Deanna regarded her frankly. "But she came across as cold and severe, right? Don't worry, once she gets to know you, she'll warm up, I promise. Ida's folks owned a factory around here. It closed about thirty years ago. They left her with enough money to live comfortably. Her husband went through some of it, betting on strike-it-rich schemes, before she caught him with a show girl from the old dinner theater that used to be out on Highway 9. Then she kicked him out. She tends to be wary of strangers, even now. Who can blame her?"

Harper mulled this over. One of the reasons she'd had lunch at Deanna's was because she wanted to get the scoop on the people she'd met. "Good to know. I'll be kind and understanding until she's comfortable with me. That is, if I ever see her again."

"Oh, you'll see her again if you get out and participate in anything. She's set herself up as the Grand Dame of Whippoorwill Gap. If there is a festival, she plans it. When there's a fundraiser, she's behind it. Well, maybe not every time, but a good chunk of the time. She has a good heart under that tough exterior. You'll see. Who else did you meet?"

Harper told her most of the apartment dwellers had been out. She'd already met Evie Adams at the Great Green Grocer's, who was pleased with the gift bag. Continuing down the street, she'd met Mike at Zippy's Hot Dogs. She chatted for the first time with Robert Kirk at Kirk's Jewelry. She'd liked his quiet, formal, and reserved demeanor. He looked to be in his early sixties, with hair turning silver at the temples, and he wore a tie and jacket. But she'd decided not to ask about music coming from his shop after hours. If it wasn't coming from him, she didn't want to know.

Deanna continued filling her in. "Mike is all business. He lives outside town and this place is strictly a job for him. He's a nice guy, but he's not as involved in the community as some of us. Evie's a good one. She mostly keeps to herself, too, but she's a sympathetic ear if you need one. There are a few stuffed shirts around who look at her sideways because of her hippie style and attitude, but she's a good person. Most of us love her for exactly who she is. And Robert? He's there when you need him, and he leaves you alone when you don't. He's always been a bit of a mystery to me. Did you meet Andrew or Chase from Take Flight Brewery?"

"I met Chase. He was coming down the stairs beside Evie's place as I was getting ready to go up. He didn't have much time to talk since he was heading to the brewery. But he did give me the run-down of their schedule. It's impressive! I introduced myself and gave him the gift bag to share with Andrew. He told me to come by the brewery for a free beer anytime. That was sweet of him, but I probably won't. I don't like beer."

Deanna slapped the table lightly. "The Take Flight Brewery has great beer! And it's a good place to get to know the locals. They have entertainment every day they're open in the summer, fall, and winter. Honestly, those guys run themselves to death. But I'd be happy to go with you one evening so you can claim your beer. Dashawn would probably join us, if that's okay with you."

Harper wasn't at all sure she wanted to get cozy with everyone in the town. But she already liked Deanna. Before she could put the brakes on, a lifetime of people-pleasing kicked in. "I'll take you up on that. Let me know when it would work for you guys."

Deanna picked up the last chip on her plate before pushing it away. "So, how're things going with the shop, Harper? Is everything moving along as expected?"

Harper knew by now that Deanna wasn't judgmental. She shook her head. "Strange things happen in there all the time. I hope you don't think I'm nuts, but I've just about decided the shop is haunted."

"Hum." From her expression, it was hard to read Deanna's thoughts. "What makes you think that?"

"Well, for one thing, everything always stays clean. I haven't hired anyone to do it for me. And I'm not doing it myself because I don't need to. Other things are done for me when I show up in the morning. Like … I'll find boxes unpacked. I *know* I didn't do it. I asked the workers, and they denied doing it. And then a week or so ago, I walked in one morning and found a bunch of fresh daisies scattered around the storage room." She stopped and shook her head. "I'm pretty sure a person isn't doing this because I've changed the locks since I got here. I know it would make the most sense for it to be a person, but I just don't see how it's possible." She looked at Deanna. "Okay, tell me I'm crazy."

Deanna kept her eyes on the table as she shook her head. "I don't think you're crazy. Not at all. Freaky things can happen. You know, Frank had only just passed away when they found him in the basement. That was a strange story, in itself. It was a Sunday morning, and the shop was closed. Robert had taken a walk in the park. When he came by Frank's on his way to the jewelry store, the front door was wide open. And it had been propped open by a stack of books. Frank *never* left the door open, even when he was working. So, Robert went in and hollered for him, but didn't get an answer. After searching around, he found Frank hunched over a table of books in the basement. He wasn't even cold yet. Now, mind you, there was nothing suspicious about the death itself. Frank was old. He had a heart attack. That's what the autopsy said."

Harper examined the beads of sweat rolling down her glass of iced tea. "You don't think something could have scared Frank or shocked him so bad that he maybe, I don't know, died of fright?"

Deanna looked out the window. "I guess that's possible, but Frank hadn't been well for almost a decade. We were all wondering when he was going to retire. But no, there were no signs of a struggle. And like I said, he was hunched over a table like he'd been working."

After clearing her throat, Deanna smiled at the birds outside the window clustered between their shops. "Maybe the robins are helping you out. Did you ever think of that?"

Harper's eyebrows shot up along with the left corner of her mouth. "No, Deanna, I'll have to admit, I've never thought of that. To me, a ghost would make more sense. Are you kidding?" She smiled to show she meant no offense.

Deanna kept watching the robins on the sidewalk between their shops. "I don't know, Harper. Like I said, I've seen some strange things in my day, too. I've come to believe anything is possible."

Harper had started to ask what sorts of things when Abby came over to tell Deanna a delivery man needed to speak with her in the back. They quickly finished their lunches, and Deanna smiled apologetically as she stood. "Try not to worry, My Friend. I'm sure everything will be just fine."

Harper felt a rush of pleasure at being addressed as "My Friend." She left a nice tip for Abby, who was working her way through college, and smiled at Walt, still sitting at his nearby table. "Nice day out, isn't it?"

He blinked at her with a serious expression before answering. "Absolutely gorgeous. I'm looking forward to spending some time down by the river this afternoon."

"Well, maybe I'll see you there when I take my walk later. The park's been stunning this spring."

"It always is, Harper. Yes, we may see each other there."

Once again, Harper felt fizzy. His voice pulled at her like an enchanting dream just on the edge of memory.

Outside the coffee shop, she glanced at the Birdsong Theatre's parking lot across the street. The Johnny and the Plowshares concert she'd attended with Gina back in the fall seemed like a lifetime ago now. While the audience at that concert had been pretty tame, she had been told that nights could sometimes be rowdy there, depending on the show playing at the theatre. The music inside couldn't be heard from the apartments, but Deanna had told her that sometimes the crowds were noisy going in and coming out. She smiled to herself. That was another reason she was pleased with her decision to place her bedrooms and living room at the back side of the building. The noise shouldn't bother her while she was cooking dinner in the kitchen, and she wouldn't be working in her office at night.

Unlike in the units across Oak Street, most of the top floors in the buildings on Harper's side had been converted to apartments. Some, like hers and Deanna's, were only accessible from inside the buildings. Others had walkup staircases from the outside.

Harper sighed happily, pleased with her day's work. While, apart from Deanna, she didn't want to be best buddies with any of her neighbors, she was happy to be friendly acquaintances with them all.

With a couple hours left in the day before it would be time to head back to her cottage, Harper decided to peek upstairs to see how the painters fared. By the time she finished answering their questions and admiring their work, it was after 4:00. She walked to the park, hoping to see Walt there, but he had apparently already gone home. But looking up at the large sycamore by the river, she smiled. The owl watched her from its customary perch in its tree.

✦ ✦

SEVERAL WEEKS LATER, HARPER inspected her completed top-floor apartment at the Robin's Nest for the last time before moving in. The late afternoon sun filtered through the open, south-facing back windows, lighting up her living room and master bedroom. The sounds and smells of the river wafted through the window screens. She'd had the walls in the living room painted a soothing shade of cream with the smallest hint of pink to warm it up. She sat down on the overstuffed blue chintz sofa, covered in a pattern of small, pink roses that she'd bought back in March. The soft pink pillows she had placed on it made her unreasonably happy. Tim had made it clear, from the time they married, that he didn't want anything that reminded him of stomach medicine in his house. But here, she could revel in pink to her heart's content. And she'd scattered it liberally throughout almost every room.

Harper stood and walked through the apartment, taking note of everything she loved about it. She glanced into the nearly empty guest rooms. One, painted apple green, already had a bed and a dresser, so she could invite Gina for a visit soon. She couldn't wait to get her friend's reaction to her new place.

Then she walked into her own bedroom, an involuntary smile spreading across her face. The walls were a soft robin's

101

egg blue, set off by floor-to-ceiling thick white muslin curtains. When she sat on the brass bed's mattress, it was soft, but not too soft. It was, as the story went, "just right." Goldilocks. I'm like Goldilocks. Not too hard and not too soft, just right. The bed was covered with a cushy white chenille bedspread, and she planned to get a white upholstered chair for the corner. She had bought a nice, 1920s-era, golden oak chest of drawers and matching dresser at the Bric 'a' Brac, the antique mall on Main Street. It all harmonized perfectly in this room.

She sat on the bed and studied the pictures on the wall. One small grouping displayed pictures of her family—one of her with her parents, one of Grandma Sophie alone, and one of Harper with Grandma. She walked over and ran a finger over her grandmother's face before turning to the other artwork. Opposite the bed hung some oil paintings she had bought from a local artist at one of the town's galleries. These renderings of graceful ballet dancers looked lovely and reminded her of childhood dance classes, when she pretended to be a swan. The wood flooring was covered with a large, round wool rug in yellow, blue, and white. Once she found the chair she wanted, this room would be perfect.

On catching her reflection in the dresser's mirror, she got up to peer at herself closely. Seriously, what was happening with her hair? Where it had been blonde and gray when she moved here, it was now sprouting black and brown streaks. How could that be happening? It was like a fun-house version of aging in reverse. She turned away and headed to the door.

On her way to the door, she glanced around with a brand-new burst of excitement as she remembered that starting tomorrow, she would end every day in this beautiful room. She padded to the apartment door where she had left her shoes. From the small table by the entrance, she picked up a note that the painters had left her.

Harper,

We enjoyed working for you! Let us know if you found everything to your satisfaction. We'll send an email in a few days with a link to our site. We always appreciate reviews! And speaking of appreciation, we'd like to thank you for hanging all the pictures in the apartment for us. We will be taking $100.00 off the final bill for the time that saved us. And again, thanks for all the snacks and coffee! If you ever need help with anything again, you know who to call.

Jane and Bill

For the second time, she frowned over the note. She hadn't hung any pictures anywhere. All she had done was place the pictures on the floor beneath the spots where she wanted them, with a note that specified how high they should be. She hated climbing ladders and wasn't strong enough to hang her artwork anyway. Yet she had found them hanging exactly as she had requested. Until she found the note, she had thought Jane and Bill were responsible.

This was the only wrinkle in her happiness. She still had no idea who or what was assisting in the shop. And now she knew whoever—whatever—it was, it came into the apartment, too. She thought of a book she had bought and read shortly after buying this building, The Bookshop by Penelope Fitzgerald. In it, a woman in an English seaside town lived alone in a book-shop that was haunted—by a poltergeist. Harper had admired the character's pluck. And she had decided that if Fitzgerald's Florence could survive a poltergeist, Harper could live with a friendly ghost.

After shoving the note into her pocket, her hand closed around her mirror. And it once again worked like a charm to calm her fear. When she descended to the main floor, she wasn't terribly surprised to hear the sound of bells faintly drifting up from downstairs. By the time she got to the bottom of the stairs, the bells had stopped ringing and everything was still.

Her gut clenched with an unsettling combination of excitement and anxiety. *Tomorrow night, I will spend the night here alone, come what may.* She glanced around the darkening space before opening the door and heading out into the warm summer night.

Ten

Harper eased out of bed a few minutes after midnight and slipped on her pink cotton bathrobe. She picked up her mirror and phone from her nightstand and placed them in her robe's pockets. Then she picked up the baseball bat beside her bed, reassured by its weight. She left the novel she had been reading, George MacDonald's At the Back of the North Wind, face down on her bed and padded to the apartment door.

Stopping, she listened intently at the closed door. All was silent for a few seconds, but then, there it was again. An unworldly music was coming from downstairs. It sounded too loud to be coming from the basement or from the jewelry shop. Besides, it was a bit late for Robert to be hanging about his shop listening to music. Undoubtedly it was coming from near the bottom of the stairs.

The music stopped only to be replaced by the sound of scurrying footsteps and low murmuring. She stiffened in dread. Looking down at her phone, she considered her options. Should she call a neighbor? Not just yet, she decided. Her phone was in her pocket if she needed it, with 911 at the ready.

With the baseball bat gripped tightly in one hand, she eased open the lock of the heavy apartment door. *I'll have to find out what this is all about sooner or later; it may as well be now.* Her heart battered her chest and her throat cinched tight, but she slid through the door and onto the landing on the other side as quietly as she could. She was relieved that the new door's hinges were soundless. Lights flashed from the floor below, though nothing about them suggested flashlight. Supercharged fireflies or perhaps disco lights winking on and off was more like it.

After standing quietly and gathering her nerves for a moment, she treaded softly down the stairs. The smell of river water, pine, and undergrowth was almost palpable. As she approached the final step, she stopped to listen again. Then, there it was. No doubt about it, something—or someone—was sliding something across the floor. Other indistinct rustlings and whispers were coming from near the front door, where small but powerful lights still flickered. Without allowing herself time to think, she turned on her phone's flashlight and aimed it toward the front door. The sight that met her eyes was so unexpected, she released an involuntary yelp.

Caught in the phone's light was a tableau featuring three miniature people, their mouths open and eyes wide with surprise. Except for their faces, they appeared childlike. One had skin the color of maple leaves in early spring, one was paper white, while the third was deeply wrinkled and the color of beech bark. Most amazing of all, one of them was hanging motionless in the air. All three wore red vests.

Harper began to say "Who—" But before her lips formed the word, she saw a pale silver shimmering cloud moving toward her so quickly, she had no time to react. The moment it reached her, she felt a burst of bliss and peace, and then everything went dark.

"I hear music," Harper muttered as she opened her eyes, finding herself tucked snugly in her bed upstairs. Well, that was a dream for the record books, she thought.

Then, turning her head towards the doorway, she saw a small person, no more than three feet tall, with brown skin and silky, straight black hair falling around enormous ears and reaching past the waist. The small visitor was holding a mug of something steamy that smelled like chamomile tea.

She bolted upright. "Dobby?"

"Dobby?" the creature responded, in an ancient but feminine voice, one eyebrow cocked. "No, Dearie, I'm not a house elf, if that's what you're thinking." She looked up at a corner as if considering the idea. "Well, not *exactly*."

"Then ... what—I'm sorry—who, are you?"

The creature held up a hand and motioned for her to lie back. "Don't fret yourself about that now. All will become clear with time. We've been worried about you. You gave us all quite a scare last night! Now sit up slowly—let's prop some pillows behind you so you can drink this nice tea."

Feeling too confused to argue, Harper leaned back in bed. As she did so, the small creature placed the stoneware mug on the nightstand and made the bed comfortable. As she bustled about, Harper inhaled the scent of honeysuckle blossoms.

"There, Dearie, lean back. I put a little sugar and milk in the tea. I hope that's okay." Its forehead wrinkled with concern. "Don't think I've been snooping, but I believe you like cream?"

"Yes." Harper sniffed the tea, hesitantly.

"Oh, go on. It's perfectly safe! I got the water from your faucet, and the tea, sugar, and milk from your supplies. A little bit will do you good. Once that settles, I'll give you a bit of the bread I've baked with butter." The creature smiled slightly with her thin, dark brown lips, but her forehead still wrinkled with tension.

Bread! So that's what was making the apartment smell so wonderful. Harper took a sip from the mug, gave the creature a small smile, and nodded. "It's good."

The little person released a breath and her forehead smoothed out. "Mind if I have a seat?" She waved toward a dining room chair that had been brought into the room.

Harper nodded. "Of course. Now, can you please tell me who you are and what's going on around here?"

The creature looked at her intently. "How much do you remember from last night?"

Harper considered the question. What did she remember? "I remember ... Wait, *last night?* What time is it now?"

"I don't keep track of time like you do, but I think you would call it late morning."

Harper took in this bit of information with alarm. "I remember being here in bed. Just before midnight, I was settling in with my book." She checked the nightstand and found the book there. That was good to see, but the bat was nowhere in sight. She swallowed. "Then I heard a noise downstairs that sounded like music ..."

The little creature nodded. "Go on, Dearie."

"I thought ... I thought whether it was people or ghosts, it was better to confront whatever it was than to keep wondering about it."

The little person sighed and nodded. "And then?"

"Well, I put my book down, grabbed my phone and my base-ball bat, and padded downstairs as quietly as I could. Where's my bat?" She put the cup of tea on the nightstand and looked around the room.

"Still on the premises. Do go on."

"When I got to the bottom step, I flipped the phone light towards the sound at the front door. And I saw ..." It seemed so absurd that to say it was ridiculous.

The creature looked at her intently with small, round black eyes, waiting.

"I saw small people. Not you. But I saw a little old man, and two young-looking ... well, they looked like children except for their faces. And one of them ... had orange hair and was floating in the air! Then I saw a sparkly mist heading my way, and that's it. That's all I remember." She sat up straight and swung her legs over the side of the bed.

"The time has come then." The creature stood up and rubbed her hands together. "It's time you met us all."

Harper clutched her gown. "Wait! Who are you? Who am I meeting? Can I get dressed first?"

The creature waved both hands from side to side. "Of course, Dearie. Go right ahead and get yourself in order. You may call me Piper. I'll wait until you're ready before I call in the others. Would you like to meet us here in your bedroom or in a different spot?"

"Where are they now? How many are there?"

"They're at the top of the steps, just on the other side of the door, I'd imagine. We are nine in all." She walked to the doorway and turned to face Harper.

"Nine?!" With an effort, Harper steadied her nerves. "I'll meet you in the living room. Are they all as nice as you?"

Unless she imagined it, Piper's look was compassionate. "You needn't fear a one of us."

Harper stood and grabbed the headboard to steady herself. In the bathroom mirror, she noticed that her eyes looked huge, like they'd been frozen in surprise. And her hair was even wilder than usual. Where many women her age seemed to lose their hair, Harper's was becoming thicker. And the streaks of black and brown were more pronounced this morning. She quickly bound it all up with a clip and splashed water on her face.

Five minutes later, she was sitting beside an open window at the corner of her couch. Before she sat, she opened all the windows wide so she could yell for help should things take a bad turn. She held her phone in one hand and her mirror in the other. She'd even tucked a flyswatter into the side cushion as an extra precaution.

Harper had brushed her teeth and put on a large, pale green linen shirt over a pair of jeans. A pair of old brown leather sandals graced her feet.

Feeling as prepared as she'd ever possibly be, she nodded to Piper, who went to the door and said in her crackling voice, "She's ready to meet us all now."

As she watched the assembly appear at the entrance to the living room, Harper gulped. One by one, the small beings made their way into the room, each of them bowing politely. With them came the renewed scent of river water and pine.

First was the wrinkled man she remembered from the night before. He removed his pointed red hat and bowed at the waist. "Pleased to meet you, Lass! Earl Grey at your service."

His formality prompted Harper to stand. "Call me Harper. It's nice to meet you, Mr. Grey."

Some of them hopped about and twittered. "Everyone calls me Earl Grey. I am what you would call a gnome," he said, with a twinkle in his eye, before moving to the window to make room for the others on the rug. Harper felt like a queen receiving a court.

Piper, standing at her side, nudged her. "Do sit down, Dearie. This may take a while. We'll take no offense at your sitting."

Harper, already feeling a bit dizzy, gratefully returned to the sofa.

Earl Grey was followed by two small ... were they men? Standing at no more than two feet tall, they were dressed in green and brown, with green caps and brown curly hair amassed about their heads. They smiled shyly as they approached. Piper continued, "Here we have what are commonly called brownies."

"Tiptoe," said one, removing his hat with a bow.

"Tarryfoot," said the other. "At your service," both announced, then together they replaced their hats and moved to stand beside Earl Grey.

Next there were the two small females she had seen the night before, one with green skin, which now glowed in the daylight. Her dark brown hair was tied in two plaits which reached her tiny waist. The one caught floating in Harper's flashlight had incredibly white skin with curly, shoulder-length hair the color of a ripe pumpkin. Both wore dresses that resembled ballet tutus or perhaps upside-down buttercups in faded shades of green and brown.

Piper moved behind them and placed a hand on the first one's head. "This is Alida." Then she placed her other hand on the flaming orange hair. "And this is Lily. They are water sprites. Alida comes from rivers while Lily hails from the deep blue sea."

"Pleased to meet you," they chirped with bell-like voices.

"You as well," Harper responded, her eyes wide.

After them, three taller beings, ranging between three and four feet tall, moved to the front of the rug. The tallest appeared to be a female, with mahogany skin so smooth it seemed polished. She nodded regally. "Ivy, at your service," she said in a clear alto, after which she glided to her place at the back of the rug.

In response, Harper nodded, equally grave. "It's a pleasure to make your acquaintance."

The second to last being, heavyset and wearing what looked like clothes from Renaissance England, bowed from the waist. "I am Hawthorne. I'm very pleased to meet you. And this"—he indicated the taller, slimmer one—"is Ash. You will find that he is quite well read." Ash, with long, straight black hair reaching his knees, looked the most like Piper. He was dressed in simple tan leather pants that were covered in a straight tunic. He bowed silently to her before taking his place at the rear.

Hawthorne continued, "You've already met Piper." Piper bowed slightly.

All fell silent as Harper took in the odd assortment of beings before her. The red vests were the only thing they all had in common.

Not sure what to do next, she smiled at them. They smiled hesitantly back at her.

She cleared her throat. "It's nice to meet all of you. Please, call me Harper. And make yourselves comfortable. Can I get you something to eat or drink? We can bring in more chairs from the kitchen if you would like ..."

"That's not necessary, Dearie," said Piper as they all seated themselves on the wool rug.

Harper suddenly felt unaccountably happy, perhaps from relief at finally knowing who was behind the odd events in the shop. But also, something about them inexplicably conjured memories of her grandmother, which evoked feelings of shelter and safety.

"I hope it's not rude to ask. But I've thought for quite a while that perhaps I had ghosts here. But you're not ghosts, are you? What should I call you? I know some of you are brownies and sprites, but what should I call the rest of you?"

Hawthorne stood. "There are many stories about our kind. We are as varied as are you Earth-dwellers. But for our Troop, those of us you see before you, we are broadly what humans call faeries. But you needn't be alarmed at that. It's true some of our kind are dangerous and most of us are mischievous." They all smiled and nodded. "But you needn't fear *us*. We've lived in this shop for a long time. And we've pledged ourselves to help the owners. Our intentions are purely benevolent."

"Thank you." She looked at them in wonder. "I very much appreciate all the help you've provided so far."

Alida flew up in the air. "You're welcome. We want to be friends!" She settled next to the tallest, dark faerie and gave her an adoring look. "Ivy here is a forest nymph." Ivy placed a gentle hand on Alida's head, smiling down at her before meeting Harper's eyes with a solemn gaze. Her bearing was strong and queenly. Harper's instincts told her not to cross this one.

Ivy spoke. "Yes, I am a wood nymph. And Ash, Hawthorne, and Piper are sometimes called common Fae. Though I hope it's plain to you, there's nothing common about any of us. We each have our gifts."

"Did the other owners, Frank and the ones before him ... did they know about you?"

Hawthorne spoke again. "Not all of them. Only Frank and one of the others. They never discussed us with other humans."

This opened a new line of thought. "Should I not tell others about you either?"

"Not unless you want to be thought touched in the head!" shouted Earl Grey with a hearty laugh.

They all broke out into bell-like sounds and chirping again. Now Harper understood this enchanting sound was laughter.

Once it died down, Harper said, "This is a lot for me to take in."

They looked at her and at one another with delighted smiles and wide eyes. Earl Grey stood. "Oh, we *are* a lot to take in. But you'll get used to us in time."

"Just one more question—I've been working here for almost six months now. I've seen what you've done, and as I said, I appreciate the help. But why have I never *seen* any of you before last night?"

Harper was surprised when the sound of bells and twittering started up again as some of them rolled or hopped about. Then she froze when they all began to chirp. It sounded exactly like the robins that hung about the shop.

"You have seen us before!" Earl Grey cried. "Think, Harper!"

Harper gasped in amazement as they transformed into robins right there in her sunny living room.

"Wait! You mean you're the robins?"

They chirped and hopped about, while a few of them took flight for a few seconds before resuming their earlier shapes.

"Yes, Dearie! We've been keeping an eye on you from the start!"

Harper suddenly felt very hot. She laid her grandma's mirror on the table beside her and wiped her forehead. Suddenly, they grew completely quiet. Several got up and came closer to get a better look. Piper looked at the mirror closely before looking up at her. "We've seen this before. Where did you get this, Dearie?"

"From my Grandma Sophie. She died in a car crash near here when I was ten. She sent me this just before she died." Harper's throat swelled, and she reached over to pick up the mirror again. Really, despite the relief she felt at having the mystery solved, she felt completely overwhelmed.

"We can see it's special to you. It would be good to keep it close." Piper exchanged a meaningful look with Hawthorne, which Harper missed.

"Yes. It means more to me than anything else I own. And it's funny. You all remind me of my grandma in some ways. I hope you don't mind me saying so, but when you're around, everything smells like her house smelled. It makes me happy."

They nodded, but this time with serious looks on their faces.

Piper moved toward the door. "We'll leave you to rest now and get adjusted to the idea of having us around. Unless you'd like one of us to stay and keep you company? You might have questions later on."

Harper didn't want to offend these creatures. But it was true she wanted some time alone to process the seismic changes in her worldview.

"Thank you, Piper. It's a relief to know who you are and that you're friendly. But right now, I'd like some time alone to think."

They all got to their feet with Harper, who walked them to the door. On the way out, each bowed to her once again, and again she returned the gesture. Earl Grey was the last one out the door. "Can we expect to see you at the Fourth of July celebrations, Harper?"

Harper nodded, surprised they would know anything about the planned festivities on the other side of town. "Yes, I plan to go. Are you going too?"

"Ah, yes, that we will. Perhaps we'll be seeing you there." And with that, they were all gone.

Back on her soft, flowered couch, she opened her mirror and looked at its clear surface. "I need your guidance more than ever. Please help me know what to do."

Unable to settle down, she wandered to the basement and pulled some books on fairies from the shelves, which she took upstairs to read. She went to bed early that night. And this time, she placed earplugs in her ears.

·✦·

TWO DAYS LATER, HARPER got ready for the Fourth of July festival by dressing in a navy blue skirt she had recently bought at S'Elena's, a store outside town that did alterations and made one-of-a-kind clothing. She paired the gauzy skirt with a white t-shirt, then tied a red scarf around her unruly ponytail. Then she headed out to Main Street where the parade was scheduled to begin at 11:00 am.

The Fourth of July parade was a smaller version of the one the town held for Christmas back in November. It started at Whippoorwill Gap Municipal, the large park on the other side of town, and made its way down Main Street before ending in the library parking lot.

Most of the entries were homemade. People pulled decked-out children and pets in equally festive wagons, all done up in red, white, and blue decorations. The high school and college marching bands played patriotic songs. A few business-es made floats. Harper saw Bryan Greene driving by in a sky blue convertible with a small girl riding shotgun, probably his daughter, she thought. They were throwing out bookmarks with seeds embedded in them. Bryan's eyebrows raised when he saw her, and he threw up a hand in recognition. Harper picked one of the bookmarks to take home and plant in a pot on her balcony.

She recognized a few people from the Chamber of Com-merce meeting threading through the crowd, distributing small American flags on wooden sticks. She had skipped their April and June meetings. Now, she moved to the back of the sidewalk, trying to avoid eye contact with any of them. But she couldn't avoid Gracie, who smiled broadly when she saw her. "Oh, hi, Harper! We're so glad you could make it to the parade. Are you coming by the park later?"

Harper frowned, expecting an invitation to stop by the Chamber booth. Though she had no intention of talking to Chamber representatives that day, her reflexive politeness took over. "Maybe, Gracie, I haven't made my mind up about that, yet."

"Well, if you do, make sure to stop by the Pies for Paws booth. You haven't lived until you've tried their pies. And they sell them cheap. Trust me, you'll thank me later."

Without another word, Gracie moved on to the next person, leaving Harper with a new flag in her hand.

After the parade ended, Harper allowed the crowd to sweep her to the park. The Whippoorwill Gap Municipal Park, commonly called "Gap Park" by the locals, was roughly ten times the size of Puckett's Park. The festival was held in a large field near its entrance.

Harper wandered from booth to booth, stopping to purchase small items that caught her fancy. She had always admired people who could make beautiful things with their hands. She bought a bright purple fabric shopping bag from a perky elderly lady in a straw hat, and she filled it with purchases of homemade dish cloths, soap, lip balm, and even Christmas ornaments. Most she would give away as presents.

She said hello to the people who made eye contact with her. Ida Barker, the short-haired woman Deanna had described as the town's Grand Dame, was there, but she didn't see Harper. Instead, she held on to a clipboard while consulting with a small group of young people dressed in red Whippoorwill Gap t-shirts.

Under a few tents, lemonade and sodas were for sale. A roped off, adult only section sold beer and wine, with wooden barrels for people to congregate around. Outside this area, large tubs containing ice and free bottles of water were scattered about. Harper was pleased they had provided water, but she'd brought a bottle of her own.

She enjoyed the mix of bluegrass and folk music a band was playing, so after making her rounds of all the tents, she found a place on the grass to listen. While she sat, she enjoyed a cherry pie she had bought from Pies for Paws. As she licked the delicious filling from her fingers, she looked up to see her very own Fae arranging themselves around her.

She quickly looked around to see if anyone was looking their way. "Well, hello," she said quietly, moving her lips as little as possible. "Aren't you guys worried about people seeing you?"

They all began chirping, and Harper felt woozy as she found herself looking at a group of robins. She closed her eyes and shook her head in confusion.

When she opened her eyes again, she was once again looking at the beings from her shop. Earl Grey addressed her. "Relax, Harper. We're just out taking in the scenery and soaking up the atmosphere. We saw you sitting here alone and decided to stop by to give you a little company. Don't worry about the people. Unless they're meant to, they don't know we're here."

Harper gave one small nod. Then she turned her head away from the crowd. "You mean, they just see a bunch of robins?"

"You've got it!" Earl Grey responded, smiling broadly while the others nodded. Harper wiped the pie residue from her hands. "Can I get you guys a snack of some sort?"

Earl Grey tossed a twig in the air. "That's mighty kind of you, but we'll be helping ourselves to all the leavings tonight. I think we may be too stuffed to even make it back to the shop. Am I right, Goodfellows?"

Harper heard tinkling bells, but a quick glance around told her no one else saw or heard anything unusual.

She watched the crowd enjoying the party on this beautiful summer afternoon. It had been a long time since she had attended an event like this without working in a booth herself. She had plenty of past experience serving up hot dogs and selling cookbooks for organizations that either Olivia participated in or Surgical Solutions supported. It was nice to be here on the periphery for a change.

But after a while, she allowed herself to wonder if things really were different here in her new hometown. Maybe the pressure she'd felt in Raleigh to impeccably perform her duty wouldn't be an issue here. It was possible she would enjoy participating in Whippoorwill Gap events. She had yet to detect any unpleasantness from anyone, apart from Bryan Greene. Perhaps she could slowly get involved and help out with a few things, without overcommitting herself.

After a while she began to feel drowsy. She lay back in the grass and closed her eyes to better take in the warm breeze and the band's music. She relaxed so completely that when she opened her eyes, the robins had gone. Shadows had lengthened and craft vendors were packing up their wares. Families were making their way back toward the entrance.

The celebration was scheduled to continue until 10:00 that night, when the traditional Fourth of July fireworks display concluded it. Harper was happy to skip the noisy finale. So she got to her feet and took the long way home, walking through parts of town she'd never seen up close before. Maybe the Fae would come by to visit that night. She thought watching the fireworks with them from her kitchen window might be fun.

Eleven

One Thursday evening in early August, Harper got dressed to visit the Take Flight Brewery with Deanna and Dashawn to claim her free beer. As always, she agonized over what to wear. Despite her best efforts, she still struggled with her childhood training.

At fifty-seven years old, she had never set foot in a brewery, so she had no idea what to expect. She'd never wanted to attend anything hinting of frat parties once she'd left them behind in college, where she felt they belonged. Before she dressed for the evening, she looked Take Flight up on the internet. From what she saw there it looked safe to dress up a little if she wanted to, but as she'd suspected, it didn't require silk or pearls. She decided to wear a pair of khaki-colored cropped linen pants topped with a loose black t-shirt and tan hiking sandals. Looking through her jewelry, she decided that a pink quartz necklace she'd picked up at the Great Green Grocer's would look nice, but casual.

Surveying herself in her bathroom mirror, she briefly wondered what Tim would have thought of her uncharacteristic foray into the world of beer drinkers. She didn't expect the evening to get wild, but she guessed there was always that chance. Olivia wouldn't approve, she suspected, but she didn't need to know about it, either. She hadn't mentioned her plans when she talked to Olivia the evening before.

Her image in the mirror looked adequate for the occasion. She didn't look young, and her outfit certainly didn't look sexy. But it all worked together, complementing her hair, which she decided to wear loose for a change. Since moving to Whippoorwill Gap, her hair looked as though it were highlighted by a demented color stylist, and the effect was more pronounced today. Maybe it was the mountain air. Her wild hair accentuated her already large round eyes, making them look even bigger. But as people in this town didn't seem to mind quirkiness, she expected to fit in fine.

When she met her neighbors out front, Deanna was wearing cropped jeans and a dark brown t-shirt reading "A Heavenly Start to Your Day: Divine Coffee," above a haloed coffee mug, with an ankle bracelet above her flipflops. Her big gold hoop earrings looked beautiful against her dark skin. Dashawn, imposing at over six feet tall with a football player's physique, was wearing a basic tee, jeans, and sneakers. He wore a single gold earring in his left ear and a trim pointed beard on his face. Harper privately thought he looked rakishly handsome enough to play a pirate in a feature film. He and Deanna made an attractive couple.

After Deanna introduced her husband and her friend, they made the five-minute hike up to the top of the hill, where they took a left onto Main Street, then walked past the Bric' a 'Brac to the brewery. The temperature had climbed to a rare ninety degrees that day, but things were cooling off before they left.

Stepping inside the brewery's cool, brick-lined interior, Harper surveyed the room. It looked a bit like her own shop but twice as wide. The worn wooden floors appeared original to the building. A huge bird was painted above the bar. Dark chocolate colored metal tables and chairs were scattered about the space.

Once they claimed a table, Chase, dressed in a light blue t-shirt with the bird above the bar and *Take Flight* on its front, came over. "Hi, guys! The neighbors have arrived! What will you have, Harper? Remember, it's on the house."

Since Harper had never liked beer, she was pleased to see a mixed berry seltzer on the menu. She pointed to it. "I'll have that."

Dashawn rocked back in his seat. "Harper. Come on. These guys have the best beer in the South and you're gonna order a *seltzer?* Give them a chance to impress you! Tell me, what kinds of beers have you had that you really didn't like?"

Harper didn't need to think about it. "Keg parties." She shuddered. "It's been a long time, but I still get sick just thinking about the beer we drank at those nasty keg parties in college."

"Is that the only kind of beer you've ever had?" Chase asked.

"Yes. But it's all pretty much the same, isn't it?"

Everyone laughed. And Deanna shook her head. "No, Harper. That's not true *at all.*"

Chase fanned himself with a menu. "Tell me Harper, do you like chocolate, or maybe coffee?"

Harper looked at him suspiciously. "I like both, but chocolate-flavored beer sounds gross."

"What have you got to lose? It's on the house. If you don't like it, I'll bring you a seltzer as a consolation gift. How about that?"

"Well then, as you say, I guess I have nothing to lose." She briefly wondered if they were planning to have fun at her expense, but considering how relaxed and happy everyone seemed, she decided she was safe.

While Chase went to get their beers, the three neighbors talked under one of the slowly rotating ceiling fans about Harper's move into the apartment. They wanted to know how she liked it so far. Harper kept things light and upbeat. She didn't mention "F-Troop," as she'd come to think of her housemates. No point in getting into that. *Not unless you want to be thought touched in the head!* she remembered Earl Grey saying. No, that was the last thing she wanted.

Chase was back in a few minutes with three beers in varying hues. A light one for Dashawn, a brownish one for Deanna, and a black one for herself.

"What *is* this?" The color was so unlike any beer she'd ever tasted, she felt leery of trying it.

Chase smiled. "It's called porter. Just take a sip and tell me what you think." They all stopped and watched as Harper took a very small taste. "Hum." She took another. "That's not bad. I'll see what I can do."

Chase nodded, looking pleased. "I'll get Andrew to come by and say hi. If you don't like it, let him know and we'll bring over a seltzer."

A few minutes later, a tall bearded man, his blond hair pulled into a manbun, wearing khaki shorts and a t-shirt identical to Chase's, came over. He said hi to Deanna and Dashawn and then looked at Harper. "So this is our new neighbor. Nice to meet you. I'm Andrew."

Harper liked him immediately. His eyes signaled an expansive, friendly disposition. "Hi Andrew." She raised her glass. "I really like your porter."

He nodded. "It's an acquired taste for some, love at first sip for others. I'm glad you like it. I'd love to stay and chat, but we're shorthanded tonight. Stop in anytime! And thanks for the cookies and the gift cards! Once your shop opens, we'll pay *you* a visit!" And with that, he was gone.

Deanna shook her head. "Those guys are great. I love them both. But they work so hard—I don't know how they do it."

Harper tapped her foot in time to the background music. The playlist contained a mix of music she loved but hadn't heard in years, including songs by The Band, Elton John, INXS, and some grunge numbers from the nineties. It made her feel young again. If she'd picked the songs herself, she couldn't have done a better job. Every now and then, a song was thrown in that she had pretended not to like—but really did—when Olivia took control of the music choices when she was in high school. She recognized one by The Offspring.

Harper's sips of the porter grew progressively larger as she drank. The walk to the brewery through the August heat had made her thirsty, and this beer was truly delicious. After a while she smiled expansively at her table mates. "This stuff is great! Where has it been all my life?" They both laughed.

Harper caught sight of Walt at the bar, watching her, his hair sticking out erratically around his head. He nodded to her and raised his glass. Harper smiled broadly and raised hers in return. When he turned back to the bar, she asked, "So, what's the deal with Walt?"

"Huh?" Dashawn looked around. "You mean Walt, at the bar?"

Harper tapped her fingers in time to the music on the table-top. "Yep. What's his story?"

"Well, he's interesting. My understanding is, he's lived here all his life. We moved here around twenty-five years ago, right Sweetness?" He placed his hand over Deanna's. She nodded. "When we first moved here, Walt was making money doing odd jobs. I'd hire him sometimes when I needed an ace carpenter. He doesn't live in town. I'm not sure where he lives, but he's in town a lot. That guy's quiet. I've met lots of reserved people—I think you're another one—but he stands out. And another thing about him is, he never seems to age. He looks about the same as he did when we moved here. He quit doing odd jobs about fifteen years ago. I don't know how he makes his money now."

Deanna nodded. "Walt's a good guy. But, like Dashawn says, he doesn't talk much." She looked at Harper and the corners of her mouth turned up slightly. "Why, Harper? Are you interested in our Walt?" She wiggled her eyebrows suggestively.

"What? No!" Then Harper watched in horror as Walt got up from the bar with a light-colored, but cloudy beer in his hand and headed toward their table. "I was just curious, that's all."

Dashawn and Deanna welcomed Walt as an old friend. Harper breathed in the fresh air scent that he brought with him, like clothes dried on a line outside. Maybe she should ask him what detergent he used. She stifled a giggle at the thought as Dashawn said, "Walt, have a seat, my man. I'm heading over to get another beer. Either of you ladies want another? Harper, you sure did make short work of that porter." Harper hadn't eaten dinner, planning to have a snack at the brewery, but now she didn't feel hungry. Pulling a ten-dollar bill from her purse, she handed it to him. "I want another one just like this." She touched the mirror in her purse briefly with her fingers before closing the bag. All at once, she felt a soaring sense of happiness.

Deanna polished off her ale. "Sure, 'Shawn. But this time, get me a stout."

"Sure thing, Baby." He headed to the bar. While waiting for Dashawn to return, Harper, Deanna, and Walt talked about the Fourth of July celebration. Deanna had worked at the coffee shop that day and had headed over with Dashawn after closing time—around 4:30. Harper had barely missed them. She was surprised when Walt said he was at the festival all day.

"I never saw you there. But then, there was a big crowd." Harper gave him a loopy smile.

Walt peered at her over his beer. "Oh, I saw you on the edge of the field under some trees. It looked like you were taking a nap, from where I sat."

Harper could feel her cheeks get warm. She hoped her face wasn't turning red.

Deanna leaned back to get a good look at her friend. "You fell asleep at the festival?"

Harper smiled sheepishly. "Well, it was warm, I was full of cherry pie, and I guess I was tired." She flashed another goofy grin.

Walt smiled down at his beer. "Hey, it's all good. We're all glad you feel comfortable here. This really is a special place."

After Dashawn returned with three more beers, they all made a toast to their lives in Whippoorwill Gap. The world outside the windows had turned obsidian black. The brewery was now full of laughing people and the playlist had ended as a band set up to play.

"What kind of owl is that over the bar?" Harper yelled over the noise. "I've never seen such a little one before. It's shaped different from most of the ones I've seen."

Walt looked at her and one side of his mouth shot up in a half-grin. "That's not an owl, Harper, it's a whippoorwill."

"Oh." For the second time that evening, Harper's cheeks grew warm with embarrassment, but Deanna came to her rescue. "I've always thought they looked like owls, myself."

Harper sent a grateful glance toward her friend. "Why is it I've never heard a whippoorwill's song since I moved here? Other birds sing like they're auditioning for parts at the theatre. I used to love to hear whippoorwills when I was a kid. But, now that I think about it, I haven't heard a single one since..."

Then everyone abruptly looked up above her head. When Harper turned, she found herself staring into Bryan Greene's blue eyes.

He looked freshly shaven and smelled of something spicy. For the first time, she noticed that his dark hair was graying at the temples. She expected him to have his wife with him, but he appeared to be alone.

His eyes settled on her. "Well, fancy meeting you here. How are things going at your bookshop?"

Walt, who had been wearing what Harper had to admit was a handsome smile, now looked down at the table with a scowl.

"Things are going great so far, Bryan." Feeling generous, she gave him a broad, happy smile.

His stare was intense while she spoke, but when she smiled, he relaxed, straightening up and smiling himself. "That's great! Good to hear. Well, I hope you all have a good evening." With that, he nodded to everyone. Dashawn and Deanna nodded back; Walt vacantly returned his gaze. Bryan turned and headed toward the bar just as the band began playing. He took a seat with his back to them.

Whoa, Harper thought, *what was that about?*

Dashawn and Walt began yelling a conversation between them, but with the indie rock band playing, she couldn't hear anything they said. Deanna tapped her foot. She seemed happy listening to the music. But suddenly, Harper felt dizzy. She'd known the porter was weaker than wine, so she'd assumed it was okay to drink it quickly. On top of that, she'd downed her two glasses on an empty stomach.

As the band launched into a White Stripes cover, she suddenly didn't want to be there anymore. She wanted to be home in bed.

Deanna yelled in her ear, "Harper, are you alright? You're looking a little green."

Harper shook her head and tried to smile. "I'll be okay, but I'm ready to leave whenever you guys are."

"Want another?" Dashawn motioned towards Harper's glass.

"Good grief! No!" Harper said, wiping her hand across her brow, as a wave a queasiness surged over her.

Deanna looked concerned. "Drink up, Dashawn. We need to get our buddy home."

They said their goodnights to Walt. And within minutes, they were on their way back to their corner of Oak Street. It was only 9:00, but that was late enough for Harper. Deanna and Dashawn said goodnight at the shop's front door. Neither Fae nor robins were around, so she made her way quietly up the stairs. As she closed the living room's windows, she heard the owl hooting in the park.

The lamp on her bedside table had been turned on for her. Beside it, a small green ceramic tray held two aspirin and a large glass of water.

Harper decided to wait until the morning to see if she needed to take the pain reliever. But then she frowned as a thought occurred to her.

How do they know I might need that? Have they been spying on me?

Twelve

⸺ ◈ ⸺

By late August, the main floor's two special collections rooms were framed in, then covered with painted drywall, providing two windowless spaces in the middle of the shop. This created a large open space in the rear, with its south-facing windows, providing light that made its way up the wide hallway to the front. The two closed rooms added interest to the space and would provide cozy reading and study spaces for the most valuable books.

Toward the shop front, the area nestled outside the smaller room formed the perfect space for a children's nook. To decorate it, Harper had bought a large, colorful rag rug, small rocking chairs, and a bright red armchair and matching loveseat. The entire front section of the shop was painted a pale shade of buttercup yellow. The open back space was sky blue, while the smaller rooms were bright spring green. The displays Harper was experimenting with in the front windows were drawing a lot of attention. As she considered her progress so far, Harper was pleased and excited by how things were shaping up. But there was still a lot to do.

For the first few weeks after they met, the faeries had given Harper plenty of space. When she'd asked about the pills on her dresser after her trip to the brewery, they found it amusing.

Earl Grey stood up and patted her lightly on the arm. "Well, you see, Tarryfoot and me, sometimes we get a hankering for beer. We head up to the brewery to breathe in the fumes, so to speak. We were surprised, but delighted, to find you there enjoying a few pints with the neighbors!"

The thought of the Fae hanging about the brewery struck Harper as amusing. And at least she knew they weren't following her around.

Even so, as they got to know one another better, Harper became increasingly concerned about her privacy. She'd moved to Whippoorwill Gap to create a new life for herself, on her own terms. She knew the faeries wanted what was best for the shop. And they seemed sincerely concerned about her welfare. While they hadn't made any effort to influence anything she'd done, she wanted to continue having the freedom to make her own choices and live with the consequences. Though she knew it wasn't fair, she found herself increasingly wary and on the alert for incursions.

She was torn about letting them do so much for her. Their habit of popping in and out of her apartment bothered her most of all. They weren't terrible about it. Some of them, like Ivy and Ash, had never once showed up unannounced. But others, particularly the brownies and the sprites, seemed to feel entitled to show up whenever and wherever they wished.

One morning, when walking out of her bathroom wrapped only in a towel, she flew into a tizzy after almost tripping over Tiptoe and Tarryfoot, who were preparing to repair a bit of crown molding on the ceiling that hadn't been nailed into the corner to their satisfaction.

And more than once, when she had been ready to settle in to read on the couch at night, Alida and Lily had popped in, wanting her to read aloud to them. They brought along their favorite book, *Folktales from Around the World.* She was impressed that the small creatures had the strength to carry such a large book. Honestly, it was endearing in its way. But while she didn't mind reading to them, she wasn't entirely pleased at their showing up unannounced.

Harper understood that it was up to her to set boundaries. But she feared offending her new friends, and that kept her from being forthright. As the days went on, she became increasingly uneasy, and sometimes resentful, about their presence. But she didn't want them to disappear entirely. Not knowing what to do about the situation, she convinced herself it would sort itself out eventually.

Early on, Harper had learned that speaking up for her needs always proved more trouble than it was worth. When she was a small child, her parents became incensed when she asked for what she wanted. As she got older, it seemed her friends and classmates didn't care when she got upset. With Tim's affair, she cemented the habit of maintaining a polite veneer of acceptance over her rage. By now it felt like the normal course of events, and she regarded her own needs with icy indifference. Harper imagined that, like everyone else in her life, the Fae would do what they would do, regardless of how she felt about it.

While mulling over the situation one morning as she surveyed the window displays, Harper remembered a long-buried experience with her father.

She had always loved the dance classes her parents' first enrolled her in when she was five. Moving around while the music played made her feel free and lighthearted. In her mind, she was a princess or a graceful swan. While she danced, all was right with her world.

Sometime around age seven, she noticed that her friend Sharon was always picked up from practice by her dad. He'd wait outside their car in the parking lot until Sharon left the building. Then she would run up to him, and he would pick her up and swing her around. When he sat her back on her feet, he would look at her with love. Then he would say, "How did dance practice go, Princess? Are you ready for some ice cream?"

After Harper wistfully watched this a few times, she convinced herself the same thing would happen with her dad if only he would pick her up from practice. Usually Harper's mom came to get her, always in a hurry to drop her off at home so she could go back to the office. Harper told herself that if her dad ever picked her up, she would run up to him, like Sharon did to her father. Then, she just knew her dad would look at her the way Sharon's dad looked at Sharon. And while the ice cream afterwards would be nice, Harper wouldn't ask for it. Instead, she would be happy with the swing and the smile.

Then one spring day, she got her wish. It was less than a week until the school's recitals, and everyone was excited. Harper was dancing the lead part in her class's performance. She had practiced the part over and over, alone in her room, and she was electric with pride and excitement. Her teacher had been especially pleased at her performance that day.

As she left practice, she scanned the parking lot for her mom's sedan. The sedan was there, but instead of her mom, Harper saw her dad standing beside it. Her heart leapt. This was going to be her perfect day. He looked so handsome in his leisure suit. To her eyes he looked better than the Six Million-Dollar Man. Standing beside him was a lady with blonde hair who was wearing a red minidress. Harper didn't recognize the woman, but that didn't matter. She knew her time had come.

She took off running toward him, but her father never turned to look at her. So she yelled, "Daddy! Daddy!" But instead of stooping down to pick her up, he frowned and held up a hand to stop her.

His jaw tightened, and he looked at her the way he did when she accidentally knocked over her milk. "Harper! Show some manners."

Then he dropped his hand, gripping her shoulder firmly. "Marie, this is my daughter Harper. Please excuse her, sometimes she gets carried away with herself. Harper, this is my new business associate, Marie Boone. We were just finishing up some business. Get in the car and wait—quietly. I'll take you home when I'm done."

Harper was mortified. From that point on, she expected nothing from her father. Life was less painful that way. A few years later, he moved out of their house to live with Marie Boone. Harper's mom, having gotten a big settlement with generous child support, was mollified. She quickly began dating again, herself. His absence made little difference to Harper at all.

Looking back, she could see why, early on, she had decided it was best to be quiet and put up with whatever presented itself. The only problem was that, sometimes, she lost her temper without warning and would inevitably embarrass herself. Along the way, she became convinced that, with social interactions so painful, she'd be safer alone. And now that she'd finally secured a refuge, it looked as though she wasn't going to be completely safe here, either.

After involuntarily screaming at the sight of Tiptoe and Tarryfoot, she had calmed down and asked them to let her know when they planned to fix something in the apartment before they came in to fix it. They had agreed to do so, although they seemed puzzled by the request.

But the two small sprites didn't just pop in unexpectedly to her apartment: they also frequently loitered about, chatting with her while she worked. Sometimes Harper didn't mind, but sometimes she needed to concentrate, and their prattle was distracting.

But, she also reflected, in some ways it was great to have them around. She still appreciated never needing to clean or to hire a housekeeper. She especially enjoyed Piper's occasional gifts of fresh wild berries and herbs, all neatly labeled for her. On a few especially busy days, Harper had come upstairs to find a loaf of homemade bread, cheese, and fruit waiting on the kitchen table. How could she object to that? But then another disturbing thought intruded. Since they could make themselves invisible, how did she know they weren't spying on her when she thought she was alone?

But with the grand opening only two months away, she had too many other claims on her attention to devote much time to this one. Harper decided to handle situations with the faeries as they came up. They clearly meant well. With luck, everything would settle on its own without too much fuss.

What she really needed now, she thought, was a trusted friend to talk to. Olivia had neither the time nor interest to be that person. She didn't really know Deanna that well yet. But there was one person who fit the bill. For the past decade or so, Gina had been her only confidant. Generally cheerful and a sympathetic listener, Gina never became overly involved or told Harper what to do. And while Harper couldn't talk to Gina about the Fae troop, she could get her friend's reactions to the shop ... and Quinn ... and Bryan Greene. She wasn't sure if she wanted Gina's thoughts on Walt.

But before she invited Gina for a visit, she wanted to discuss her concerns with Piper. It wouldn't do for them to flit in and out during the visit. Even if Gina only saw robins, it would be awkward to try to explain why birds were in her kitchen.

While working downstairs one afternoon, she spied Piper sitting atop a shelf with a book in her hand. She invited the Fae upstairs for a glass of homemade lemonade. Piper smacked her lips in appreciation. "I haven't had any of this since the shop first opened. A little girl used to have her mother leave this out for us sometimes. I do miss the old days every now and then."

It pleased Harper to make Piper happy. She laid out her concerns. "Do you remember when I first came to look at the shop?"

"Oh, yes, Dearie, I do. You were with that plump, cheerful looking lady with the long wavy black hair."

Harper smiled, gratified she remembered. "That lady's name is Gina. She's an old friend of mine. I'd like to have her visit for a few days. But—"

"But you would like all of us to be scarce," Piper finished for her. "Don't you worry, Dearie. I'll tell the others. We'll be completely invisible. As you know, we always look like robins to those who shouldn't see us."

"Yes, but Gina might be surprised and upset to find robins inside my shop and apartment."

Piper laughed. The twinkling sound never failed to make Harper smile. "Yes. I do see your point. But you need never worry about that. Not with your guests and not with your customers. Remember, we've got lots of experience with this sort of thing, we have. To tell you the truth, we're very good at hiding when we want to."

Harper nodded. Her firsthand experience had proved Piper right.

Piper turned her round, black eyes to Harper's hazel ones. "In fact, we can stay away from the shop altogether while your friend is here, if that's what you'd like."

Harper hadn't known this was an option. She assumed they always stuck close to the shop. She thought for a second. "No, Piper. I trust you all to be discreet."

After nodding her agreement, Piper began to chatter away, relating the most amusing recent adventures of Tiptoe and Tarryfoot about town. Thus occupied, the afternoon passed pleasantly for them both.

Gina excitedly accepted Harper's invitation for the weekend before her fall community college classes were to begin. She said a trip to Harper's would give her a chance to unwind before starting the new semester. Though she offered to stay in a hotel or inn, Harper insisted she stay in one of the guest bedrooms in the apartment. By now, she had decorated and furnished both rooms, making them nice for company.

The following Friday evening, Harper had the pleasure of seeing the apartment afresh through her friend's eyes.

"Harper, this is so *you*!" Gina walked around with unmasked enthusiasm. "I love the bright colors and the sweet, old-fashioned furniture! It's all so cozy. It makes me want to redo my place. I never thought you belonged in that big house in Raleigh. It was too formal for you."

Harper laughed out loud. "Thanks, Gina! I agree with you about that! And you're welcome to visit here anytime. Bring Jim if you can talk him into it. There's always a lot going on. We could have lots of fun!"

Gina's eyes sparkled. "I know Jim would love to come. We'll do that sometime. But we can have a great time without him along. I'd love to get to know this place while the weather's warm. It was nice back in November, but now we can explore all of it without the shivers. I brought my walking shoes and my appetite. Could we walk the trail around the town again tomorrow? It would be nice to see it with the leaves still on the trees!"

"I love that idea! As a matter of fact, I haven't walked it since that day, either. It will give me a chance to play tour guide and share everything I've learned about the place since I moved here." Harper grinned as she led the way to her balcony. "The whole place is decked out in pink, white, and purple Crepe Myrtle right now, so it should be gorgeous. But now let's decide on a place for dinner tonight. Do you like beer?"

"Yes, I do. But unless I'm thinking of the wrong person, you don't." They settled into the green- and red-striped cushions on the steel mesh chairs on Harper's balcony with glasses of iced tea.

"To my amazement, I've discovered since moving here that not all beers are the same. If you don't mind pub food, I know just the place to have dinner tonight. I've made reservations for the winery tomorrow night."

Gina held up a tall glass of tea. "I'll drink to that!" They clinked their glasses together in the warm summer afternoon air.

At the Take Flight that night, Bryan Greene came in alone again and stopped by their table on his way to the bar. Harper was beginning to wonder if she was wrong about his marital status. Not that she cared, she told herself.

He tipped his ball cap. "Harper."

Gina smiled at him as Harper introduced them. "I remember you! Harper and I stopped by your shop in November!"

"I'm sorry, we were awfully busy that day. I do remember meeting Harper. You were with her?"

Gina nodded, no less enthusiastic. "You can't be expected to remember everyone."

"No, unfortunately not." He turned to Harper. "How's the shop coming? Any idea of when you'll be ready to open?"

Harper looked at him with what she hoped was a vacuous expression. She didn't want to talk shop, or anything else, with him right now. "Fine, Bryan. It's coming along. Unless something goes wrong, I plan to open during the weekend of the Whippoorwill Gap Mountain Folklife Festival."

His eyebrows shot up and he looked impressed. "Well, that should start it off with a bang. Do you realize how busy that weekend will be?"

She raised one eyebrow and nodded. "That's why I picked it. I wanted to get the word out that the shop was open. I figured the more people who see it then, the better."

Gina was all ears. "When is the Mountain Folklife Festival? I've heard of it, but I don't know anything about it."

"It's always the third weekend in October." She looked at Bryan. "Isn't that right?"

He pursed his lips, nodded, then looked at Gina. "Harper will be too busy for a visit, but if you can get a hotel room or a camping spot, you'd probably enjoy the event. It's quite a party. Well, I won't keep you from your dinner. Have a nice night."

He made his way to the bar as Gina turned to Harper and grinned. "I still say he's *cute*!" She took a bite of a pub chip. "But there's someone else in here who doesn't seem to like you talking to him."

"Who?" Harper turned around just in time to see Walt turning back toward the bar. How had she missed seeing him there?

Gina smirked at her. "The lumberjack-look-alike guy at the bar."

"Oh, Gina! Don't be silly. That's Walt Howell. Believe me. He has no interest in me. And even if he did, I don't care." But Harper's smile belied her words.

Gina kept her eyes on her plate. "I wouldn't be so sure about that. He looked pretty interested when we walked in, and he's been turning around to look at you ever since."

Despite her protests, Harper's stomach did a loop-the-loop. Suddenly, she wasn't interested in eating her steak wrap. Walt never walked over though, and he didn't turn around when they left.

As the two women finished their walk at Puckett's Park the next afternoon, Gina said, "Will you look at that!"

Harper's eyes followed the direction of her friend's finger and saw all of them: the gnome, the brownies, the sprites, the nymph, and the three other Fae, playing what looked like a ball game under a nearby maple tree. She felt the color drain from her cheeks. But before she could say anything, Gina added, "Where are all these robins coming from? I remember seeing a bunch of them around here back in November. I guess it makes sense for them to be here this time of year, though. And look at this big boy." Earl Grey broke away from the others, hopping toward them. "Hi there, Good Fellow!" she said cheerfully.

Earl Grey nodded politely. "Good afternoon, Madame."

Harper almost choked. But Gina looked at her and smiled. "I swear I believe he's chirping at me."

Just then they heard a "Whoo-who-who-who-whooo ..." from the riverside. Gina straightened up. "Harper! Is that the same owl we saw here last fall?! It is, isn't it?! What is this, an enchanted park?"

Harper turned her head thoughtfully toward the sycamore tree. "He always seems to be here when I am."

Gina grinned. "Maybe he's watching out for you. And it seems like he's not the only one. Now, let's go get a muffin at the coffee shop! I've been wanting one of those since I saw them last fall."

Harper turned back towards the row of buildings with a happy sigh. "Sounds good to me! While we're there, I can introduce you to my friend, Deanna."

As they approached the park entrance at the corner, she turned back to look at the group in the park. Earl Grey caught her eye and gave a salute.

Thirteen

❖

After breakfasting on Harper's homemade oatmeal–blueberry pancakes and bacon, Gina left for Raleigh on Sunday around noon. Now that the workers were finished with remodeling, Harper had nothing to distract her from the heightening pressure the approaching grand opening had spawned.

Early Tuesday morning, she got an unexpected call from Olivia, who had decided she wanted her father's Eagle Scout memorabilia after all. Not only that, but she wanted to have it shipped to Toronto as soon as possible. While Harper didn't specifically remember what she'd done with Tim's patches, memory books, and assorted trophies, she did remember offering them to her daughter, who had turned them down. There was a possibility she'd stored the collection in a storage unit she'd rented outside of town, but she had no idea in which box to look.

What prompted Olivia to change her mind was a mystery. But with all Harper had to do to get the shop ready, it was annoying that she wanted it now. When she'd suggested Olivia come down to visit, see her new place, and search the storage unit herself, Olivia had gotten angry.

"Really, Mom? You're *there* and I'm in *Toronto*! I'm taking classes right now. Couldn't you take a few minutes to see if you could find it for me?"

Harper had tried to remain calm. "Olivia, I don't understand the rush to get this. I've got more than I can do right now. I'll go look for it after the shop opens and everything settles down, or you could come down before then and look for it while you're here."

The call had ended with her daughter acidly pointing out that Harper was always too self-absorbed to consider Olivia's feelings. Harper, as usual, had come away stunned and hurt. She wondered if she had been as hard on her own mother. Maybe she had. But if so, she doubted her mother ever let it bother her.

Already agitated, she stood in the small special collections room trying to switch her attention to the dilemma before her. She had already decided to put the folklore books in the larger room. What sort of collection should be placed in this room? Several options presented themselves: one was a creative arts collection, another was cookbooks, and still another was nature writing. This last option, she thought, would probably make the most sense. People who came out to hike and kayak in the surrounding mountains might be interested in buying those kinds of books. The problem was that nature writing wasn't one of her primary interests.

When she'd discovered the shop came with a ready-made folklore collection, she thought it would be fun to add another collection to serve as a passion project. Collecting rare and valuable books on a topic she really cared about would give her the opportunity to learn more about the topic and then, if all went well, to sell the collection when she retired. In so doing, she hoped to leave an endowment to a cause she cared about. It was important that it be something she created through her own efforts.

From the beginning, she'd wished to have this room ready for the grand opening. That way, she could leverage the crowds who visited during opening weekend. Maybe some of these customers would provide leads for finding more of those types of books. But right now, only empty shelves lined the room's walls. Time was growing short, and she was increasingly frustrated with her inability to decide.

To distract herself, she turned her attention to the large folklore room across the wide hallway. She surveyed this room with satisfaction. Lined floor to ceiling with shelves and double-sided, three-foot shelving units in the middle of the floor, it contained plenty of room for the folklore books still stored in the basement, waiting for the trip upstairs in the elevator.

Let's do it, she thought to herself. Heading to the basement, she loaded a few boxes into the elevator and wheeled them to the doorway, where she left them outside the room. Then, though it was still early, she decided to call it a day. Hoping to make up with Olivia, she drove to the storage unit to see if she could locate Tim's Eagle Scout collection. While she was at it, she'd mull over what to put in the small room. With any luck all would become clear after a good night's sleep.

Fortunately, she found the Eagle Scout collection without too much trouble. She called Olivia, who was happy to hear she'd be getting it soon.

She sounded contrite. "I'm sorry I blew my stack, Mom. But I wanted to show my new academic advisor Dad's collection. He's a former Eagle Scout himself. I thought it would be a good way to bond with him."

Happy she had settled one issue, Harper planned to take the box of memorabilia to the post office after lunch.

But when she made her way downstairs, her composure evaporated as she realized she was no closer to a decision about the new collection than she had been the day before. No longer merely concerned, she was becoming agitated over her indecision. How was she supposed to run a business if she couldn't resolve something this simple? Her entire body was taut with anxiety.

In this frame of mind, she became aware that the books she'd left in the hallway had already been removed from the box and neatly arranged on a shelf near the folklore room's doorway. She hadn't yet decided where she wanted to place these books on the shelves. And, as they say in the South, that fixed it. She heard herself asking in a waspish tone, "Who shelved these books?"

Alida's dark head popped up over a table. "I did!" She beamed at Harper as if expecting praise.

Harper gave the little sprite a stony stare while exhaling a long, loud breath. "Alida, could you please find the others and have them meet me in the back of the shop by the windows?"

Alida's smile faded as she nodded and disappeared. By the time Harper walked the short distance to the back, all the faeries were waiting. They looked at her expectantly. She began venting her frustration. "Look. Don't think I don't appreciate all the help you've all given me, but from here on out, I'd prefer it if you'd *ask* me before you change or help with anything." Rather than taking wind from her sails, expressing her annoyance only seemed to increase its strength.

Her volume rose as she plowed on, "And would it be possible for you all to actually knock on my door upstairs, and wait for me to invite you before you come in? I need my alone time. It makes me nervous when folks show up unannounced." Now on a roll, she continued without pause. She looked at Alida and Lily. "And I can't think with you guys gabbing at me when I'm trying to work. Maybe it would be best if you let me work by myself, at least until the grand opening is behind me." The two sprites hung their heads. But Harper still wasn't finished.

Later, thinking back on it, she had no idea what possessed her to say what she said next, but it was out of her mouth before she thought it through. "Honestly, if I had known you were here, I probably wouldn't have bought this place at all." As soon as these words were past her lips, she heard a small gasp.

She stopped speaking and waited for their response. When none of them moved after her speech, she grew alarmed. Was she missing something? She had only expressed her understandable feelings. But they all just stood there, staring at her wide-eyed for a long moment. Then Hawthorne responded gravely, "We will do whatever you wish. But you must remember we've considered this shop our home for over a century now. It won't be easy to change our habits. Everything we do is intended to help."

Most of them, except for Hawthorne, Piper, and Ivy, looked at the floor as they nodded. They reminded her of children who had been chastised. Harper thought back to the times her father had gotten angry with her when she had only meant to show her love. Suddenly, she felt mean and petty. If she had been honest with them from the beginning, this whole scene could have been avoided.

She was especially chastened to see that Alida appeared humiliated. Her little green cheeks were tinged with gray. She burst out, "It's all my fault. I'm sorry!" She placed her face in her small hands as Ivy moved behind her and placed her arm around the sprite's narrow shoulders while glaring at Harper over her head.

Harper, recognizing that she had offended them, desperately cast about for some way to soften her message. "Maybe that came across too harsh. But wouldn't you all like a break from working now and then? Listen, I've been thinking about making a space for you all under the stairs in the basement. Would you like that? We could put cushions in there and whatever else you'd like. I'll bring food to you."

The room was completely hushed for a few more seconds. Then, ignoring what Harper had just said, Ivy looked her in the eye for a moment before elevating her chin. "Yes. Of course. It is your shop. You bought it without knowing about us. You had plans for it. And of course you're free to run it as you see fit. But Alida was only trying to help. She and Lily talk with you because they like you. If we had known our help wasn't wanted and that our company wasn't appreciated, we wouldn't have offered it. If you don't want us here at all, say so. We can go."

"No!" Harper felt icy when the import of her last statement fully hit her. "No! I *do* want you here. I just want ... to be in charge, that's all." Her chest began to ache, and she was having trouble thinking. "Please don't be angry. I didn't mean that I don't want you here." She looked at their downcast faces.

They nodded with somber expressions. Then, in pairs, they left the room. They didn't simply disappear, as they sometimes did, especially when they were happy. They walked away. Finally, the only one left with her was Hawthorne. He stood there looking at her with his fathomless, inscrutable eyes.

He spoke plainly. "You need to remember you are not dealing with humans. We do not live by your rules. If you had made such a speech to many of our kind, you would have already found yourself alone with no hope of a return."

She met his gaze with misery. "I didn't mean to sound so ungrateful."

"There are things you need to understand. First, we *never* mean offense to anyone who owns this shop. But we have, all of us, pledged ourselves to be of help here. If we can't help, in the best way we see fit, there is no reason for us to stay. You see, if we consent to do only what you ask us to do, and nothing more, we are little more than unpaid servants. The one thing we value above all else is our freedom...our agency. What you are asking would deprive us of that."

Harper looked out the window, a knot forming inside her throat. "I had hoped you stay here because you like me."

He gave a small chuckle. "Our *feelings* about you do not matter overmuch. Some of us *do*, in fact, *like* you, very much. Not one of us dislikes you. We understand your need for privacy. It may not seem so to you, but we've tried to be mindful. Changes can be arranged. From today forward, we will wait to be invited to come to join you upstairs, unless you change your mind. But you must understand—if we are not allowed to freely serve here with joy, we will leave, and we won't come back until our efforts are welcome again."

Harper felt as though her brain had turned to lead. All her life, she had been unable to think when people were angry with her. She searched miserably for a way to put things right. "I expressed myself too strongly. I didn't mean to offend any of you. But I see I have. Tell me how I can make it up to you all."

Harper became increasingly uneasy as he stood mute and unmoving for a few moments more.

Then he sighed. "We will discuss the situation among ourselves. I believe you are not totally at fault. You need to learn some things about us. And there are crucial matters you need to understand about *yourself*. I will let you know what we decide. I promise we won't leave for good without saying goodbye."

Harper nodded, too stunned to speak. Even though she regretted hurting their feelings, before Hawthorne had left the room, she was already defending herself in her mind. They were overreacting. Why they took her request so gravely made no sense. She may have been a bit harsh in her delivery, and she regretted her last statement about not buying the shop, but her request wasn't unreasonable. After all, it was her shop. Naturally, she wanted to be in control. She decided they were being oversensitive. They would get over it with time, she thought as she stood up and made her weary way back to the folklore room.

As she walked through the doorway, her foot caught on something and she crashed to the floor. After catching her breath, she saw that the box of books she had left out the night before had been repacked and placed barely inside the room's doorway. She sat still for several minutes waiting to see if anyone would offer to help her up from the floor. When no one did, she made her way slowly to her feet and placed a hand on her shin. She could feel the bruises forming already.

Fourteen

A WEEK SLUNK BY before Harper saw any of the faeries again. None were outside the shop as robins, neither were there signs of them in the building. Dust began to pile up on the furniture, food was no longer waiting for her, and one morning she realized her bathroom needed cleaning. She hadn't encountered a dirty bathroom since she left her rental cottage. The smell of the river and pines faded, then disappeared. The building lost its feeling of enchantment.

Even worse, she began to feel lonesome. She pulled out her mirror every night, with no clue how to stop the mist encroaching its surface once again. She yearned to have Piper leave her something—anything—to eat. She yearned for the sprites to unexpectedly appear for an evening's read aloud.

By the time Hawthorne finally knocked on her door, Harper had spent many hours reflecting. Now some of Olivia's grievances made sense. Yes, she had always done everything she believed a mother was expected to do. She'd attended ballgames and competitions. Without fail, Olivia had the equipment and clothes she needed. Harper had thrown birthday parties for her that featured clowns when her daughter was small and bands when she was a teenager. She'd joined parent–teacher organizations. She read to her daughter for as long as Olivia wanted her to. She had done everything she knew to do to be a good mother. But most of it had been done from a sense of duty, not deep affection.

For the first time, Harper realized in her own quiet way, she kept people, even her husband and daughter, at a distance. And now, with a chance for a do-over, she was following the same entrenched path in Whippoorwill Gap. Even though most of the people she'd met had been friendly, she jockeyed to keep herself secluded.

She ignored Quinn Ellis when he knocked on the door, and Bryan Greene rankled her ... okay, maybe that wasn't unreasonable. But shouldn't she give him a chance? He always tried to talk when they ran into each other. Maybe the aversion that she sensed came, not from him, but from her. And after the trip to the brewery, she had even avoided Deanna. And now, with these faeries who wanted nothing more than to make her happy, she'd done the same with them. The question was why.

While mulling this over one evening on her balcony, with only the notes of the katydids to keep her company, it dawned on Harper that perhaps she should be a little more open in her relationships.

The very next day, just as she finished her lunchtime yogurt and granola, Hawthorne knocked on her door. Elated to see him again, she invited him to join her for tea at the kitchen table.

As they settled down with their cups, Hawthorne got right to the point. "We've talked it over and formed a plan. Having received approval, we have a proposition for you."

"Approval?" She wasn't sure she liked the sound of that. Who could they need approval from? "I thought you guys were independent agents."

He fixed her with a grave stare. "As I told you before, that is the problem. There is much about us you do not know. Speaking of matters you know nothing about, have you looked into your mirror lately?"

It was a surprising question, so she pulled it from her pocket. "I look in it every day. Why? What does my mirror have to do with anything?"

He cleared his throat and looked down at her rug for a moment. "Have you noticed any changes in your mirror?"

She frowned and showed it to him. "It's starting to mist over again."

"I'm not surprised. It will continue to mist over until you learn more about our circumstances. To begin with, and as you no doubt suspected, we are not native to your world. To stay here for very long costs effort. We come from another place. You can call it the Faery Realm. But what you call it isn't important.

"We belong in *that* place. It is our home. We, those of us who share this space with you, choose to come here to be of service. But we do not have enough spare energy to stay with someone whose wishes and vitality are not attuned to ours. To do so would drain our life force dry. An important personage in our world has told us that it is essential you understand about where we come from. For that to happen, we need to take you to that other place—the Faery Realm."

The feeling of curiosity that swept over Harper was followed closely by foreboding. "I don't understand. How would we get there? Is it safe? I mean ... why can't you just tell me what I need to know? If I get it, maybe I won't need to go there after all."

Hawthorne's eyebrows rose into an arch. "No, I am afraid we cannot 'just tell you about it.' All will become clear after we pay our visit. Rest assured; this will only be a visit. You may return here when you wish." His teacup landed in its saucer with a clatter and he wiped up the resulting spill with a napkin.

"If you agree to go, Ivy and I will escort you. Once we have returned, you will decide the terms on which we stay. You may wish to break all contact with us, but you may also decide you want us to stay. But to make a wise choice that comes from your truest self, you need to understand what you may gain and what you may lose."

She wanted to argue that she had already thought about it, that she already understood what they meant to her. But after looking into his bottomless eyes once again, she admitted to herself she knew nothing.

"Will I be in danger?" She hated her cowardice, but she couldn't help herself.

"Everything in life presents danger of one sort or other. Yes, there are dangers for humans who visit our land. In fact, for most, the journey would be impossible. Some would call where we are going another dimension. That's not entirely accurate, but it gives you an idea of the difference between that realm and this. With Ivy and I to guide you, the danger is minimal provided you do as we tell you. And you are expected there. That is all I can say at present."

That grabbed Harper's attention. "Expected? Who would be expecting me in another world?"

He didn't answer. Instead, he pointed to her mirror. "That gift you treasure is more valuable than you know."

She wrapped her fist around it and clutched it to her chest. "I'd like to take it with me for luck."

His head swiveled from side to side. "That won't be necessary. In fact, it is not desirable. And, with us as your guides, you will not need it. But I repeat, you must follow our instructions, even when you don't wish to."

"Okay." Harper glanced around her cozy pink and green kitchen nervously, a sudden compulsion to scrub it down seizing her. "When will we go?"

Maneuvering his square form solidly from the chair to the floor, Hawthorne stood. "There's no time like the present."

Standing in response, Harper stammered, "Now?! What should I wear? Is there anything I should do to get ready?"

He took in her pajama-and-bathrobe-clad figure. "Wear whatever you like, though comfortable shoes are recommended. It would be good to take a jacket in case of chill. As I said, leave your mirror and your keys here. We will make sure you get back inside when we return. Oh, and bring a water bottle. You may get thirsty, and drinking anything there is unwise."

"Will we be gone long?"

"It's hard to say. Time functions differently there. We may seem to be there for many hours, but only seconds may pass here." He began tapping one foot pointedly on the floor, his eyes never leaving her face.

"Okaayy." She drew out the word, wanting to stall but not knowing how.

"Meet us at the park, down by the river, near the owl's tree." With that, he turned and walked out the door. Harper wondered briefly why he'd said, "the owl's tree," but the thought quickly evaporated. She knew the one he meant. She opened her mirror and looked inside. It was already completely misted over but hadn't begun to tarnish. She gave it a squeeze and held its cool surface to her forehead before laying it gently in the drawer beside her bedside table.

After changing into a long-sleeved t-shirt and hiking pants, she wrapped a fleece hoodie around her waist and donned a pair of sneakers. Then grabbing a bottle of water from the fridge and a small book she had found in the shop, she headed out the door.

Before locking the basement door behind her, she glanced toward the river and saw them all gathered under the owl's sycamore tree. For once, the owl was nowhere in sight. As Harper approached, none of them said a word, but they all gave her dignified nods.

Without considering whether people nearby might hear, she burst out, "Hey! I've missed you all so much!" She hurried over to Alida and got down on one knee. "I'm sorry for being so irritable with you. I *do* appreciate your help. Here, I brought you a present." And she handed over a copy of a little book, Fairies of the Trees by Mary Cecily Barker.

As Alida held out her slim little hand for the book and looked at it thoughtfully, she said, "Thank you, Harper. I wasn't mad, just a little sad. I'll share the book with Lily."

"Of course. I hope Lily enjoys it, too." Convinced that her offering wasn't enough, Harper stood glumly until Earl Grey caught her eye and gave her a wink. She smiled gratefully before looking timidly at Hawthorne and Ivy, who were standing apart from the others, silently waiting for her. Ivy stood straight, looking regal, in green pants, a white shirt, and her red vest. "Do you have your mirror with you?"

"No, Hawthorne said ..."

Ivy's hair whipped in the rising wind as she bestowed a small smile on Harper. Her eyes looked a shade warmer than they had the last time Harper had looked at them. "Good. We mustn't chance your losing it. Come with us if you are ready."

The two Fae turned and led her down the small path she had avoided since that scary day when she'd gotten lost back in January. But unlike its previous confounding track, today it quickly led them to the riverside, where they turned left and walked a short distance to a large granite rock. Here they stopped and turned to her again.

Ivy faced her. "This is your only chance to turn back if you wish. We caution you now that you may feel enchanted by what you see, hear, and feel when we get to the Faery Land. You will likely feel as though it is a place you've known before but cannot remember. You will encounter things that may shock you. But if you are willing, we are ready to escort you now."

Harper swallowed her frigid terror, determined to do whatever it took to get her friends back for good. She straightened her spine and raised her head, ignoring the pops and cracks in both as she did. Her answer held all the dignity she could muster. "Yes. I'm ready, please lead the way."

Ivy raised her hands to the riverbank, and the honeysuckle vines parted to reveal the entrance to a dark tunnel. Once inside, Harper had only inches above her head to spare, but the tunnel was wide enough for all three of them to walk side by side. She and Ivy followed Hawthorne.

Once inside, she felt more physically comfortable, sheltered from the whipping wind. The tunnel smelled pleasantly of earth, and its bottom was completely covered in soft, fallen leaves, which muffled the sound of their steps. Though the floor was smooth, the walls and ceiling occasionally revealed tree roots poking through. Her nose detected notes of plowed garden and ancient pipe tobacco. She found herself yearning to move forward, like she was heading toward some sublime joy. A line from Yeats entered her mind unbidden: "Come Away, oh human child."

After walking along the tunnel's twists and turns for twenty minutes or so, she noticed high windows off to the left letting in a diffuse, pearly light. Where had the light in the tunnel come from before the windows appeared? With a start, she realized it came from her two friends.

She stopped, straining to see out one of the windows, but Hawthorne shook his head. "It would be best if no other beings here see you. Don't be frightened, but neither should you draw attention to yourself."

Despite his reassurances, Harper's hair began to rise, and her serenity cracked. She asked quietly if they could slow down so she could put on her jacket. The two made eye contact before they stopped. Her jacket felt substantial and comforting. By habit, she reached into her pocket and was momentarily disoriented when her hand closed around emptiness instead of her mirror. She forced her legs to move forward again to keep up with her companions.

After continuing for what Harper guessed was another twenty minutes, they came to a large chamber with earthen walls that held an old desk and chair, tables, chests, and shelves of very old, leather-bound books behind glass fronts. *Merlin's office.* Fascinated, she asked if they could stop and look at the books, but her escorts shook their heads no, and they continued to a tunnel opening in the opposite wall.

A short while later, they emerged into an open field. When they'd entered the tunnel, it had been late summer in Whip-poorwill Gap, but here it appeared to be the height of autumn. Forests formed a ring around a large field, overgrown with tall yellow grass, with gently sloping hills stretching to their left. An old barn and wagon stood, seemingly abandoned, near the top of the hill.

Despite the wild, deserted landscape, or perhaps because of it, Harper felt an unreasonable surge of happiness she hadn't felt since she was a young child. Fall was her favorite season. A homey smell of woodsmoke hung faintly in the air along with the heady scent of grapes and honey. Something tantalizing dangled on the edge of memory, but she couldn't grasp what. It was as though the air itself was rich with possibility. Taking a deep breath, she suddenly felt more intoxicated than she had after that first glass of porter—expansive, happy, and in love with everything. This is where I belong, she thought. I could stay here forever.

Fifteen

IVY MOVED AHEAD, TURNING left to descend the hill. Hawthorne and Harper followed close behind. While Ivy kept her gazed forward, Hawthorne, forehead furrowed, peered this way and that while sniffing the air.

Nothing about the environment caused Harper qualms. As Ivy had foreseen, she felt as though she had entered the land of her earliest dreams, when all was secure, and worries didn't exist. She remembered taking long walks with Grandma Sophie in the fall, stopping to gather pinecones in the forests and pumpkins at local farms, while admiring the beautiful leaves. And though not the October blue she remembered from her childhood, this luminous, pearl gray sky struck her as unaccountably lovely.

And it wasn't just the sky; everything was bewitchingly beautiful. On the edge of the field near the trees, she saw a little cream-colored cottage that reminded her of pictures in fairy tale books. Like the barn, it appeared to be abandoned. Ripe red apples lay scattered beneath a gnarly old tree to its side, while languid bees skirted leisurely from one rosy sphere to another. For a moment, she felt compelled to examine the structure's interior. If only she could convince her companions to let her peek into its windows.

She was about to ask when a stiff breeze began to blow, and she became distracted by the turmeric- and toffee-colored leaves that flew from the trees. The three figures made their way down the hill through the overgrown, dry-roasted grass that released a scent like freshly baked butter cookies as they stepped on it. Harper's heart began to ache with a yearning she didn't understand. She became increasingly convinced that *this* was where she had always belonged. She felt a pleasing mellow warmth at her back, though she could detect no sun. The sky itself seemed to radiate serenity. She turned her head to gauge how far they had come. Hawthorne glanced at her. "Don't look back, Harper. Keep your eyes to the front. You never know what may be lurking about over the hilltop."

Unperturbed, Harper returned her attention ahead. There, she saw a massive beech tree standing at the edge of the wood. As a child, she'd spent happy hours playing house underneath beech canopies while Grandma Sophie rested on their friendly roots. She realized with piercing sadness that she hadn't seen one of these trees up close since her grandma had died. The grief of losing her grandma hit her with an overwhelming wave of anguish as though it had just happened. Tears filled her eyes as she remembered that she never got a chance to say goodbye.

Then other trees towering around the beech drew her attention as the wind romped joyfully through their branches. Harper had never seen such majestic trees, their bright lemon-yellow leaves rattling in the wind. She pointed to them. "What are those?"

Hawthorne tilted his head up at a ninety-degree angle, straining to see to the tops. "American Chestnuts like these used to grow all over the east coast of your country. Ink disease and chestnut blight wiped out most of them. Your forests still mourn the tragedy. But, as you can see, their counterparts thrive here."

Harper looked at them in wonder until she was under their large branches. Her sadness forgotten, she only wanted to sit down and soak up the enchanting atmosphere. But Ivy continued her steady pace, taking them further into the wood. A little further downhill, Harper heard running water. As they walked on, the sound grew to a roar.

Ivy curved right, leading them through an assortment of hardwoods and evergreens of enormous height. The air became flooded with the bracing smell of pine. Then, Harper saw another magnificent beech right ahead, but instead of golden leaves, this one was crowned with royal purple. To its left, a path wended its way down to a thunderous river, where it ended at a cascade of silvery waterfalls. Everything about this place looked embroidered with gold. Once they reached the beech tree's trunk, Ivy halted. "We'll stop here. If you would like to drink some of the water you brought with you, it's safe to do so."

Harper sat down at the base of the mighty purple-clad tree, soaking in the surroundings. Light filtered through the treetops, and the air was laden with an intoxicating mixture of fallen leaves, earth, spices, and river water. The sky felt like a great soft gray blanket overhead, persuading Harper that all was well. The sound of falling water, and of music, the likes of which she had never heard, filled her ears with an enchanting symphony. Gradually, Harper understood the music was singing. It came from the trees, the river, and even from the rocks and the ground beneath her. She closed her eyes to immerse herself in the vibrations.

After a while, she realized all of it—the vibrations, the music, and even the light—was building in intensity. In response, her soul felt lifted and stretched somehow, as though she were becoming a part of it all. Hawthorne was sitting on one side of her; Ivy was on the other. Suddenly, both of them stood. Hawthorne touched her shoulder. "Stand. Brush off your clothes."

Ivy reached over to pick a few leaves from Harper's thick, unruly hair. As instructed, she opened her eyes and got to her feet. She could see silver light, edged in gold, growing across the river as its source approached through the trees. As it drew closer, she saw that a tall column of light was surrounded by smaller beings that resembled her Fae friends. They, too, had a light that seemed to emanate from within. All were dressed in simple but elegant robes in vivid hues Harper couldn't place. As she watched, they crossed the water on a stone bridge that had materialized when they reached the river's edge.

As they made their way up the hill toward the trio underneath the beech tree, Harper's heart leapt wildly, beating much faster than before. Her heart whispered that a joyful reunion was at hand.

When the light reached the edge of the giant tree's canopy, Hawthorne removed his hat. He and Ivy bowed low to the ground. "Queen Sophia."

Harper followed their lead and lowered her head. As the light grew closer, she felt a hand on her head and heard a clear, melodious voice saying, "Harper."

As she looked up at the being, the light faded, and she gasped.

In front of her stood Grandma Sophie. But instead of the sixty-five-year-old woman Harper remembered, she more closely resembled a picture of Grandma at age twenty-one, taken before she had married Grandpa Al. Her unlined face was lovely. Oddly, Grandma seemed as tall as she had when Harper was a child. Her auburn hair was crowned in a wreath of purple leaves.

Finding her voice, she exclaimed, "Grandma!? You're not dead? Are we in heaven?" She looked around for Hawthorne and Ivy, but they had disappeared, along with Grandma's attendants.

Harper found herself swaying in shock. As her knees buckled, Grandma caught her. "Have a seat, Harper." Instead of falling to the ground, she sank into an evergreen silk-covered sofa, which, like the bridge, had materialized from nowhere.

Overcome, she began crying hysterically. The intense light around Grandma faded as she reached into her robe and handed over a soft linen handkerchief. Then she waited silently until Harper's sobs turned to sniffles, then finally ended.

Harper sat still and waited for Grandma to explain herself. But as the quiet unwound itself interminably, she realized she would have to speak first. Her voice shook as she asked, "Is it okay if I give you a hug?"

"Of course, Darling!" Her grandma smiled and held out her arms. When Harper let go, she leaned back and drank in the sight of Grandma Sophie's face.

Then, with a rush, her questions came tumbling out. "Why did they never find you? Why are you here? Why did you give me that mirror before you died? Why didn't you tell me you were going to Whippoorwill Gap? How do you know Hawthorne and Ivy? Tell me everything!" She paused for breath, her chest tight.

"Is that all you want to know?" Her grandma leaned over with a smile and tucked a lock of Harper's hair behind her ear.

"Darling child," she said, her voice as clear and strong as Cate Blanchett's when she played Lady Galadriel. "I didn't want to leave you the way I did. But I had no choice. There isn't enough time to tell you everything right now. You, being mostly mortal, can only stay here a brief while. But I will tell you the most important things for you to understand right now."

Harper nodded; her overstuffed brain rendered her unable to think.

"Are you familiar with the word changeling?"

Harper remembered a poem in her literature textbook she had been obsessed with as an eighth-grade student. She even remembered parts of it: "On the wings of an owl I take my flight ... "[1] But what did it mean? It was one of those times when she knew the answer, but it wouldn't come to her.

She looked into her grandma's unearthly bright-green eyes, a sight that left her more confused. Grandma's eyes had been hazel, like her own. She shook her head. "I've heard the word *changeling*, but I don't know exactly what it means."

Taking Harper's hand in her own, Grandma continued. "In old times, people used to believe faeries were unfriendly characters. For good reason, too, because some of us *are*. As the stories went, the Fae would sometimes want a human child for themselves. When they found one they wanted, they would substitute a faery child for the human one. The human parents would be left with an alien being." She frowned. "Dreadful things sometimes happened when parents suspected their child had been stolen by the Fae.

"The stories weren't entirely false. Right before your tenth birthday, when I was sixty-five, I was visited by some emissaries from this land. And I was told, to my complete shock, that I, myself, had been a changeling child." She watched Harper, gauging her reaction.

Harper shook her head. "But that doesn't make sense. If faery children were strange, then you couldn't have been one, Grandma. You were the only person who ever made sense to me." She looked down at her grandmother's beautiful gown, which looked as though it were made of spiderwebs glistening with

---

1. Leah Bodine Drake, "Changeling." https://www.poemi st.com/leah-bodine-drake/changeling

morning dew. It made a spectacular contrast to the polyester pantsuits she wore in Harper's memories.

"Always remember, Harper, most stories you hear are only *partly* true. In my case, no human child was stolen away from the Earth Realm. I was in imminent danger when I was born. To save me, some of my people left me on the steps of an orphanage in Whippoorwill Gap, North Carolina. The orphanage is no longer there." She smiled at Harper's budding protest. "Yes, I know you've been researching me."

None of this made sense. Harper cast about for what confused her most. "But you were raised in Winterfield—that's over a hundred miles away from Whippoorwill Gap."

"Yes. Your great-grandparents in Winterfield wanted a child, but they were unable to have one. They had relatives in Whippoorwill Gap who checked with the orphanage there to see if they had any newborns available for adoption. When I had been there less than a week, they told your Great-Grandfather Bob and your Great-Grandma Sally about me. The couple drove over right away in their Model-T Ford, adopted me, and took me to Winterfield. They raised me there, and they were good parents. No one, except me, ever suspected I was different from everyone else."

"You thought you were different?" Harper studied the purple leaves forming the crown on Grandma's head.

"Yes, I did. From a young age, I could see creatures no one else could see. I often had visitors at night. They told me how the universe works, and other things most humans never guess at. They explained that there were other places, even right where I was, that other people couldn't see. When I was small, I would tell my parents about these beings, but it upset them. As I got older, they told me not to talk about it, ever again, to them or anyone else. They said I was too old for such foolishness." She smiled sadly as she shook her head.

"After that, my nighttime visits ended. But I kept seeing little people in bushes and trees, birds and animals changing into people—that sort of thing. After I got married and had children, those sightings became less frequent, too. But after you were born, I sensed you were different like me. I always felt our connection. But you never saw other beings until recently, did you?"

Harper's eyes dropped from the leaves circling her grandmother's head, to those carpeting the ground at her feet, and back up again. "Yes! I did, when I was very small. Sometimes I would look outside, and little people would be dancing on the back lawn in the moonlight. They waved at me sometimes. But I never told anyone. And after a while I stopped seeing them, too. I told myself they were imaginary. But I saw one a few times outside my home in Raleigh after my husband Tim passed away. And then, of course, I see them in my bookshop where I live now. And—wait a minute—how do you know Hawthorne and Ivy? Did they call you a queen a little while ago?"

Sophia straightened herself so that she now towered over Harper. Her voice gained power, echoing in the forest around them. "As you've no doubt figured out, I am, as some people say, Fae, a faery. Hawthorne and Ivy were correct to bow to me, and you were too. Indeed, I am a Faery Queen." Then she resumed her previous size and so did her voice. She put a hand beneath Harper's chin, lifting her face to her own. "And it's time you knew that you, yourself, have inherited a magical gift."

This was more than Harper had bargained for. She wasn't sure she even wanted a magical gift. "But what about Mom and Uncle Buddy? Did they have magical gifts, too? What about Beverly and John?"

At that, Grandma Sophie threw back her head and gave a hearty chortle. "None of my children, nor any of your cousins, inherited my magic. I'm certain of that. Their DNA was one-hundred-percent human."

"Did Mom and Dad know any of this about you, or about me?"

The beautiful head shook conclusively. "Oh Gracious, no. Your parents were so wrapped up in themselves, they had trouble seeing beyond their noses. They had no idea what was going on around them—not only about you and me—but about most things. Now, any more questions before I tell you about your new friends?"

Harper didn't want this meeting to ever end. "A million questions, Grandma! Why did you send me the mirror and then run off to Whippoorwill Gap to disappear like you did? I've been sad, ever since." Once again, her voice caught. "Did your accident hurt?"

"What accident?"

Harper's brows squeezed together in confusion. "They found your car after it ran off that cliff. But you were never found. I always wondered if you suffered."

Grandma put a hand to her forehead. "Oh, Dear. Poor Sadie. She was such a good sedan. No, I didn't know they did that to her. I guess it makes sense, though. There needed to be a cover story."

She looked back at Harper. "When I arrived in Whippoorwill Gap, a committee of Fae met me at a little park at the edge of town. I believe it's near your shop. Some of them came here with me while others stayed behind. I just assumed they left my car in the parking lot."

Harper sniffed. "Apparently not."

Her grandmother patted her shoulder. "My dear, dear child. I knew it would be hard for you. But I had no choice. I was told I must go to Whippoorwill Gap only a day after your family left for your beach trip. They gave me the mirror and told me to bring it with me. But instead, I sent it to you because I hoped it would make you feel a little better. I meant it to be something you could remember me by. I've been told since then that giving it to you was a grave mistake. But I don't regret my decision."

Harper leaned over and picked a bright purple leaf from the ground. "So, that's why I'd never seen it before."

"Yes, once I understood that if you had it, I could watch over you telepathically, that's what I planned to use it for. But then it quickly became so misted and tarnished, I couldn't see or hear you at all. I was pleased when you started coming through again when you moved to Whippoorwill Gap." She leaned over and blew softly on the leaf in Harper's hand, which instantly turned into a bouquet of leaves the color of purple cabbages.

Harper smiled in delight. "I knew it. I had a feeling you could hear me." She felt the leaves vibrating in her fingers. Opening her hand, they turned to bright, long-tailed violet butterflies and flew away.

Her grandmother watched them as they grew smaller, then disappeared. "Yes, let's try to keep the surface clear from now on." She turned her now plum-colored eyes to Harper's hazel ones. "I'll tell you the secret—stay true to your heart. Allow others to do the same. And that brings us to your new friends."

Harper looked around. "Where did they go?"

"They'll return when it's time to leave. Now, you must understand something about your friends. They are a special group, Harper. They possess, I suppose the best way to put it would be exalted spirits. You may think all of us here are like them, but you'd be sadly mistaken. Your friends are made of finer stuff, and desire, above all, to help inhabitants of the Earth Realm. Service rings true to their hearts. And I'm delighted to say, they come from my corner of the Fae Realm. But no Fae, no matter how noble or well intentioned, can help a human without their consent. Our natural law forbids it. They want to help you. Will you let them? If not, they will find another place to serve."

Harper knew she had been foolish, and she needed to explain herself. "I *don't* want them to leave! I admit I got angry with them. But I was already in a bad mood that day. I was afraid they were trying to control my life. I've struggled my entire life to live the way I want to. Now I'm confused. I was only being honest about my feelings at the time. Is it bad to want to be in charge?"

"Are any of us completely in charge of our lives? What you need to understand is that your friends don't want to tell you what to do. They want to help achieve what *you* desire in your heart. That's a very different thing from trying to control you. Do you see the difference?"

Harper nodded slowly. She didn't completely grasp why her small mistake was so grave. But then again, she wasn't dealing with fellow human beings here: Grandma had called them "exalted spirits." So they were definitely different from humans. "They just want me to be happy. And now I know that having their company makes me happy."

"That was good for you to learn. Who knows? Maybe you can help them one day. And that would be a blessing—for you."

Harper looked at the cascading water. "You said I have a magical gift. Is my gift seeing the Fae or something else?"

"Seeing the Fae—yes, that is a gift. But you also have another that is more amazing. Once you find it, it will change your life forever." She patted Harper's hand.

"Can you tell me what it is?" Harper was startled to see her grandmother's eyes had shifted color once again, now shining burnished gold.

Her grandmother chuckled. "No one can tell you what your gift is. You must discover that for yourself." She stood. "My time with you is done now. You must go back."

Her light grew piercingly bright, then in less than the time it takes to wink, Harper found herself standing at the edge of the massive forest, below the tunnel's entrance. Hawthorne and Ivy were waiting for her at the top of the hill. Harper looked around for Grandma Sophie, but she was gone, and the pearl gray sky was deepening into a charcoal twilight. In a daze, she made her way up the hill to her waiting friends.

Ivy and Hawthorne wordlessly bowed to her, then they all turned toward the tunnel. None of them spoke until they emerged at the riverbank. Harper felt a chill in the air. It would soon be fall here as well.

As the tunnel disappeared once again behind a covering of thick vines, Harper turned to her friends. "I want you all to stay. Grandma explained how things are with you. I'm honored you want to help me."

The two Fae smiled at her. "We know."

Back at the Robin's Nest, Harper felt ravenous and exhausted. She thanked Hawthorne and Ivy and said goodnight at the bottom of the stairs. Then she made her way up to her apartment on shaky legs.

Once inside, she was grateful for the pot of warm passionflower tea waiting on her kitchen table beneath a pink and white toile tea cozy. Beside it lay a spread of hummus, fresh bread, olives, and pears. Before she sat down to eat, she went to wash up. The bathroom was pristinely clean. Taking her jacket into her bedroom, she found the bedside lamp was on and the covers on her bed pulled back. Pulling her mirror from the nightstand drawer, she saw that it was crystal clear. "Thank you," she said gratefully. Then she went back to the kitchen table and sat down to her supper.

As she bit into the sweet, juicy pear, she heard the owl's call drifting in through the open living room windows.

Sixteen

"No, no, no!" Tiptoe shook his head decisively. "We'll have none of that! You may be pleasantly surprised at how skillful Tarryfoot and I can be with a needle!"

Tarryfoot stomped one foot in accord. "Just so."

"Well, okay, if it suits the two of you, it suits me." Harper had gathered them all together and shown them an online fabric catalog. Then she had each of them pick out fabric for their own cushions. On the day the bolts of cloth arrived, she met them all downstairs near their new room, the spacious closet under the stairs. Once she had their approval, she gathered up the cloth to take to a seamstress in town.

But when the brownies understood that she intended to pay for the labor, they were incensed. They insisted they would do the work themselves. They each whipped out a packet of needles in varying sizes and held them out for Harper's inspection to prove their fitness for the task. Harper gave in willingly. After handing over the cushions the fabric was to cover, she left them to their work.

That settled, she asked again about providing food for them. They'd responded yes, they would like food, if she didn't mind supplying it from November 1 through May 1. Unless something unusual was going on, during the rest of the year, they preferred to eat whatever nature itself offered.

The room was to be ready for them before November 1, a big holiday of theirs, when their winter season officially began. Harper had asked one of the carpenters who had worked on the shop to make a table, low to the ground, for them to use as they wished. She had chosen a forest green woolen carpet to cover the concrete floor. Harper asked about the stories that if you offered clothing to faeries, brownies in particular, they would leave and never return.

"That is correct." Tarryfoot chirped, pleased that she knew of the custom. "Emphasis there is on *clothing*. You're not planning to offer us little breeches and jackets now, are you?"

Harper assured him she wouldn't dare.

"Well then, it's not a problem, is it?" he asked as he cartwheeled away from her.

Harper was busy and happy, but also tired. While the visit with Grandma Sophie had been comforting, it was also a shock. She felt overrun by emotions and memories. Her worldview had undergone a complete overhaul. Since she was ten years old, she had convinced herself that she was nothing special and that her life was destined to be dull. It was no longer possible to believe that. Now she felt exhilarated on the one hand and exposed on the other. In addition, she feared the shop could not possibly be ready to open by the Whippoorwill Gap Mountain Folklife Festival—only six weeks away—as she had planned.

One impossibly bright September morning, Harper was rehashing what to place in the smallest bookroom when she heard a knock at the front door. She took her time in looking to see who was there, expecting it to be Quinn Ellis again. That man was alarmingly persistent, and Harper had gotten used to ignoring his visits. No one from the department had told her not to work with Quinn, but she decided he could wait until opening day to see the shop.

But when she got to the entrance, ready to shake her head and mouth "not now" at him, she saw, with surprise, that Bryan Greene stood at the door. Harper's stomach clenched. While Quinn proved easy to brush off, Bryan still intimidated her. And she wasn't exactly sure why. Lately, he had been sending her emails requesting they get together for a chat. She had ignored them. Ever since their conversation at February's Chamber of Commerce meeting, Harper had dreaded talking with him about the shop. She wasn't afraid of him, but for some reason, she found it difficult to think when he was around.

The next Chamber meeting was in a couple of weeks. Since it was the last open meeting before the festival, she planned to attend this one. She knew she'd see him then, and that was soon enough for her. But here he was, waving to her through the display window and pointing at the door. Now that he'd spotted her, it was too late to sit down behind the counter and hide. So, suppressing her annoyance, Harper opened the door.

"Hello, Bryan." She granted him a small, tight smile. "What brings you over today?"

He gave her a quick, compressed smile in return, which did nothing to take attention from the curly dark hair hanging above his startling blue eyes. *He's too young for me.* The involuntary thought made her face hot.

"Harper, have you read any of the emails I've sent you? I know you're opening them because I've set them to notify me when you do."

Sensing that this conversation might best take place in private instead of on the street, Harper stepped out of the way and motioned him in. She didn't ask him to have a seat. Instead, she moved behind the checkout counter, wanting something solid between them. She returned his stare with an expressionless one of her own.

"Do you remember when we talked at the Chamber meeting last winter? I asked you if you wanted to continue the arrangement Frank and I had." Harper noted his speech was abnormally rapid. He paused and swallowed. "He bought some of my leftover merchandise to sell here at a discount. I've been waiting to hear back from you ever since."

She looked down at the countertop for a few seconds and then looked back up. "I haven't decided. I think I told you then, I'd rather decide after I open the shop."

"Why wait? I've got plenty of stock you could use right now." He looked around as if to indicate that, obviously, her shelves were shamefully bare. "It will look better if you have a bigger inventory when you open. You know, there's a lot to running a bookshop, even a used one. And with no experience you may be surprised at the problems that can pop up. I could help you out in all kinds of ways."

Despite his confident tone, Harper detected an undercurrent of nervousness about him, making her suspicious. She looked over his shoulder. Earl Grey was standing at the top of the basement stairs, making an obscene gesture at Bryan's back. That relieved the tension, and Harper choked down a laugh. Seeing her smile, Bryan frowned, his face turning pink.

"Well, maybe you think that's funny, but I have decades of experience in the bookstore business. I can keep you from making lots of mistakes."

For a second, Harper wondered if she was being stubborn and silly. Maybe she could use a person with experience to help her run the shop, at least in the beginning.

But then she glanced back at Earl Grey, now joined by Ash and Ivy. While Ivy was looking on with narrowed eyes, Ash was wearing a tight-lipped smile, while shaking his head. Their message was clear. She looked Bryan straight in the eye.

"You may be right, Bryan. But I want to run the shop for a while before I make agreements with anyone. You're not the only one trying to get me to make decisions about the shop that I'm not sure will suit me."

"Who else …?"

She interrupted. "It doesn't matter who else. Thank you for thinking of me. I do want us to get along. Maybe we can work together at some point. But I need time to figure out what works best for me. If I make mistakes, I'll learn from them like everyone else does. I hope you understand."

Behind him she saw the three Fae join hands and begin rising in mid-air, dancing a silent reel. She smiled again, despite her anxiety.

Bryan shook his head, but to her surprise, he returned her smile. Even more unexpected, his smile was pleasant. "Okay, Harper, I've done my best. I'm glad you're keeping the door open to possible collaborations. Can I help you with anything before your grand opening? If you have any printed up, I could put out signs and give out postcards or bookmarks printed with your business info."

Harper felt blindsided; she hadn't expected this generosity. Sensing her reaction, he continued. "Here in Whippoorwill Gap, businesspeople help each other out. We aren't all best friends, but we do support each other. So, whether we work together or not, I will support you and I hope you'll do the same for me."

Harper examined his handsome face and noted the crow's feet around his eyes. Maybe he was older than she thought? "That's a good idea. I'll make some posters and bookmarks and I'll get some to you. Of course, I'll be happy to return the favor."

His shoulders relaxed for the first time. "Here's my suggestion. Order them today and hand them out at the Chamber meeting this month. People will be happy to advertise for you."

"I'll do that this afternoon. I do appreciate the suggestion. Forgive me for not answering your emails, I've been focused on getting everything ready."

He nodded and knocked twice on the countertop before turning towards the door. Seeing that her friends had disappeared, Harper breathed a sigh of relief.

He stopped at the door. "I'll see you at the Chamber meeting, then?"

"Yes. I'll be there. See you then." As she locked the door, he turned back as if to say something else, but she pretended not to notice and walked to the back of the shop. When she glanced back at the front door, he was gone.

That afternoon, she made a trip to the local printshop where she'd had her building's sign designed and produced. The sign, which hung above the entrance, was a replica of the shop's original sign from 1923. The seafoam green background highlighted a charming painting of robins in a nest, with a little gnome holding a basket of books out to them. Happy with the printshop's design, Harper ordered a generous supply of bookmarks and small posters with the same image, as well as her address and phone number.

Excited by the day's events, Harper invited all the Fae to her apartment for an evening of snacks and conversation. After popping popcorn, she closed the curtains so no one passing by would see them zipping through the air.

Earl Grey entertained the others by mimicking Bryan Greene from earlier in the day. "And then he said to our Miss Harper here, 'I can keep you from making lots of mistakes.' The nerve of that jackanape!"

Tarryfoot looked over at Harper, arms crossed, with a serious expression on his diminutive face. "Would you like for me and Tiptoe to go over to his shop and give him some of the 'help' he deserves?"

Alarmed, Harper started to shake her head, and they all broke out into peals of bell-like laughter. "Give him some 'help,' that's a good one!" Lily piped as she zipped around the sofa. Then Harper realized this was their way of being supportive. She laughed with them in delight.

"At least I know you're on my side! But I think you missed the part where he really did give me a good idea. Maybe we're being too hard on him?"

"Pshaw!" Earl Grey responded heartily. "Can't be too hard on him. The man needs to listen!"

Before they left for the evening, they introduced her to a favorite tradition of theirs. They told her it began when they first came into the shop over a century ago. Each of them would read or recite a passage from a book of their choice. Some read poems. Ash read from Black Elk Speaks. Hawthorne recited a soliloquy from Shakespeare's Henry V. His intonations made Harper shudder. It was a good night.

Things were going so well that she was puzzled when she checked her mirror before turning out the light. To her bewilderment, the mist was encroaching again. Maybe her nervousness about the shop opening was causing it. "Grandma, I'll have to admit, I'm scared. What if I make a fool of myself over this shop? What if no one wants to shop here?"

She knew, in the grand scheme of things, it didn't matter if everything turned out badly. Other options were available to her. She could always rent the shop to someone else and live upstairs, like Ida Barker above the CPA. She could also leave Whippoorwill Gap and start over somewhere else. But she wanted to stay here. In the short time she'd lived here, she'd come to love the town.

She had to admit, most of the people she'd met hadn't been pushy—they had been welcoming. The town was lovely. Almost everything she wanted or needed was within walking distance of her apartment. And there was F-Troop. She smiled again, thinking back over their support that day. As a matter fact, she thought, if she was to leave, she'd even miss the owl in the park.

"I'll do my best. It will all be alright." Then she closed the mirror and turned out the light.

But in the days to come, Harper frequently found her palms sweating and her heart beating fast. She cast about for ways to increase her inventory. Thinking it was a great deal, she ordered the entire stock of a liquidating used bookstore in Connecticut. But on the truckload's delivery, she found many of the books were moldy, and they all smelled of cigarette smoke. The purchase agreement specified the books would be received "as is" with no returns or refunds.

To her dismay, they were beyond salvage. She didn't want to bring them into the shop because the smell would transfer to the rest of her stock. She looked through one box for the odd book or two she could possibly save with fumigation. But before she could make it to the bottom, she began sneezing and developed a sinus headache.

She checked with the public library, the college library, the Bric 'a' Brac, and local shelters, but no one wanted any of the books. Worse, no one had suggestions for disposing of them. She asked the Fae if their magic could freshen up a load of books, but they shook their heads sadly. These books were beyond their ability to repair. So with a heavy heart, she spent an afternoon driving loads of them to the municipal dump.

That night, while nursing her sore back with a heating pad, she discussed her fears with Piper. She asked if she should delay the shop's opening until next year, maybe until spring. Piper asked if Harper would run that idea by the others to see what they thought. Harper wearily consented.

When they all joined her in the storage room the following morning, they asked what was bothering her. Harper looked out the door to the cheerful basement with its bright yellow paint. She pointed out that the shelves were too empty. She still had no plan for the smaller special collections room. And on the main floor, only the green folklore room was in good shape. All the furnishings and décor looked nice, but Harper felt the sparse inventory would make a bad impression on anyone who came in.

Earl Grey shook his head. "Don't let that Greene Man get to you, Harper, My Lass. Why when the shop first opened in 1923, it contained fewer books than you have at present." The other faeries nodded vigorous assent.

Then Ash stood and said quietly, "Ever since we've been here, when I read a book in the shop, I put it back when I'm finished. When Frank was alive, he got most of the books he sold from his customers. He paid people for some of them, but most were donated. He kept what he needed and found ways to get rid of the rest."

"Yes, thank you, Ash. Those are all good points. But I don't have any customers yet."

"Once the shop opens, you won't need to worry about that. People will bring you books. But if you need books now, why not ask for donations? Put up signs in the front window asking for unwanted books. Call organizations around town and ask them if they can help. Then, in appreciation for the donations, promise to run a storewide sale sometime before the holidays."

Of course! Harper wondered why she hadn't thought of that sooner. "That's a great idea! It sure won't hurt to ask. Thank you!"

Ash gave her one of his rare smiles. "We can help you go through the books and get them ready." They all chimed in with their agreement.

By that afternoon, Harper had a sign in the window requesting donations. The next day, she placed copies of the sign in the coffee shop, the library, around the college, and at her Tai Chi and yoga studio on the other side of town. She spent the afternoon contacting businesses and churches. Most said they would be happy to help.

Almost immediately, boxes of books were dropped off at the shop. She found them waiting under the porch awning on the front stoop and by the back entrance to the shop. Within a few days, she had more books than she could process. They filled her downstairs storage room, spilling out onto the shop floor.

Ash was as good as his word. Braiding his long silky hair into a ponytail, he took charge of the book processing, saving Harper valuable time. He proved that his well-read reputation was no myth. Since he was the quietest of the Fae, she never suspected the knowledge he'd accrued from reading everything he could get his hands on for over a century.

He quickly made piles: to keep, to discard, and to ask Harper about. The to-keep piles were then divided into the sections in which they were to be shelved. He asked everyone to leave these alone until Harper could approve the choices. Once she did, he assigned each Fae a section to arrange. Within a couple of weeks, the shop was well-stocked and organized. And Harper felt much more confident.

Now she spent her days bustling about, getting the checkout counter ready for the opening. She expected business to boom during the first week, but after that, she had no idea what to expect. If things slowed down, she decided to use the time creating a digital inventory of every book she had. Within a year, she wanted to be selling books online.

Even more exciting, she had decided on a collection for the small room. But she told no one, hoping to keep it a surprise. Locking the room's door, she made the Fae promise not to enter it until she told them it was time, not even to dust. She ordered stock and asked them not to open anything shipped in from out of town. She wanted to process those books herself. It was to be a surprise for them all.

By the next Chamber meeting, Harper was enthusiastic to attend. This time, she showed up in brown work pants, a red sweatshirt, and work boots. While the first Chamber meeting had only thirty or so attendees, Harper estimated two to three hundred people were at this one. Everyone was excited about the Whippoorwill Gap Mountain Folklife Festival. Before moving to town, Harper had never heard of this event, but at the meeting she learned that people made the trip from the entire Appalachian region and beyond. She was astounded to learn that the celebration had an international reputation.

The college folklore department held storytelling events on campus. The major streets uptown and downtown, including the one in front of the Robin's Nest, were closed to traffic. Demonstrations of Appalachian crafts were scattered around, as were craft booths and food trucks. The Birdsong Theater had live entertainment, both inside the building and outside in the parking lot. Puckett's Park hosted Cherokee and settler's reenactments. Shuttle buses ran between parking areas at the college and around town to the festival site, and back. The town's population typically quadrupled on the big day. And it swelled well above normal for days before and after.

Learning all this thrilled Harper. She could not have picked a better date for the shop's grand opening.

During the open comment portion of the meeting, Harper steeled her nerves and stood. "Thank you all for welcoming me to Whippoorwill Gap. I'd like to know if there is anything I can do to help get ready for the festival."

Someone yelled, "Yes, Harper, there is something you can do! Make sure your shop is ready and that you get some rest beforehand. We're all rooting for you!"

Everyone applauded. Someone else yelled, "Is there anything we can do for *you*, Harper?"

"Well, Bryan Greene at Whippoorwill Gap Books suggested I make posters and bookmarks to help spread the word. I'll leave them on this table. You're all welcome to take as many as you'd like to distribute. I'd be grateful." She spread her items quickly, then looked around the room. Bryan stood by a side wall. He gave her a nod and a thumbs up. By the time Harper left, all her signs and bookmarks were taken.

For the first time, she relished being part of the business community. After the meeting, she dared to believe the shop would be successful.

But when she checked her mirror that night, she found not only mist, but troubling spots of tarnish. Uneasy and confused, she asked, "What's the matter, Grandma? I seem to be doing okay."

As she turned out the light, she promised herself she'd ask her friends tomorrow morning what could be amiss.

Seventeen

❖

BY THE NEXT MORNING, Harper had forgotten about the increasing haziness of the mirror's surface. Still excited from the Chamber meeting, she called Olivia to ask if she and Jeremy would like to come visit during the opening. Olivia begged off, saying they were too busy at work to make it down that soon. Harper, though disappointed, had expected that. But she was elated by Olivia's enthusiasm.

"Maybe we can make it down in the spring, Mom. But I wish you good luck. We'll be rooting for you. Keep us posted on how it all turns out!" She also thanked Harper for taking the trouble to find Tim's Eagle Scout memorabilia and shipping it to her. Even more amazing, a few days later, Harper received a silver bracelet hung with book charms, each with a different classic title, shipped from Toronto. It was the most thoughtful present Olivia had ever given her.

On the Monday evening before the grand opening, Harper invited Deanna and Dashawn for dinner. She wanted to show them the shop and thank them for their support.

With Piper's help, she made a hearty fall dinner, featuring chili with cornbread and cheese served with a kale and pomegranate salad. For dessert, they whipped up an apple crisp made with local Braeburn apples Harper had picked up at Thompson's Orchard Stand outside of town. It was a simple dinner, but she hoped her friends would like it. Thanks to Piper's counsel, her cornbread was nearing culinary perfection. She'd picked up the salad recipe from Scrumptiously Clean, a YouTube channel she enjoyed watching.

When her guests arrived, they brought a bottle of champagne, and they each sipped a glass during Harper's guided tour of the shop. Basking in the couple's compliments, Harper led the way upstairs. At the tour's conclusion, Dashawn begged off sit on the balcony while Deanna and Harper got dinner on the table. "You ladies excuse me. I don't believe I'd add much to the dinner preparations. And Deanna can tell you I like to spend time under the full moon when I can, and a beautiful Full Buck Moon is going to rise over those trees soon. From here, I'll have a perfect view."

Harper already knew Dashawn, like herself, was a practitioner of the fine art of balcony-sitting. On more than a few evenings they'd kept each other's silent company on their respective perches. "Of course, Dashawn. It's chilly out though. Would you like a cup of decaf or some tea to warm you up while you sit?"

"No, thank you. I just want to breathe in that river mist and enjoy some peace and quiet. I'll let you and Deanna enjoy some lady-talk."

Harper walked him to the balcony door. As soon as she re-entered the kitchen, her eyebrows flew up. Lily was sitting boldly on the countertop, right beside Deanna, who was mixing the salad. She caught Lily's eye and shook her head.

Deanna caught the motion and smiled. "It's all right, Harper, Lily and I are old friends. I hope it's okay with you—I asked her to stop by for a short chat while I was here. This seemed like a good time. I guess this might also be the right moment to confess that I've known what was going on in your shop all along."

Lily gave Harper a rueful look. "I hope you don't mind, Harper. There's a good reason." Then she peeped at Deanna with bright eyes, bit her lip, and smiled mischievously.

"Of course, Lily. I didn't know you and Deanna are acquainted. I'm surprised, that's all." She turned to Deanna, her arms crossed and a mock frown on her face. "You've known about them all along? Why didn't you tell me?"

Deanna flashed a roguish grin. "Oh, yeah. I know all about your little robins. They've been friends of mine since I moved in next door. They don't come in my shop, but we talk out back in my little garden plot and sometimes they keep me company when I'm alone on the balcony. I didn't tell you about them because I figured you'd think *I* was crazy. I knew it would all come out when the time was right."

"Does Dashawn know them too?" Harper asked, as it occurred to her that maybe everyone in town knew about them. Had she been the butt of a community-wide joke?

"'Shawn? Nah, he's oblivious. He's got the soul, but he don't have the sight. We'll keep this between us, okay?" She finished tossing the salad with Harper's wooden forks.

Harper pulled the butter from the refrigerator and set it on the table. "Sure. But I don't understand—why they don't come into your shop?"

Lily jumped from the countertop to the floor. "Deanna doesn't need us. She's got her own helpers, don'tcha, Deanna?"

Deanna placed a hand on the orange curls then pulled one lightly. "You got that right, Little Missy," she said with a smile. "I've got two helpers, and I don't know how I would get everything done without them. One of them helps my hubby out too sometimes, but 'Shawn don't know it."

Harper's forehead wrinkled. She wondered if this place would ever stop surprising her.

When they heard the balcony door open, Lily flew off the floor. "I'd better be leaving now. 'Bye Deanna! 'Bye Harper!"

She disappeared as Dashawn walked into the kitchen. "My old buddy, the owl, is out there tonight. He's always good company. Man, it smells great in here!"

"What's the deal with that owl, anyway?" Harper asked, leading the way to the dining room table with the pot of chili in her hands. Then she headed back to the refrigerator. "Is beer from Take Flight okay? I have wine, iced tea, and decaf if you'd rather."

Both her guests said beer would be great. Harper had made sure to get the types they ordered the night they went to the brewery together. Of course, she'd gotten porter for herself. As they sat down at the table, a lull in the conversation allowed them to hear the owl's "Who-who-who-who-whooo" drifting in through the cracked windows.

"To the owl!" said Harper, raising her glass.

"To your shop!" said Dashawn in return.

"To friendship!" said Deanna.

They clinked their glasses and continued their evening of food and laughter. As she straightened up the kitchen after they left, Harper felt blessed and happy. Now that she understood Deanna knew about the Fae, she felt relieved, and less lonely.

But the good vibes disappeared completely when she reached for her mirror before turning in to discover that now the surface was completely buried in tarnish. It looked as bad as it had on the day after the Mulhennys' dinner party. Dismayed, she called Piper's name and was gratified when the faery materialized at her door.

Harper held up the mirror for her to see. "I don't understand, Piper. Grandma said if I were being true to myself, the mirror would stay clear. I meant to tell you all about it days ago, but

I forgot. It doesn't make sense—I've never been happier. I'm starting to get worried. What could be the matter?"

Piper took the mirror from her hand and scrutinized its surface with a serious look on her thin face. "I'm sure I don't understand it either, but I'll tell the others. We'll help you get it all sorted out. Now, you get a good night's sleep, Dearie. You've got a big week ahead!"

Harper felt weak with gratitude. How had she ever lived without the Fae's support? "Thank you, Piper. It's so wonderful to have you here."

Piper ran a hand along the bed's footboard. "Well, Dearie, I feel the same about you!" With that, she popped out of sight.

Harper laid her head on the crisp white pillowcase. The mirror on the nightstand was the last thing she saw before she fell asleep. Confident that the faeries would help her resolve the issue, she enjoyed her last peaceful night's sleep for quite a while.

Eighteen

"WHY DIDN'T I THINK of this sooner?" Harper put a palm to each temple in despair. "Everyone in town is probably already committed that day! Can you think of anyone who might be willing to help?"

Deanna opened an oven door in Divine Coffee's kitchen and placed a huge tin of apple butter muffins inside. It was 5:30 am on Wednesday morning. Harper had woken up in panic after dreaming of an insanely busy opening day with people wrecking her shop while she was swept out the door by the crowd, unable to force her way back inside.

When she'd stepped out on her balcony to clear her head, she'd noticed the lights were burning in Deanna's shop kitchen. So she'd called to ask if she could come over. She needed Deanna's advice, and a cup of coffee would be nice, too.

"Well, there's Walt. I don't know if he's already committed to helping anyone, but I'll ask. He's cool-headed and strong. He'd be great in an emergency. He likes books ... Oh! And there's Nate, Abby's little brother." She chuckled. "He's sixteen, old enough to help. He likes to read, too. He might be able to lend a hand, at least for part of the day. He helps take care of his grandmother on weekends, but maybe he can get away for a while. You'll know him if he shows up. He'll probably be the only tall, skinny kid with blue hair in the shop that day."

"I thought colored hair wasn't fashionable for young men anymore."

Deanna started the mixer for a new batch of blueberry muffins. "It is for Nate."

Harper took a sip of her coffee, basking in a trifecta of warmth: from the kitchen, the coffee, and Deanna's companionship. The thought of having Walt in the shop all day made Harper's nerves buzz with excitement. Merely being within sight of him threw her off-center. She wasn't sure if that was good or bad. And she didn't know how he felt about her. For all she knew, he found her as annoying as she found Quinn.

As for Nate, what harm could he possibly do? She agreed because she didn't have any better ideas herself. She figured Nate must be a pretty good kid if he helped take care of his grandmother. Deanna promised to ask Abby when she came in for work that afternoon.

The only other person Harper could think of who wouldn't mind helping was Quinn Ellis. But he would probably be required to work the college storytelling events and wouldn't be available. Besides, she wasn't sure she could trust Dr. Ellis to refrain from rearranging the folklore room or helping himself to items he wanted. No—of the two adults, Harper preferred Walt. She'd just have to stay busy to distract herself from those eyes of his.

Another entire day went by before it hit Harper. She hadn't seen her Fae friends in days. That morning, when she brushed her teeth, she'd noticed her bathroom needed cleaning. Where could they be? She assumed they were as excited about the opening as she was, possibly more. As she thought back over the past several weeks, her conscience pricked her. She'd been so busy, she'd neglected them.

Thinking carefully over the last few days, she realized she hadn't seen any of them since the night Deanna and Dashawn had come over—three days ago. The last one she'd talked to was Piper, when she'd shown her the mirror. She had planned to talk with all of them the next morning, but they hadn't shown up, and with so much to do, she had forgotten. Her heart squeezed with regret as she wondered if she had offended them.

Later that afternoon, still with no sign of them, Harper went over to Divine Coffee and sat down to a bowl of butternut squash stew and a cup of decaf coffee. While there, she caught Deanna as she walked by. "Have you seen any of my small friends lately?"

"Why no, Harper, not since I chatted with Miss Lily at your place the other night. I thought they were all busy helping you. Goodness knows, you need their help now."

"I haven't seen any of them since the night you guys came over to eat. I'm afraid I may have offended them." Harper stared out the window, trying vainly to glimpse a robin landing on the sidewalk.

"I seriously doubt that." But Harper detected a note of concern in her tone. Deanna glanced over at Walt, who was sitting by the door, and lowered her voice. "On a different topic, Walt said he would be happy to help you this Saturday if *you* asked him." She smiled and headed back to the kitchen.

Harper didn't finish her stew. She quickly wiped her mouth with a napkin and approached Walt's table. "Hi, Walt. Deanna says you might be willing to help me with my grand opening this Saturday?"

Walt raised his enormous gold-flecked eyes to hers. "That's right." He took another sip of his coffee.

"Do you want to come over and see how everything is set up? I could show you around as soon as I finish my lunch, or any time that works for you."

"How about tomorrow morning? Unless you have something that needs fixing around the shop. I could come over now if you do." The corners of his mouth raised slightly. "I know my way around a hammer. And I excel at lifting heavy boxes." He peered at her over his mug. She looked at his broad shoulders and thought he was probably right about that. She silently cursed herself as her face grew warm.

"Umm. Anytime tomorrow morning would be fine, Walt. I appreciate your help. It shouldn't be too strenuous. I don't believe I'll need a lot of hammering or heavy lifting."

Harper immediately wanted to kick herself for that last comment. She could feel the sweat breaking out on her forehead. Why couldn't she think before she spoke? But he didn't bat an eyelash. Instead, he slugged back the rest of his coffee and stood, looking her in the eye.

"It's going to be all right. It's all going to work out fine." Harper felt as if a heavy backpack she'd been unaware of carrying had dropped from her shoulders. She swallowed, touched at his show of compassion. How did he know she was worried?

She rewarded him with a grateful smile. "Thanks, Walt. I'll see you tomorrow."

That afternoon she drove to the big box store on the outskirts of town. She was surprised to find posters for the Robin's Nest going in, going out, and at the checkout counters. The place was mobbed with people. Some she recognized, but many she didn't. The atmosphere radiated pre-party euphoria. All the talk she overheard pertained to the festival. The inns and motels for miles around were completely booked; so were the campgrounds. The enthusiasm was contagious. Despite her worry about the faeries, she couldn't help feeling fired up.

After she got home and put away her supplies, she looked the building over, inside and out. Seeing no signs of the Fae, she called their names, thinking maybe one of them would turn up. When none did, she headed over to Puckett's Park to scout around. People were building temporary displays for the reenactments in the cool mountain afternoon, but no robins or Fae were in sight.

Running out of ideas, she slipped down the unmarked path to the riverbank. The only thing that greeted her there were fallen leaves and drying reeds. She walked to the spot where she had entered the portal with Hawthorne and Ivy only a few weeks ago. Now thick, impenetrable vines covered the spot, and Harper wondered briefly if she had only imagined it. Overhead in the large sycamore tree, the owl watched her closely, surrounded by gold and brown foliage. She looked up at it. "Do you know where they are?" In response, it blinked its eyes and turned its head to look at the spot where the portal had been.

In bed that night, when Harper opened her mirror, she examined the dull gray, brown, and green mottling. It was as though the reflective surface had been completely devoured.

"Grandma, I hope you can hear me. I don't know where my friends have gone. Did they decide I don't need their help? If they thought that, they were wrong. And even if I didn't need their help, I would want them with me anyway. They make me happy. Can you tell them that for me? Please? I want them to come back."

She looked at the mirror for a few moments more before closing it and turning out the light. Between anticipation of working with Walt the next day and worry over the Fae, it was a restless night.

The next day, Harper had little time to think about her missing shop mates. She tried to make herself look nice, even going so far as to apply makeup. She pulled on a gauzy black top that she hoped would hide some of the extra weight she had put on around her middle since moving to town. After trying unsuccessfully to style her hair with a curling iron, she tied it up in a messy bun that didn't look too bad. When Walt came in that morning, she observed appreciatively how nice he looked in faded jeans and a blue t-shirt covered by a flannel shirt. Tearing her eyes away, she turned her attention to the good luck cards and wishes that had been plastered all around the door, along with several additional boxes of book donations.

Walt brought the boxes in for her. Then she showed him around the shop, except for the small special collections room. Its door was locked and labeled with a sign that read, "Surprise Special Collection—Opening Soon." Walt didn't comment on that or much of anything else. As her nervousness grew, she reminded herself that he was a quiet person. He examined everything with apparent interest. He merely nodded approval when she showed him the elevator. After lingering in the folklore room, he pointed to a section of shelving. "I see you kept the A.E. Crowe novels Frank had collected. That makes me happy. Have you read any of them?"

Harper looked at the shelves of novels, all based on Appalachian folklore. "No, I haven't. But I did my research. I know they have a good reputation in the fantasy and folklore communities. Do you recommend them?"

He turned his chestnut-honey tinted eyes to hers. "For what it's worth, yes."

She cleared her throat. "Well, then, for what it's worth, I'll give them a try. Which would you recommend I read first?"

He handed her a book titled A Call from the Forest. "I'd start with this one. It should give you a good idea of the writing style and the subject matter."

"Thanks! Help yourself to anything you'd like for helping me out, by the way. And I want to pay you. Does twenty dollars an hour sound okay?"

In response, he shook his head as he ran his fingers over a table display. "No need to pay me. I consider helping you an honor. But I will take this book if you don't mind." He picked up a guide to Eastern North American birds.

After he left, with a promise to be back about thirty minutes before the 9:00 opening the next morning, she hurriedly processed the boxes of books he had brought in for her.

Just before sunset, Harper rested on her balcony bundled in a heavy jacket, with a blanket and a glass of Pinot Noir, watching the activity in the park. Despite the prodigious noise, the owl also watched it all with her from his sycamore limb. After the sun fully set, she went back inside for an Epsom salts bath, which she followed with reading the novel Walt had recommended, in bed. But neither the bath nor her mug of lavender–chamomile tea calmed her fidgets.

At one point, she put down the novel to examine the tarnished mirror. "Grandma, this is it. I won't ask for magic. But please wish me well. I'm so nervous about the opening tomorrow." She swallowed. "And I still want my friends back. If you see them, please tell them for me."

To her relief, A.E. Crowe's novel proved engrossing once she got into the story. The intermingled Cherokee and local folklore kept her spellbound. Since it was set in the modern world, she found it easy to put herself in the story and get caught up in its magic. And so, thankfully, the night passed quickly. She fell asleep around 3:00 am but was up and dressed by 6:30 that morning. She padded downstairs hoping to find the Fae, but the shop was empty of life, save her own.

She went back upstairs to drink a cup of strong black tea while wrapped in a blanket on the frosty back deck. Dashawn, sitting on the deck next door, was equally bundled. He raised his mug to her, and she returned the gesture. Neither spoke for fear of waking the people camping in the park. Looking past Dashawn, she was disappointed to see the owl was missing. *He needs to eat too; he's probably out hunting.* Draining her cup, she went inside and dressed for her big day.

In keeping with the festival's theme, she had bought a cream cotton blouse and a loose, wool smock jumper in steel blue to wear that day. Harper paired them with cream-colored tights and black lace-up boots, then pulled the front section of her wild hair back, clasping it with a silver barrette. For the second day in a row, she polished off her preparations with a light coat of makeup. She studied the effect in the mirror. No one would confuse her with a twenty-five-year-old, but for someone in her late fifties, she was happy with her reflection.

Even though the sign on the storefront said the shop would open at 9:00 am, by 8:00, Harper could no longer stand the wait. She unlocked the door and flipped on all the lights. Today, no matter what came through that door, she was ready to meet it. And only ten minutes later, Walt walked in with two large cups of coffee and a couple of pumpkin cream cheese muffins from Divine Coffee.

"I was going into the coffee shop when I noticed your lights were on, so I thought I'd bring you some breakfast. You're going to need extra energy today," he said as he handed her the coffee.

"Thanks, Walt! I've been too nervous to even think about breakfast." She pulled napkins from beneath the checkout counter and passed one his way.

He unwrapped his muffin. "Supplying good ideas is my objective for being here." Shaking his head with a smile, he added, "I expected you'd be too nervous today to think clearly."

She smiled gratefully and took a sip of strong, dark coffee. How did he know she took it with cream and no sugar? Deanna must have told him.

Before they finished their muffins, Quinn Ellis walked through the door, decked out in blue jeans and a red and white checked shirt with red suspenders and a black flat hat on his head. "Hi Harper ... Walt. I thought I'd get here early and be the first in line. I need to be at the college to help with the storytelling at ten-thirty. But since you seem to be open, is it okay if I come in?"

Harper looked into his eager brown eyes and smiled. For the first time, she felt genuinely happy to see him. He'd stressed his expertise in folklore so often that she was now curious to know what he'd think of her collection. "Sure Quinn. Come on in. Feel free to look around."

He rocked forward on his toes as if eager to start a race. "Any place off limits?"

"If it is, it's locked. The shop is on this floor and in the basement. If you can get to it, it's open. But you may want to start at the first door on your left." She pointed down the hallway.

His eyebrows reached new heights when he saw the "Folklore Collection" sign hanging above the door, and he quickly disappeared beneath it. When he emerged, it was almost time for his shift at the college to begin. He reminded her of a giddy teenager when he brought several thick reference books to the counter.

She rang him up. "I'm glad you found something!"

"Yeah, I really need to be going, but wow! I like what you've done with the place! I don't know where you found some of that stock, but you've got some good books in there! And once again, I'm happy to help you out part-time."

Harper was too relieved by his praise to be annoyed with his never-ending offers to work for her. "Thanks, Quinn! You're welcome to come back any time I'm open. But I don't think I'll be needing any help for a while."

He looked at Walt, who was talking with an elderly woman in the children's section. "Oh. Is Walt working for you, then?"

Harper shook her head. "Just for today. I may hire someone at some point, Quinn, but not yet." She placed his books in a large robin's egg blue bag with The Robin's Nest stamped on the front.

"Have fun with the storytelling!" she called as he turned toward the door. He threw up his hand at her before melting into the crowd outside.

After that, the door opened and closed with such frequency that Walt propped it open. Several visitors told her they came to the festival every year and were thrilled to see the Robin's Nest open again. A woman from Ohio told her, "We missed this place when it was closed last year. It's always been a big part of the Whippoorwill Gap experience for us!"

While most were pleased with the changes she had made, a few high school and college students lamented her decision to get rid of the comic books. Harper nodded sympathetically. She had expected this. She offered them a free cup of spearmint- and lemon-infused water that she'd made after breakfast and asked them to take their time looking around. Some of them, after a bit of exploration, discovered books to purchase.

Later that evening, with her feet propped up on her blue living room ottoman, she reflected over the day. As it wore on, the shop had become increasingly busy and muggy. She had set the thermostat to seventy degrees, and she heard the air conditioning flip on more than once. During brief breaks from answering questions, she reflexively looked out the windows to see if the robins were on the sidewalk. But the crowds were so thick, there was no room for a robin to land.

By 11:00 am, the shop was filled with people. Harper never imagined so many people could fit into Whippoorwill Gap. The customers kept her so busy, she forgot all about lunch. Around 2:00 pm, Walt went out and came back with corned beef sandwiches and homemade chips from O'Malley's Pub Fare, the food truck across the street. The sandwiches were delicious, but so big that Harper saved half of hers for dinner.

After she sold several of the A.E. Crowe books, she went back into the folklore room and pulled a copy of each of his novels off the shelves and put them behind the counter to keep for herself. A customer had told her that vintage copies of his hardbacks were highly collectible.

Shortly after Walt polished off his sandwich, he stationed a tall, slim young man with blue hair at the shop's doorway to serve as gatekeeper, only allowing one group to enter as another left. That was the first time Harper saw Nate. For a while, there was a line to get into the shop. The crowds began thinning out after 5:00, and around that time, Nate disappeared. Minutes before the 6:00 pm closing time, he emerged from the basement.

"It's a mess down there—would you like me to stay and help you straighten it up?"

Harper looked up at him and nodded gratefully. Even though she was exhausted, she knew tomorrow morning everything needed to be neat before she opened.

Walt asked if Harper wanted to close on time. Harper, her energy tank nearly depleted, nodded yes. He locked the door then stood beside it, only unlocking it to let people out. It was an hour past closing time before the shop emptied of customers.

Harper tried again to pay him for his help. He staunchly refused, not even letting her pay for the food he'd bought for her. "Seriously, Harper. This has been a great day for me."

He began to straighten the books around the disheveled front section, and Harper made her way downstairs to check on Nate. The shelves were already as neat as they had been early that morning, though a bit emptier.

Nate stared at the sci-fi books, his back to her. His remarkable hair was the bright blue color of cobalt. "Take any of them you'd like." He jumped.

"I didn't hear you come down. You have some good books here. They're in better shape than Frank's paperbacks. You have a couple of Asimov books I haven't read."

"Take them. I appreciate your help ... Nate, isn't it?"

"Yeah, I'm Nate. I would have introduced myself when I came in, but you were busy. And I'd be happy to help you anytime. This place was always my idea of heaven. I started hanging out here with Frank back when I was old enough to ride my bike across town alone. Frank was a great guy. I've missed this place."

"Well, Nate, you're welcome to come hang out here any time I'm open." He carried the books upstairs and laid them on the counter. Then he joined Walt in the folklore room to help restore order.

After Nate left, happily carrying his Asimovs and some cash Harper gave him for his time, she removed the money from the cash register. Walt finished sweeping the main floor and joined her, checking behind her accounting. After subtracting the beginning total, she was surprised to find over a thousand dollars in the till. Adding that to the amount her credit card account reported, she discovered she had made almost three thousand dollars that day.

"Not bad for one day's take in a used bookstore," noted Walt.

"You're right! And I'm surprised because I sold more rare folklore books than I expected to." Harper was tired, and she was happy to be sitting on the stool behind the counter, giving her feet a break.

Walt appeared thoughtful. "That makes sense though, this being a folklife festival. Do you want me to come back to help tomorrow?"

"Only if you'll let me pay you."

He sighed. "Okay, I'll let you buy my lunch and give me another book. How about that?"

Too tired to argue, she smiled. "You've got it! And tomorrow, we won't open before ten."

As she climbed into bed that night, she was too exhausted to worry over the mirror's tarnish. She picked it up without opening it. "It was a good day, Grandma. But I still want my friends back." Once she flipped off the lamp and her head landed on the pillow, she knew nothing more until her alarm woke her the next morning at 8:00.

Nineteen

"THANK YOU, BRYAN, THEY'RE lovely!" Harper reached out for the enormous pot of magenta chrysanthemums he'd delivered.

Bryan grinned. "I heard you got off to a great start! So I thought congratulations were in order."

Harper stood awkwardly in the doorway. While she appreciated the flowers and felt flattered by the attention, something about him still made her wary. Then she remembered the help he had given her.

"Thanks again for the tip about the posters and the bookmarks. I think that had a lot to do with my success."

Bryan nodded, a hopeful look in his eyes. He was evidently waiting to be invited in, but today was Tuesday and the shop was closed. He had knocked on the door while she was working on a harvest-themed window display. She made a mental note to stay away from the ground floor on the days she was closed. When people saw her through the glass, they felt free to interrupt whatever she was doing.

Today, after finishing the displays, she planned to comb the park and town for signs of her friends. "I'd invite you in, Bryan, but I have a lot to do today. Can you come back one day when I'm open? I'd be happy to show you around."

Bryan nodded and looked at the hours posted on the door. "Okay, I'll come back on—Thursday, is it? Yes, Thursday afternoon. I'll be back then. I'd like to see what you've done with the shop. You know, you haven't been back by my store since you moved to town. You're welcome to come by any time."

Though she was taken aback at his slightly hurt tone, she was too preoccupied to give it much thought. She wanted to begin searching for her friends. "I promise I'll come by as soon as I get a chance. Thanks so much for the flowers. I'll see you when you come on Thursday."

And with that, she closed the door and pulled down the shade. She watched as he headed up the sidewalk toward Main Street. Something about his posture as he walked away made her feel guilty. She wondered if he was lonely. Really, she knew very little about him. Was it possible he wanted to be friends?

She turned and looked glumly around her shop. She had been so excited about this place for so long. But now that the opening was over and her friends were gone, it no longer held the same charm. Perhaps she was simply tired. But with the fresh river scent absent from the shop, the feeling of peace it had given her was also gone. The atmosphere now seemed sterile and empty. Without the Fae, she wasn't even sure she wanted to run it anymore.

For the rest of the morning, she looked in vain for signs of her friends. Their little room beneath the stairs was neat and tidy. The cushions Tiptoe and Tarryfoot had sewn were stacked in a colorful column in a back corner, exactly as they had been the last time she'd checked. Everything else in their room was neat and tidy, though covered with a thin layer of dust.

She trekked over to the park, walking all the trails. She took the side path to the spot where she had entered the portal and slowly walked back and forth, under the gaze of the owl, examining every stalk and tree. His closeness no longer bothered her; she had given up her fear of him long ago.

"Have *you* seen them?" The owl blinked at her several times before hooting softly. After leaving the park, she passed Deanna's door on her way home—she had planned her days off to coincide with Divine Coffee's. So she wasn't surprised when the basement door to Deanna's place opened. "Hi Harper! I was just getting ready to go for a walk in the park. Wanna join me?"

"Sure, Deanna." Harper wanted to sound upbeat and happy, but feeling as she did, like an empty windsock, she couldn't pull it off.

"Why're you looking so down? I know you've been super busy since the shop opened. That must make you happy." Deanna looked at her friend, her dark eyes softening to concern. "Tell me. What's the matter?"

"They're gone, Deanna," Harper burst out, her eyes filling with tears. "All my Fae friends are gone. I haven't seen them since the night you and Dashawn came over. I keep hoping they'll show up, but they're gone. What did I do wrong?"

Deanna looked her over. "You're shaking! First, have you had anything to eat today?"

Harper swallowed against her tight throat. "No."

Deanna pulled her arm and led her up the backstairs to her apartment. She instructed Harper to sit at the table in the cheerful, bright yellow and orange kitchen. "Let me get you something to eat. Anything can be handled better with a well-fed stomach. I have leftover chicken salad. How about a sandwich?" She pulled out a bag of croissants and some lettuce.

"Thank you, Deanna. That would be great."

Harper slumped in her seat while her friend bustled around, making her a sandwich, which she placed beside a sliced apple and some red grapes. She served the plate with a steaming cup of tea and a slice of lemon.

Harper picked up the tea, almost choking as she took a sip. "Oh my God, that's Earl Grey, isn't it?" She burst into tears which quickly turned to wailing sobs.

Deanna looked momentarily stunned. "Oh, I didn't think of our buddy Earl Grey! Forgive me."

"It's okay." Harper took a ragged breath. "It's just that, I've come to care about them, you know?" She hung her head. "I'm really sorry, Deanna. I know I'm too old to be carrying on like this."

Deanna looked out her window. "I don't know what I'd do without my two. You're exactly right—they aren't only help, they're family. And I'm sure the last couple of weeks have been exhausting for you. Never apologize for how you feel."

Harper nodded, miserable yet gratified. "That's exactly it. They *are* my family. I know it sounds crazy, but I've come to love them just as much as my daughter, and more than the rest of my family. Both my parents are dead. And did I tell you my grandmother ... well, she disappeared near here? I really don't have anyone else."

Deanna watched the owl sitting on its branch in the park. "When we get back from our walk, I'll ask my two friends if they know what's happened. Maybe they've heard something. I'll let you know what they say. How does that sound?"

Harper finished up her sandwich and picked up a slice of apple. "Yes, that sounds good. Can I meet your friends sometime, Deanna?"

Deanna looked at her from the corner of her eye. "I think that can be arranged at some point, yes. But I'll leave the timing up to them. Now, how about that walk?" She picked up Harper's empty plate and placed it in the dishwasher.

Harper stood up and put on her jacket. "Do you mind if I share something sad with you?"

Deanna shook her head as they walked out the door. "Not a bit. Maybe one day, I'll return the favor."

Harper walked quietly until they approached the river. "When I told you I think of my friends as family, I remembered something I hadn't thought of in a long while.

"I was an only child. Neither one of my parents talked to me much. They both worked—it seemed like all the time. They owned a real estate firm. And, I think it's fair to say, they liked to party. Most of their big parties were on weekends. When they had those, they usually sent me to stay with my Grandma Sophie. And I was glad about that. I loved my grandma, and I hated to be home when they had their friends over. I could tell you another story about that, but not today. If Grandma wasn't busy doing something else, they were happy to have me go." She released a small sigh.

"But even on weeknights, they sometimes had people over for 'a few drinks,' as they called it. I hated that, too. I stayed in my room and locked the door. But I could still hear their music. To this day, I hate the songs they played ... Tom Jones, ugh. And I hated all the loud laughing. I didn't understand a lot of what I heard them say, but I had a feeling I didn't want to, either."

Deanna nodded. "I hear you."

"They paid me to clean up after those parties. I guess I was around six or seven when they started giving me a weekly allowance to clean up the bottles, glasses, and worst of all, the ashtrays, from the night before. I could do this anytime the next day. We had a dishwasher, so it wasn't too hard, but I had to run soapy water in the sink and wash the ashtrays by hand. I really hated that. The smell turned my stomach."

Deanna wrinkled her nose. "Doesn't sound like a fun job for an adult, to me."

"Well, I don't want to make things sound *too* bad. My parents weren't abusive. It's not like they were making me bust rocks or dig ditches. And they did pay me. But I still hated doing it."

She looked over at the river. "I guess I remembered that because, while I was washing those ashtrays, I always wished that I had a brother or a sister to talk to while I did it. It would have been nice to have another kid around. Maybe then I wouldn't have been so lonely."

She grew quiet then, and the two friends walked side by side, accompanied by the sound of their sneakers on the asphalt pavement and squirrels chittering in the leaves. It was a breezy afternoon, not cold, just chilly enough make them glad their jackets had pockets.

As they circled back within sight of the buildings, Deanna said, "You don't need to be lonely now. You've got friends here in Whippoorwill Gap and not just the Fae. No doubt we may be annoying sometimes, but we're not such a bad bunch. Like I said, I'll talk to my own friends and see if they might know what's going on with yours. I'll call and let you know when I find out. I don't see them every day, so it may be a day or two before you hear from me. But call me if you need anything or just want to talk."

After they said goodbye, Harper found herself energized enough to stay busy cleaning for the rest of the afternoon. She called Olivia that night. Her daughter seemed sincerely pleased the opening had been such a big success.

On Thursday, as she was heading downstairs to open the shop, Deanna called her with worrying news. All Harper's friends had been seen heading to the Faery Realm a few nights before the grand opening. Now they were apparently trapped there, held against their will. That's all that Deanna's Fae friends would reveal.

Deeply troubled, Harper went downstairs to open the shop. She hoped they were okay. What could "they were trapped" mean? Did that mean they wanted to come back, but couldn't? Was *Grandma* holding them there against their will? She couldn't imagine that was the case. They had warned her nefarious beings existed in that realm. Could it be that some of these others had harmed them? The longer she thought about it, the more distraught she became.

She felt she had no other option than to go there herself to find her friends. The longer she waited the less likely they were to come back. How long such an expedition would take was anyone's guess. She needed a plan that would give her enough time. Her next day off was Tuesday, which, as luck would have it, was Halloween. It wasn't ideal, but she couldn't think of a better alternative.

Her friends had told her Halloween night was a big celebration for the Fae. The barriers between the realms became thin, and many beings from that dimension, realm, frequency—or whatever someone wanted to call it—made their way over to this side, the Earth Realm, seeking mischief. While some of it was in good fun, not all of them had friendly intentions. Halloween, as Alida had so charmingly phrased it, was when "the horrid hordes" rampaged in that world and this. Harper didn't know if there was anything to these stories or not, but she knew that, no matter what happened, she had to make that journey.

Hawthorne and Ivy had been cautious about her safety on the last trip. This time, she'd be entering the Faery Realm, on Halloween, alone. The thought terrified her, but she made up her mind to try.

Both Bryan and Quinn made it by the shop that afternoon. She was too distracted with her upcoming journey to be disturbed by anything they said. Bryan looked around while trying to make small talk. She tried hard to be pleasant, and she was grateful when he didn't mention them working together. She promised to make a trip to his bookstore before Christmas.

Quinn insisted on offering, yet again, to work for her in exchange for books. She flatly told him no: any unorthodox payment arrangements were off the table. If he wanted to work for her, it would be for hourly wages only. And she told him, for what seemed like the thousandth time, she wasn't interested in hiring anyone yet. When he asked when she would be, she almost laughed out loud. "When I make a decision to hire someone, Quinn, I'll let you know."

As the next four days creeped by, Harper found she could manage the workload on her own just fine. But she also understood that, if the Fae didn't come back, she would need to cut back her hours or hire someone else to help with the housekeeping and in the shop. She had completely underestimated how much labor was involved in keeping a bookstore stocked and attractive. Her pre-opening vision had been of herself sitting behind the desk while reading and drinking tea until a customer needed tending. Now that idea struck her as hopelessly naïve.

In her spare moments, she formulated her plans for her solo visit to the Fae Realm.

The day before Halloween, Deanna dashed through the pouring rain after closing the coffee shop to check on Harper.

Harper stared out the front windows at the rain. "Have you ever been to the Faery Realm, Deanna?"

Deanna's eyes bugged out. "No, I've never been there! My companions told me people like us can't even get in there without one of them at our side. It's a bad idea, Harper. Even if you get in, you might never return. You could be hurt. They told me it's dangerous for humans to travel there."

None of this made Harper feel better. But neither did it change her mind. "I have to try."

She invited Deanna upstairs for a cup of tea, but Deanna shook her head. "I'm sorry Harper, I've got to get Halloween treat bags ready for tomorrow evening. You do know that the merchants in town always hand out treats to the kids on Halloween, don't you?"

Harper groaned. "No, I seem to remember hearing something about it, but it didn't register. I guess I'll have to miss it this year. It may not matter anyway."

"I'll check and see if Abby and Nate can stand in front of your shop and hand out candy for you. How does that sound? At least that way all the townspeople will know you were thinking of the kids."

Harper gave her head a listless bob. "That'll work. I'll run out now and buy some bags of candy. I'll put them in buckets and drop them by your shop. How much should I pay them?"

"Pay them? Abby and Nate? They'll do it for free! Teenagers and college kids beg to help with this. Trust me, they will have enough fun to make it worth it. I'll give them each a bag of treats to take home to pay them for their help. And Dashawn and I will be in front of the coffee shop handing out treats too. We'll keep an eye on them, if that makes you feel any better."

"Sure. That all sounds good. But I'm not worried about Abby and Nate. I think they can be trusted." Harper turned to the water running down the sidewalk in front of the shop. "I wonder what the weather is supposed to be like tomorrow."

"Rain in the morning followed by a partly cloudy and windy afternoon and evening. The kids should bundle up because it's going to be chilly."

"I guess I'd better wear a jacket then." Harper bit her lower lip.

Deanna gave her a stern look. "I wish there was something I could do or say to stop you. But I know there isn't. I asked my friends if they could escort you there, but they told me no.

They need a specific type of bond, whatever that means, with someone to take them safely. I guess their rules are different."

Harper knew she had an advantage over most humans. She'd been there before, and her grandmother happened to be queen. While this gave her a small store of confidence, it felt unwise to tell Deanna about her grandmother or her prior visit to the other side.

After Deanna left, Harper threw on a rain jacket and walked to the Great Green Grocer's, where she bought honey sticks and individually wrapped cacao candies. Then she loaded them into buckets and took them over to Deanna's. Back upstairs, in her apartment, she wrote a farewell letter to Olivia, which outlined how to find her will so she could claim her property and other assets. She'd leave the letter on the kitchen table in the morning, just in case.

That night, when Harper pulled out her mirror, she spoke to its dull surface. "I'm coming to see you. I want my friends back. If they don't want to come back, I want to say goodbye to them. I don't know what's going on and I'm scared. Please guide me, Grandma."

The rain let up during the night, but an ominous dark red sunrise greeted Harper through her kitchen windows on Halloween morning. The winds picked up speed as more rain clouds rolled in from the west. The last remaining leaves on the trees were ripped from their tethers, scattering across the parking lot behind Harper's apartment. Harper ate the most substantial breakfast she could manage that morning—oatmeal with pumpkin butter and black walnuts. She drank a cup of regular coffee and packed herself a water bottle with a package of trail mix in a small black backpack. On her way out the door, she grabbed her grandma's mirror and shoved it in her hoodie's pocket.

Then, heart pounding, she made her noiseless way into the park, her footsteps muffled by the sodden leaves. As she crept down the little path to the river, she felt relieved to hear the owl hooting. At the river's edge, it perched on the low limb of a hornbeam tree right above her. This was the closest she had ever been to it. She peered at it through the curtain of hair the wind had ripped from her ponytail. Then she looked at the riverbank to where the portal had been. Closing her eyes, she clenched the mirror in her pocket, breathing deeply to steady her nerves. When she opened them, to her astonishment, the portal gaped open before her, exactly as it had on the day she entered it a few months before.

She remembered Hawthorne's warning to leave the mirror behind. Pulling a black bandana from her backpack, she wrapped the mirror inside it. She carried it to a spot underneath an overhanging rock that jutted from the riverbank and looked up at the owl. "I'm going to leave this here for a while. Will you watch it for me and make sure nothing happens to it?"

In response, the owl hooted, holding her gaze. It was an intense look. Harper turned back toward the portal. But to her horror, it had disappeared; thick vines covered the spot where it had been. Looking at the spot, it was impossible to tell an entrance had ever been there.

Oh no! Harper thought desperately. Once again, she looked at the owl. But instead of looking at her, he was looking at the spot where the mirror was lying. He left his branch and flew down to it. He turned his head to look Harper in the eye, then abandoned it there and flew back to his branch, hooting loudly. Harper went back to the rock, picked up the mirror, and unwrapped it from the bandana. His message was clear.

Going back to the spot where the portal had been moments before, she clutched the mirror and closed her eyes. When she opened them, the portal had reappeared. She looked back up at the owl.

"I have to take it with me?" It blinked at her. "Who-whoooo."

Harper nodded, pushed the mirror into her pocket, and stepped inside the tunnel.

Twenty

THE MOMENT SHE WAS entirely inside, Harper heard rumbling behind her. Turning back, she saw an earthen wall at her back—the portal was closed. She stopped for a moment and inspected the solid expanse. Would she ever see the other side again? Unable to resist the urge to try, she slipped the mirror from her pocket and closed her eyes, thinking *open*. But when she looked again, the wall still stood, a solid sentinel blocking her escape. With no choice left but to see it through, she marshalled her fraying nerves and began walking.

The tunnel seemed darker and colder than before, and its atmosphere harbored a festering sense of menace. In pulling out her phone for light, Harper found it dead. She frantically wrenched the mirror from her pocket and discovered, with relief, that it provided a subtle golden glow, allowing her to see a few steps ahead. The carpet of leaves lining the floor muffled the sound of her sneakers.

After creeping down the lonely, unnerving tunnel, for what she judged to be an hour, she approached the chamber she'd dubbed *Merlin's Office* on her previous trip. This time, instead of the heavy, nearly sacred silence, she heard grating, high-pitched, raucous laughter, an annoying buzz, and ... what sounded like the footsteps of an army of small creatures. With it came the scent and oppressive atmosphere of an electric fire.

She scurried to the bend where the tunnel curved just before the room's entrance. Then, dropping to the floor, she pressed her full length as tightly as possible to the inside of the curve. Facing the wall, she pulled her hood over her head, placed her hands in her pockets, and became as motionless as a rock. There she waited, tense and cold, her hip cramping in agonizing spasms.

Just as she felt she couldn't lay there another second, the racket reached a fever pitch and erupted from the chamber's entrance like an exploding cannon. A wild river of insect-like creatures whooshed past her like shrapnel. She kept her breaths shallow for as long as she could, though none of the beings were moving slowly enough to notice her. After roughly five minutes, the shrieking, locust-like horde passed her by, the noise dimming as they moved down the passage, and all became quiet and dark once again.

Harper lay immobile, listening intently, for a few minutes more before opening her eyes. When she did, she found what looked like drab blue and iron-gray glitter sparkling on the walls and floor of the tunnel. After gingerly sitting up, she reached down to rub her aching hip and saw with horror that she was covered in it herself. Now that her chances of entering the realm unseen were diminished, she needed to hurry.

Cautiously, she peeked around the corner into the chamber. The formerly dignified room was in shambles. Chairs were overturned, ancient books lay scattered on the floor, grimy cups and saucers were dispersed among windowsills, tables, and even the floor. Puddles of spilled drink surrounded islands of dropped victuals. And all of it glowed blue and silver.

Harper froze when she saw the back of a small figure with straight black hair inside the room. The figure was muttering, while apparently tidying up the tremendous mess. As she began to back slowly into the tunnel again, the being suddenly straightened up and turned to look directly at her. To her shock, she found herself looking at a familiar face.

"Piper!"

Eyes wide with alarm, Piper held up a slim hand. Then she whispered, "Quiet Dearie! The next group will be arriving soon. They mustn't see *you* when they do!"

At that moment, Harper detected the sound of heavy chimes coming down the tunnel from the Fae Realm entrance, like church bells pealing in a hurricane. Piper hastily opened a small wooden door in the wall that Harper had never noticed, then motioned for her to crawl inside. Harper sat on the floor of the closet-sized space and wrapped her arms around her legs, breathing in the ancient, dusty scent of the wood, worn smooth with age. But when she tried to fit herself deeper into the space by burrowing beneath some shelves, she dislodged some pottery. The resultant clatter prompted her to freeze.

Then, with explosive force, another group of Others hit the room. Peeking through a small crack in the door, Harper saw more of the shimmering substance, but this time in shades of sewer green and tarnished bronze. These larger creatures, close in size to baseballs, shrieked as they entered the room, eating and drinking from the same half-empty plates and cups left behind by the previous contingent. She watched a round, heckling being, the color of a storm cloud, pull Piper's hair as another behind it laughed. After ten minutes or so of the maddening din, a sound like a gong being struck mushroomed from the entrance. Suddenly, as though a cork had burst from an agitated bottle of champagne, they rushed for the entrance, flying over and under each other in a frenzied race for the tunnel.

Once they were gone and all was silent again, Piper opened the closet door. Her usually sleek black hair now lay arrayed in tangles and heaps about her head, and her shirt was torn near the shoulder. Loads of sticky glitter clung to her like a second skin. As Harper left the closet, she shivered. The room felt much colder than before.

Piper's thin lips formed a tense straight line. "What are you doing here, Dearie? Never mind. You picked a bad day to come, you did! Don't you know it's the first day of our winter? Our rougher sort cavorts in your world this night."

Harper stretched with a groan. Her hips and knees objected strenuously to their confinement. But Piper gave her no time to tend them, grabbing her hand and pulling her toward the exit.

"Hurry, Dearie! The next group will be here soon. And each group is more fearsome than the last!"

As Harper remembered, the room lay very close to the tunnel's entrance from the Fae side. Piper's speed conveyed the urgency of their flight, and Harper scuttled behind her as quickly as she could manage.

Harper fleetingly wished she had spent more time running and less time practicing Tai Chi. She gasped for breath while her mutinous knees and ankles threatened desertion. "Piper! I can't move this fast! Can't we slow down a little?"

Piper didn't look back. "No time, no time! Come along, Dearie, do keep up, we're almost there!"

Just when Harper's knees gave their resignation notice, they emerged into the large field Harper remembered from her previous visit. This time, the sky was a thunderous gray, tinged with red, the ground covered in a flinty frost. Above the leafless trees circled large vulture-like birds Harper had never seen. Piper pulled her behind the old wagon where they quickly burrowed into an ancient pile of hay.

Piper kept a tight grip on her hand as Harper felt, rather than saw, another swarm of creatures emerge over the crest of the hill they had descended only moments before. The energy this time felt decidedly murkier and more ominous. The smell of rotting vegetation preceded it. With her free hand, she clung desperately to her mirror. A sneeze was threatening thanks to the dusty hay tickling her nose. But the chaotic roar was so loud it went unheard when it came. *Where are you, Grandma?* she thought in despair.

Once the tunnel absorbed the stampede, Piper pulled her hand again. They emerged from the haystack to race quickly down the hill to the now-barren beech and chestnut tree forest where she had met Grandma Sophie before. Once hidden by the tree trunks and undergrowth, Harper allowed her shoulders to detach from her ears.

Behind a thicket of holly bushes, Piper stopped for a moment and sniffed the air. Then she took Harper's hand once again. "Quick now, Dearie. We must find a place to hide you."

As they approached the spot by the river where Harper had chatted with Grandma, she was astonished to see a small village on the site. It looked archaic, like she imagined a village inhabited by peasants would have looked a century or more ago. Where had that come from? Then she spotted Earl Grey as he emerged from a doorway carved into a massive white oak trunk. Her fear and fatigue forgotten; she ran up to him, yelling, "Earl Grey! I'm so glad to see you!"

She stopped short on discovering that instead of joyful, he looked positively nettled to see her. "You shouldn't be here, Lass—today of all days! You're in great danger here."

Taking her hand, he jerked her to the doorway he had only just exited, then opening the door, he stepped aside. "Quickly now, in you go."

She forced herself through the small doorway and, on her hands and knees, crawled down a tight tunnel beneath the tree. She groaned. *Why didn't I think of wearing knee pads?* Earl Grey ignored her whimpers of distress.

Finally arriving at a small door, she pushed herself through it to find herself in a snug room, wider than it was tall, with a ceiling too low for her to stand upright. It was filled with plain wooden furniture: chairs, benches, and tables. Looking around, she saw they were all there: the brownies, the sprites, Ivy, Ash, and Hawthorne. She drank in the sight of them. But something was clearly wrong. Instead of happy, they looked scandalized.

What was going on? Wasn't she safe here from the Others? "I don't understand. I've missed you all so much! Didn't Grandma tell you?" She paused to look imploringly at each of them in turn. "I told her that I want you to come back. I *do* need your help. But it's more than that! I want your *company*. I realize that now. If I did anything to offend you, I'm sorry. Just tell me what it was, and I won't do it again."

The intolerable silence stretched out for a few more moments.

"Didn't Grandma tell you?" she whispered. Her throat suddenly grew very tight. "Don't you want to come back?"

Ivy stood so abruptly that her chair clattered to the floor behind her. "Queen Sophia no longer rules here. You shouldn't have come."

Twenty-One

"I DON'T UNDERSTAND," HARPER repeated wretchedly.

Hawthorne got to his feet and faced her, his expression grim. "We will hide you until First Night, or Halloween, as you call it, is over. After that, we will try to help you back to the Earth Realm"—he glanced at the others—"if we can."

"Please tell me what is going on! Where is Grandma? Why isn't she still queen? Please, can't someone tell me what's happening?" She was thankful she hadn't bothered with mascara that morning. In her confusion and fatigue, tears welled up, threatening an overflow.

"I'll do my best to explain. But first, we must make sure you are safe. Everyone else wait here." He motioned to Harper. "Follow me."

Hawthorne led her to another door in a far wall, barely visible to her eyes; through it, she followed him into another cramped tunnel. After descending a shallow incline, the two emerged in a small, underground chamber with no windows and no other exit that Harper could detect. One corner held a pile of potatoes, and several barrels lined the back wall. Hawthorne turned on a lantern hanging by the doorway that burned with a flameless light.

"You should be safe here. I will explain what I can quickly, then I must get back to the others. Do you know why your grandmother was placed in the Earth Realm at birth?"

Harper blinked. "I know she was in danger, but that's all I know."

His words came rapidly. "Your grandmother was born to Queen Dewberry, hours before the queen was killed by her own sister, Lady Lockspur. Your grandmother's aunt has always fought to rule this realm. She's a menace to us all.

"Lady Lockspur murdered your great grandmother, Queen Dewberry. After that, your grandmother, Queen Sophia, was spirited away to the Earth Realm, where she could live unmolested until Lady Lockspur was defeated. Once that was accomplished, word was sent for Sophia, our rightful queen, to return. She was given the object you treasure—your mirror. It was her only reliable defense against her aunt. But instead of bringing the mirror back with her as instructed, she chose to leave it with you. Once Lady Larkspur regained strength and returned, shortly after our last visit here, your grandmother was at a severe disadvantage."

Harper grasped the mirror tightly. "Where is Grandma now?"

His answer was dour. "Imprisoned. Now I must return to the others. Spies have no doubt reported your entrance into the realm." He looked pointedly at her black hoodie and yoga pants, which gleamed blue and silver. "She will be hunting you. And she must not find you. Rest here. Tomorrow, we will attempt to get you back to your home."

"But I want to help!" Harper pulled out her mirror and held it out to him. "If this can save Grandma, I'll give it back! Please Hawthorne! I need your help. I don't know my way around here. Where can I find this Lady Lockspur?"

Hawthorne shook his head miserably. "Trust me on this. You would likely die, or worse, yourself. Stay hidden. It's the only way to survive." And with that, he stepped back through the door, closing it behind him.

She had not come here to be cosseted and protected by her friends like at home. They and her beloved grandmother were in danger. She couldn't live with herself if she hid until she could be safely spirited away. That decided, she needed to find a way out of this chamber.

Harper listened intently. Hearing nothing, she dug through the potato pile and moved the barrels, hoping to find another secret door, to no avail. With no other option, she crawled back up the tunnel. Once at the door to the larger room, she could hear them arguing over what to do. After an intense discussion, they decided their best option was to head outside, separately. Alida argued it was too dangerous to leave Harper alone. But the others thought Lady Lockspur and her soldiers would never imagine that they would leave her behind. Thus fooled, the presumptive queen and her minions would be led further away on wild goose chases.

After they left, Harper listened for several minutes to make sure all was quiet. Then, closing her hand tightly around the mirror for courage, she eased the door open a tiny crack. Seeing no one, she slipped out of the tree's doorway and into the pewter twilight, where she made her way to the river.

Once there, she went to the bridge her grandmother had used to cross the river before, which was now covered in dark green moss and black soot. Looking up, she saw a reddish light expanding over the top of the hill like a hostile sunrise.

Harper crept to the center of a thick laurel bush, where she quickly burrowed in the black dirt to hide the glitter still stubbornly clinging to her hoodie. Then, through the laurel's dark green leaves, she watched the light draw nearer. A tall being, who reminded her of her grandmother but dressed in a beet red gown, descended the hill, surrounded by several menacing attendants. Where her grandma's retinue had given off silver and golden light, these gave off a dull foreboding red and gray glare. They smelled noxious, like burnt hair.

Before them, they herded two small beings at lance point. As they drew near, she recognized Piper and Earl Grey. She watched, stone still, as they crossed over to her side of the river, where she could hear them speak. Though they weren't speaking English, Harper found she could understand their exchange.

With a voice like a rusty nail scratching a metal surface, the tall woman wearing a crown of hemlock leaves said, "I can smell her. There's human blood nearby with the taint of my niece about it. I've heard sickening stories of your troop and humans. I know you flatter yourselves that you 'help' them. And I know the lot of you dared bring this one here, to my lands, before I took care of your beloved queen. Now tell me—where is she? She's very close. You don't want to know what will happen if I find her without your help."

Harper watched Piper and Earl Grey walk by, looking straight ahead with blank expressions on their faces, saying nothing. She was amazed to realize that, even in the gathering gloom, she could see them as though it were broad daylight, with every detail in sharp relief.

Enraged, Harper's blood began to careen through her veins, and she felt a surge of strength and power. Her limbs ached with the desire to fight. But she forced herself to stay still as the group continued its climb toward the village. When they crested the hill above her, Harper found herself lifting off the ground and breaking through the branches of the massive laurel bush. Turning her head left, then right, she saw to her astonishment that her arms had transformed into spectacular brown and black wings, tipped in white.

Turning her attention to the group ahead, she opened her mouth to yell, but her ears filled not with her voice, but with a terrifying shriek. She swooped down at Lady Lockspur's crown, tearing it from her head. Then she landed at the top of the hill, defiantly staring down the assembled Fae.

Lady Lockspur turned a hate-twisted face her way. "Kill her!" Her attendants, lances aimed at Harper's chest, rushed up the hill toward her. Harper lifted off, spreading her wings again. As she swooped over them, she grazed the first with her talons, and blood poured from the gash she left along one cheek. Within seconds, she found herself at the top of a tree. The attendants flung down their spears and quickly grabbed Piper and Earl Grey, pulling them back. Now, instead of lances at their backs, the pair had knives at their throats.

"What's your name, Hybrid?" Lady Lockspur spat. "Never mind. Let me explain your position. Come closer so we can chat, unless you want to find out what color blood your friends shed." Her lips unfurled in a nasty smile. "I won't give you time to guess the color first."

Seeing no option that wouldn't imperil her friends, Harper landed. On touching down, she found herself in human form once again. "Where's my grandmother?"

"Your *grandmother*?" the woman croaked. "Oh, you mean my weak-blooded, brainless niece Sophia? Let's just say she's in a safe, but inaccessible place. I can take you to her if you'd like. But first, let's talk things over. I get the feeling that you and I may have more in common than you think."

She gestured to her soldiers. "Drop your knives."

Her attendants lowered their arms, then shoved Piper and Earl Grey to the ground. Harper dashed to them. After seeing they were unharmed, she stood up, eyes blazing toward her great-aunt. "Okay, if you want to talk, we'll talk. But let them go."

In response, her aunt leered. "Not quite yet. So, you know we are relations. Yes, your grandmother is my beloved niece. What a pleasant surprise! I hadn't realized Sophia had literally gotten herself mixed up with humans. But *you* have inherited a Fae gift, I see. We value your kind here. You could be of great use to me."

The smirk disappeared and she lowered her voice as though attempting to convince Harper she could be trusted. "We could work together. Between the two of us, we could rule our realm forever."

Harper snorted with disdain. "I don't want to rule anything with you or anyone else." She drew herself up and glared at this imposing Fae with all the venom she could muster.

"My, what big eyes you have!" Lady Lockspur smiled with mock sweetness. "Oh, I think you'd prefer working with me to the alternative." She turned and nodded to the attendants standing in formation behind her before barking, "More of these vermin are hiding behind that big rock down by the river. Run and fetch them for me."

The henchmen made their way quickly down the hill. Even though it was now completely dark, Harper could still see clearly. She watched as Hawthorne, Ash, and Ivy appeared from behind the boulder. They were out-sized and out-armed. Her rage threatened to overcome her ability to think as they made their gloomy march up the hill, weapons at their backs.

Harper's friends were thrust to the ground before their hands were bound behind them. Lady Lockspur regarded her with scorn. "Don't even think about it. While impressive, I think you'll find that your gift is no match for mine. I suggest you listen to what I have to say. Otherwise, I promise you will regret your obstinance."

"Fine," Harper spat, returning her hands to her hoodie pockets. "I'm listening."

Lady Lockspur took a small object from a fold in her gown and held it out for Harper's inspection. With it came the nauseating scent of blood mixed with metal. "This is an old family heirloom. Come closer and have a look. If you join with me, it will be yours forever."

Harper's eyes gave an involuntary roll. "How dumb do you think I am? Your whole schtick sounds like something from a bad novel."

Lady Lockspur's eyebrows shot up, and she tilted her head to the side. "Sass! I like it! Maybe we have more in common than I dared hope. Here!" She threw the object at Harper, who caught before it hit her in the face. It was a mirror, identical to her own, except that this one was heavier, and a dull gray, covered in blood red vines.

The tone of Lockspur's voice changed once again, becoming softer, almost hypnotic. "Open it. The deepest secrets of your soul will be revealed when you look within."

Harper knew it was crazy to trust this wicked being. But another part of her felt compelled to look. After all, she'd just discovered she could fly. What else might be revealed in this mirror? The longer she gripped it, the more irresistible the thought of peering within it became.

Harper placed her thumb on the latch and pressed. As it clicked open, she looked down toward the glass, but just before her eyes connected with its surface, it went sailing from her hand, knocked away by an invisible force. In response, Lady Lockspur roared while shooting a blaze of laser-red light from her fingertips. Harper felt nothing, but she heard a sound like a dying songbird. Suddenly Lily, the orange-haired water sprite, materialized beside her on the ground, gasping for breath, a wide wound in her shoulder.

Harper screeched, but before she had time to react, she heard the rising clamor of shrieks and beating wings bearing down through the treetops. Then a maelstrom of claws and feathers descended on them all in a great screeching cacophony. Harper saw owls, dozens of owls, some swooping down at Lady Lockspur and her followers, others clawing at the ropes binding her friends' hands behind their backs.

Harper ran to Lily, who, with an effort, gasped out, "Harper! Your grandma's mirror ..."

In an instant, Harper grasped what must be done. She quickly jerked her grandmother's mirror from her pocket and ran over to Lady Lockspur who, distracted by the owls diving at her head, was frantically shooting sparks from her fingertips. Harper reached her at the same moment a very large owl, identical to her own owl from Whippoorwill Gap, landed on Lockspur's head and took off again with its talons full of dull hair.

While her great-aunt screamed curses at the owl, Harper grabbed Lockspur's chin in one hand and thrust her grandmother's open mirror before those soulless eyes, which grew round and black, the irises dissolving as they focused on the glass. Lady Lockspur cried out as she realized, too late, what had happened.

At the same time, a huge burst of silver light, intertwined with gold, rushed from Harper's mirror and surrounded them all like heat lightning on a summer's night. With a final howl of despair, Lady Lockspur faded into a red and gray mist that was rapidly sucked into Harper's beloved mirror with the efficiency of a retractable vacuum cleaner cord. The captured queen's soldiers dropped their weapons and fled over the hill from where they'd come. Closing the now much heavier mirror quickly before shoving it into her pocket, Harper joined the others who, now freed by the owls, had gathered around Lily. The owls, their cries now silenced, melted away into the trees without a trace.

Harper's friends dropped to one knee and bowed. But Harper, distraught over the now unresponsive Lily, didn't notice the genuflections until she felt a touch on her head and heard a familiar voice.

"Well done, Harper."

Looking up, she saw Grandma Sophie smiling down at her in a way she remembered so well from her childhood.

Twenty-Two

<hr>

GRANDMA'S EYES GLOWED WITH a golden flame. She reached over and placed a hand over Lily's wound, which closed cleanly, leaving only a small scar to commemorate her heroism. Lily opened her eyes and saw the regal figure leaning over her. "Oh, it's you." She smiled serenely and closed her eyes again.

Harper picked up the small sprite, holding her close. "Thank you, Grandma." Suddenly, the familiar, haunting sound of faery music arose, as it had on her last visit, seeming to swell from the ground below, the sky above, and the trees all around. From nowhere, a crackling fire appeared, surrounded by an open pavilion.

Then other Fae, Grandma's former attendants, arrived, armed only with thick blankets and warm drinks. One of them took Lily from Harper and laid her gently in a small bed closer to the fire. Remembering their previous warnings about eating or drinking here, Harper regretfully declined a steaming mug when it was offered. She was hungry and thirsty, but in the day's confusion, she had lost her backpack, her water bottle and trail mix with it. Her grandmother smiled at her. "Now that you've claimed your inheritance, there's no risk involved for you to eat and drink as we do, Harper."

She picked up the hefty earthenware mug and tentatively took a small sip of the most delicious warm drink she had ever tasted. She could detect chocolate, roses, sweet cream, and something herbal that she couldn't identify. After drinking it, she found herself feeling uplifted yet peaceful, as though she had enjoyed a substantial meal followed by a long night's sleep.

She basked in the bliss it bestowed while the others were tended. Soon enough, her grandmother turned to her. "Well, Darling, you showed up just in time. You were plucky and brave. We're all proud of you."

Only then did Harper realize what she had accomplished. Though she had never thought herself a weak person, ever since Grandma had gone away, most her of energy had gone into protecting herself. But today, she had thrown aside her own welfare for those she loved. Once that sunk in, she felt pleased with herself, too.

She looked around at all these beings she adored. "Thank you. I'm still shocked it happened at all. None of it seems real. So, that woman in red and gray—she was your aunt?"

"She *is* my aunt, Harper. She's your great-aunt. And she's not gone, at least not forever. The last time you were here, I didn't have time to tell you of the whole history. I'll tell you a bit more now." Harper snuggled deeper into the soft, snug blanket, eager to listen. The attendants had taken seats and were settling in with drinks of their own, their faces turned to their queen.

"Eons ago, when our kind first came to this corner of the realm, the being you met tonight, Lady Lockspur, had a twin sister, who was my mother, Dewberry. They were not born royals. For many lighthearted centuries, the two Fae sisters were playmates, best friends, and protectors of one another. But at some point, their people, who had been free for all of memory, came under attack from some of the Others. Humans today might call them demons or aliens ... it depends on one's perspective and experience. They are a specific breed—fierce beings. And they wanted to control us and our sphere."

"Those were the ones we barely escaped today," Piper whispered in her ear.

"The sisters' father, my grandfather and your great-great-grandfather, Granitejaw, led the defense of our people and managed to defeat the invaders. But that's a story for another day. From that time to this, they haven't bothered us. For a long while, they've stayed in their area, and we've stayed in ours. You could say we now peacefully coexist."

"To peaceful coexistence!" muttered the surrounding Fae, raising their mugs.

"In gratitude for his leadership, our kind wanted to make my grandfather a king, and his wife, Difflefled, who fought bravely beside him, their queen. From that point on, Lockspur and Dewberry grew apart. You see, my mother wanted our Fae to remain free. She wanted no part of royalty or rulership, preferring to let everyone follow their own star, so to speak.

"But Lady Lockspur felt differently. Traumatized by the attacks, she believed that to protect ourselves, we should keep company only with our own people. In time, her caution turned to hatred. And once she saw the power that royalty gave her parents, she wanted it for herself." She paused and took a sip of her own drink, contained in a golden goblet, studded with enormous pearls.

"Rather than wait for her parents to die a natural death—yes, we do move on eventually—she learned to practice forbidden magic, which she regretfully used to hasten her parents' demise.

"Once she'd accomplished that, the only thing preventing Lady Lockspur's supreme rulership was her sister Dewberry."

Here Queen Sophia held up the heavy gray and red mirror that Harper had dropped. "Both sisters had been given magic mirrors when they were born, a gift from their 'faery godmothers,' if you will. Lockspur secretly put a spell on her own mirror, making it a snare for anyone who peered into its surface. But one of the faery godmothers, Betsy..."

"Betsy?!" Harper said in surprise. It didn't sound particularly Fae-like to her.

"Betsy," her grandmother affirmed, "discovered her wicked scheme. While she couldn't remove the spell from Lockspur's mirror, she borrowed Dewberry's mirror and placed a counter spell on it, making it capable of ensnaring a soul as well. The difference between the two mirrors was that Dewberry's was enchanted only to trap a soul who meant its owner harm."

Harper felt into her pocket and pulled out the mirror that she had cherished for decades and moved to sit on the sofa's edge.

"In time, my mother learned of her sister's treachery. And thus, thousands of years of conflict between the sisters began. Both had loyal backers. The tides of battle continued to turn until just after I was born. Then Lockspur, threatened by my birth, was determined to rid herself of my mother once and for all. She had both my parents fatally poisoned. Once they were gone, my mother's followers spirited me away to the Earth Realm where I would be safe from my aunt until I was old enough to fight her." She turned her beautiful eyes to meet Harper's.

"I grew up with no idea of my lineage. As I've told you, my human parents told me I was adopted. I believed I was human and led a human life. Then, right before your tenth birthday, I received a visit from a hauntingly familiar and compelling being. After he convinced me he was Fae, the being gave me the mirror. He instructed me to bring it with me to Whippoorwill Gap the following week. He told me I was needed in my homeland. As I held the mirror, visions of this realm came to me. I knew I would be leaving the Earth—and you—behind." She sighed softly and placed her goblet at her feet.

"You and your parents had already left for the beach. And I knew that you would be devastated to lose me. My daughter was such a self-centered creature. That's why I sent you the mirror. I intuited that it would connect us. I still don't regret it, though it did place me at a disadvantage. I hadn't a clue why I really needed it until I got back and was instructed more thoroughly."

Harper finally comprehended the price her grandmother had paid for her welfare. "The mirror got me through some of the darkest days in my life. I've always treasured it. But I would have given it back right away had I known you needed it. And I think it's only right to give it back to you now." At that, she took the mirror and rested it on her grandmother's palm. Queen Sophia stopped speaking for a few moments as though overcome with emotion. Then Harper leaned over and gave her grandmother an impulsive kiss on the cheek before returning to her seat.

The queen continued. "I learned that I had the ability to watch you through my internal connection to the mirror once I got here. And I did keep an eye on you until the connection became too muddied. But I've also had other ways of keeping up with you." She looked at the group of faeries around them and nodded. "We never know how we'll benefit when we're open to other places and ideas."

They had all been sitting quietly, listening to Queen Sophia's tale. Now Hawthorne spoke up. "So, you see, Harper, we wanted to come back to you. And your grandmother wasn't holding us back. We came here the very night you told Piper about the troubling new cloudiness on your mirror. It didn't sound right to us, and we wanted to investigate. And," he added, glancing around at the rest of the troop, "we also hoped to bring you a present from this realm."

Alida piped up. "We thought it might give you confidence when you opened your shop."

Hawthorne nodded and continued. "But when we arrived here, we found power had just shifted back to Lady Larkspur for the first time since your grandmother's return. We tried to give aid, but soon after we arrived, Queen Sophia became imprisoned in Lockspur's mirror. Your great-aunt closed the portal to the Earth Realm. Once she accomplished that, her subjects could return here through the portal, but we could no longer leave. Your mirror was our only hope of defeating your aunt. Nevertheless, though we knew you could, we hoped you wouldn't come. It was too dangerous. Then today—there you were, mirror in hand."

"There you were," they all repeated, looking at Harper in wonder.

Harper's brows furrowed. "Where is Lady Lockspur now?"

Queen Sophia nodded toward the silver and gold mirror Harper had given her. "She was imprisoned inside our mirror as soon as she saw herself in its surface."

"Okay. I figured something like that would happen when I held it up to her." She got to her feet again. "Well, that's good, isn't it? Now, we'll just bury it or destroy it, and she'll never bother any of us again. And while we're at it, we'll destroy her mirror, too. That way, no one will ever be trapped there again."

Her grandmother shook her head. "I refuse to kill or destroy another being. Underneath her accumulated false ideas, Lockspur is still one of us. But for now, and probably for a good long while to come, she will be incapacitated. We can all enjoy a well-earned rest."

Harper looked at her with doubt. "But wouldn't it be better to put a stop to her craziness now?"

Her grandmother shook her head forcefully. "No, Harper. I have neither the wisdom nor the right to destroy her. But I have a feeling, given enough time, she will destroy herself. In the meantime, we must all live up to our highest standards while appreciating the ability to do so."

Queen Sophia looked around at the others. "And I think we can all agree that, from here on out, our Harper will be fine. She's discovered amazing things about herself today, hasn't she?"

They all rose, as if at some secret sign, and held up their self-replenishing mugs. "To Harper!"

Earl Grey stepped forward, removed his cap, and bowed before the Queen. "Forgive me, Queen Sophia. But perhaps we should be making our way back to the Earth Realm. I've left behind some friends I've been missing."

The queen inclined her head toward him and stood to her full height. The gold and silver light began to twinkle around her as she beamed a beatific smile at him. "Dear Earl Grey. Yes, I suppose you should." She reached over and placed a hand on Harper's thick striped hair and looked deeply into her eyes. "Always remember, My Child, you are descended from Fae. You have magic in you. Never settle for a life without it."

With that, she pulled out a soft handkerchief and handed it to Harper, who wiped her eyes, blew her nose, and laughed. "I love you, Grandma. I'll look forward to seeing you again."

Then Queen Sophia's light became so bright that Harper could no longer look directly at her. Her powerful voice rose and echoed through the forest, replacing the music that had emanated from it before. "You have done well, my child. My love is with you always." And with that, she disappeared completely.

Twenty-Three

◆

HARPER STARED AT THE space where her grandma stood only seconds before, a sense of loss pervading her heart. Then, she felt a small tug on her hand. She looked down to see Alida smiling up at her. Behind her, the rest of the Troop were laughing, clasping and high-fiving one another. Harper leaned down to hug Alida. Then, one by one, the rest of them approached her for hugs of their own.

"Good job, Lassie!" said Earl Grey, the last to reach her.

Letting him go, Harper inspected the now velvety-black sky above. "What now? Should we head back, or is it still too dangerous with the Halloween festivities?"

They all gathered around. Piper answered, "Well, Dearie, the First Night celebrations should be over by now. Most of the Others are back in their lairs, sleeping off the party. A few of them will move back and forth between here and the Earth Realm for the next six months. They get energy from the darker months. But we needn't fear those tonight."

The rest murmured their assent. "Is it still nighttime in the Earth Realm? I'm confused because you told me earlier that time moves differently between here and there."

Earl Grey shook his head. "No, tonight our time is the same. There are only two times a year you can count on time lining up between our lands. One is April 30 and May 1—what your culture calls May Day. And the other is October 31 and No-vember 1, or what you call Halloween and All Saints' Day. On those days, our times are identical."

"Got it." Harper glanced around the clearing. "Do you need to take anything back with you?" The quaint little village, along with the doorway into the tree, had disappeared.

They responded with twittering laughter. "Why, bless you, no! What could we possibly need?" one of them shouted.

"As I said earlier, we were going to bring you a present, but we never had time to collect it. At any rate, it doesn't seem you'll need it now," Hawthorne said, moving to her side.

Intrigued, Harper asked, "Do you mind if I ask what it was?"

"Not at all! We planned to bring you a golden feather from one of your fellow Owl-Souls. The feathers are quite beautiful. It was to be a riddle for you to solve with time. We suspected it would serve as a clue, helping you discover what your gift might be. And in the event it didn't, it would have made a lovely decoration! Sadly, we never had a chance to find one with all the troubles. But now that you've discovered your gift, you won't be needing it after all."

Harper's eyes widened with wonder. "You knew about my gift?"

Hawthorne chuckled. "Let's just say we've suspected it."

Their trip back to the tunnel was joyful. Her friends soared through the air, tumbling about as they discussed who in the Earth Realm they planned to visit first. Apparently many birds, mammals, and other Earth creatures, including humans, com-prised their social circle.

They questioned Harper about the shop's opening, and she happily filled them in. A short way down the tunnel, they re-en-tered the room where Harper had encountered Piper the day before. While it had been in disarray at the time, Harper could see that it was worse by magnitudes now. The unpleasant scent of sulfur lightly suffused the air. It was as though the space had been recently vacated by an out-of-control high school chemistry class. "Why were you bothering to clean up in here earlier, Piper?"

"Well now Dearie, even if they are a bunch of bogies, hobgoblins, and demons, I wanted to make things nice as I could for their big night out!"

Harper was speechless with astonishment, but the others continued striding down the tunnel like Piper's was the only sensible sentiment. "Don't worry, Lass. Some of our kind will restore it to its former state of decorum in short order."

They continued along the way and, in what seemed only a matter of minutes, they were all standing on the river's edge again. Harper could see the lamp she had left burning in her apartment shining over the bushes. As the portal disappeared behind them, Harper heard the familiar hoot of the owl and looked up. It perched on the same branch where she'd left it the morning before, close enough to reach up and touch.

She was startled when the Fae removed their hats and bowed low. Earl Grey straightened his form. "Walter! Thank you for your help back there! You showed up in the nick of time. I'll look forward to catching up later over a pint." Harper's eyes grew wide as they hurried her on by him.

"Wait!" She stopped short. "Did you say, Walter?" They twittered quietly as Harper turned back to the owl. But in place of the owl, she saw Walt with his messy, multi-hued hair, sitting on a bench underneath the tree. He silently raised a hand to her. She blinked just once, and Walt was gone. Once again, the owl sat upon the branch.

Before she had time to react, Tiptoe grabbed one of her hands and Tarryfoot took the other, whirling her around. And with that, the troop escorted her jubilantly back to the shop.

Once inside the building, Harper left her friends at their private room to check it over. Warning them that she had removed some things with good reason, she asked them to meet her at the back of the main floor when they were done. There, she had set things up before she left the shop, in hopes of a happy return. Their cushions lined the back of the room. Small plates, goblets, and napkins waited on a table. The refrigerator in her apartment held a feast of berries, nuts, and cheese. Crackers and homemade oatmeal cookies waited on the table. She also had a pitcher of cream, a bottle of wine, and a growler of beer she had bought from the brewery.

Harper closed the blinds and lighted beeswax candles. Then she went upstairs to retrieve the feast. Later, after hours of laughter, talking, eating, and drinking, they all grew quiet, as their fatigue and full bellies overpowered them. Finally, Hawthorne rose and asked if anyone had anything to share or recite to honor the occasion.

Harper was ready. She cleared her throat and recited the first three verses of "A Friend's Greeting," by Edgar A. Guest. She finished it with the final lines she had altered for the occasion:

"And could I have one wish dear ones, this only would it be:

I'd like to be the sort of friend that you have been to me."

She turned red when done, sure they'd think her silly.

But when she was done, they clapped and whistled. Small instruments materialized, and some began playing joyful music while the others danced. When the music and the laughter died down, it was only a few hours until dawn. Harper stood and motioned them to follow her to the small special collections room.

She removed the cover from the sign beside the door. It read, "The Good Folk," with a painting of a being that looked much like Piper on it.

As she unlocked the door to the room, they crowded in to see what she had done. All four walls were covered with beautiful hand-painted murals. On discovering Nate was a budding artist, she had paid him to complete these renderings of Fae folk through the seasons. They marveled at the accuracy of his work. Harper wondered at how quickly he had completed it. Snug, cheerful upholstered armchairs were tucked in available spaces. All the books in this room were about the Fae in one way or another. There were children's fairy stories, folk tales, books of modern Fae sightings, and many others besides.

An antique, glass-fronted cabinet contained older, more valuable books. Harper held up a key to the locked case. "I'll hang this inside your room under the stairs. You can use it whenever you like."

They all buzzed with excitement as they flitted from one shelf to another exclaiming at what they found there.

Ash walked over, took her hand, and bowed over it. "You could *not* have pleased us more." And Harper, worn out with care, worry, excitement, and joy, burst into tears.

"What? What's the meaning of this, then?" Earl Grey said, as Ivy walked over and looked at Harper gravely.

"I'm just so happy! I never in my life expected to feel this happy. I'm so glad you like my gift! But I have to admit, I also don't think I've ever felt so tired. Please, all of you, stay for as long as you'd like. Enjoy the rest of the food and drink. Look around to your hearts' content. But right now, I must go to sleep. Thank goodness tomorrow is Wednesday, and I have the whole day off!"

They looked at her with faces that sparkled with inner light. "Sleep as long as you can, Dearie. We shan't disturb you."

She climbed the stairs to a riotous chorus of good night wishes.

In her room, she found the lamp on, and the bed covers turned down. Magic ... she thought, smiling to herself. From habit, she reached for her mirror and felt sad, for only a brief second, before she crawled beneath the blanket and quilt and closed her eyes.

Around noon the next day, Harper woke in her bed with no memory of how she'd gotten there. The last thing she remembered was leaving her bed in the gray light just before sunrise and walking out to her balcony. Once there, she paused, allowing her lungs to drink in the crisp, still, pre-dawn air. Then she reached up to free her hair from its ponytail elastic before climbing onto the railing. Spreading her wings, she lifted off, sailing through the sky. She headed for the park, where she was joined by another owl, who swooped first above her, then below. Finally their paths united as they soared wingtip to wingtip over the treetops, following the path of the river toward the full moon.

About the Author

L.C. Maxie pursues a magical life. After the former librarian published two guides to excellent nonfiction books, *Library Lin's Guide to Superlative Nonfiction* and *Library Lin's Biographies, Autobiographies, and Memoirs*, both featured in Booklist, she ventured into paranormal women's fiction. Her first novel, *The Robins Nest*, the first in The Whippoorwill Gap series, is set in the city of Whippoorwill Gap, North Carolina where faeries cavort alongside the human residents. When she's not writing, L.C. bakes goodies and takes walks in Virginia's Blue Ridge Mountains with her husband Roger and their captivating canine, Dusty Marie.

Connect with L.C. Online:
https://lcmaxie.com

facebook.com/LibraryLin

youtube.com/

pinterest.com/

Acknowledgements

⸺◦◈◦⸺

WHILE I'M EXTREMELY GRATEFUL for the support of many people, I cannot thank the following people enough for assisting me with *The Robin's Nest.*

First, as always, I thank my husband, "Big Rog" for his emotional, psychological, and financial support during the writing of this book and all the others. He makes me laugh and helps me keep my sanity. This book would never have been written without him.

To all the folks at Bryan Cohen's Ad School and Best Page Forward. The amazing blurb on the back of this book is their work. Without their helpful encouragement and sound advice, I'd have likely have given up on the project before completion.

In addition, I'd like to thank the awesome folks who were willing to beta-read for me. Garry and Eydie Clifton bravely read the first draft and had wonderful suggestions and ideas to help improve the work. Their expertise in the worlds of folklore and Fae added immeasurably. And I'm grateful to Rebecca Flippen and Emma Babbit for their opinions on the first revision. Both made me think more deeply about the characters and plot.

A lot of credit goes to the wonderful editor, H. Louise Sianni. Her thoroughness, patience, and persistence proved invaluable.

And finally, I thank you, the reader, for sticking with the book to the end. A book is useless without an audience and I sincerely appreciate your time. I hope you found it enjoyable.

Cover Design by: Karen Dimmick at Arcane Covers

Editing by: H. Louise Sianni at Sianni Editing

First edition 2024

ISBN 979-8-9859234-4-5 (paperback)

979-8-9859234-5-2 (ebook)

Divided

A Memoir Of A Family I Never Knew

Published by Double A Publishing 2024.

Contact

Email: <u>abneyandrew81@gmail.com</u>

Facebook: <u>https://www.facebook.com/profile.php?id=61561318201455</u>

This book or any portion thereof may not be reproduced or used in any manner whatsoever without the express written permission of the publisher except for the use of brief quotations in a book review.

Dedication

This book is dedicated to Darlene Mazon because without her this book may not have ever been written. She opened my eyes and gave me the courage to pursue answers to questions that plagued me my entire life. Although she was confined to a wheelchair she stood up straight for what she believed in. She encouraged me to find the truth no matter where it took me.

Table of Contents

Foreword

If you want to ruin or awaken your life simply order a DNA test kit and wait for the results to come back. People take DNA tests for various reasons. Some think it's cool to find out their family heritage while others are searching for something more. For me it was to find the truth of who was my biological father. Whatever your reasons are prepare yourself before you go down that road because the truth you thought may not be the truth you find or was looking for.

In this book, you are not merely a reader but a witness to the personal journey of someone who has chosen to peel back the layers and offer a raw, unvarnished view of their world. This is my story of salvation and redemption and how one day a phone call suddenly changed my life forever.

My story is common yet unique. My story speaks to millions of people who thought their lives and upbringings were dysfunctional but came to find out that their life was quite common as compared to others in similar situations.

There is something profoundly powerful about stories that come from lived experience. They remind us that while our paths may differ, the essence of what we seek-purpose, connection, and meaning-remains universal. As you turn the pages of this book, prepare to be moved, inspired, and perhaps, see your own story reflected in the narrative. This is not just the author's tale, but a reminder that we all carry within us stories worth telling. In this memoir, truth and vulnerability are the guides. May it stir something within you.

The Beginning

When we are born two of the most powerful feelings I believe we experience is love and rejection. Those two feelings will have a powerful impact on you for the rest of your life and how you manage them will determine the direction of your life.

My life started in February of 1964 in Waterbury, Connecticut, a midsize town of approximately 115,000 people located southwest of Hartford, the state's capitol. Waterbury was known as the Brass Capital of the World for its high-quality brass and copper product production during the 19th century.

The identity of my biological father was something my mother never wanted to talk about for some reason. Some folks had their speculations of who my biological father was, and those speculations were surrounded around a single man, David. This was the same man whom my great grandmother had once told me when I was young was my biological father. Over the years though I had my doubts.

Before she told me who he was she said, "everyone should know who their parents are." After telling me who she believed was my biological father she made me promise not to tell anyone that she had told me. I kept that promise not to tell for the next fifty years.

My great grandmother has since passed, but little did we know that even our secret had a secret. I had already vowed to myself to never go looking for my biological father or family. Not because I didn't want to know, but because I didn't want to disrupt or hurt anyone else with this secret. Upon finding out the truth of my biological father, my story brought out a range of feelings in me that I never felt before, some that I didn't even know existed. It made me question everything I thought I ever knew about my mother and my life.

It's difficult for me to forgive my mother for not telling me the truth because before forgiveness can be given, responsibility must be accepted. Taking responsibility is something my mother has never done and probably never will. Through all of this I learned that you can't think about vengeance and do the work that needs to be done.

In order to truly know your future, you must know your past and exposing old lies can be very uncomfortable for some people.

To better understand my story, I had to track down as many people as I could and bring their stories back to life. Stories from people who are alive and stories of some who have long since passed. I made sure that their voices would be heard from the grave. My regret is for the people who have since passed. They did not get the opportunity to know the truth.

In order to know how this all started I have to start with the person who is at the center of it all, my mother, Sallie Mae Abney. My mother must have been a magician because she sure pulled off one hell of an illusion for a long time. I once heard that that the greatest illusion the Devil ever did was make people think he didn't exist. I'm not saying my mother is the Devil, but she sure knows some of his tricks.

Sallie Mae

Every story has a beginning, and this one starts with my mother. My mother was born Sallie Mae Green in March of 1940 in Saluda, South Carolina. Although she went by the name Sallie Mae Abney for most of her life, this was not her birth name. My mother's father was Willie Green. Although this was my grandfather he was a person I never heard of or knew growing up. Just like my biological father, my mother for whatever reason, chose not to tell me about him. This journey not only uncovered who my biological father, siblings and family were, it also uncovered who my grandfather and his family were.

My mother never told me anything about her father, not even his name. I just learned about my grandfather a few years ago when I did the DNA test. This might lead some people to think that maybe something bad happened between my mother and her father, but no. She was in contact with him and his family her entire life, I just wasn't included. His family knew about me, but I just didn't know about them. I don't want to get ahead of myself, so we'll get into my grandfather's story later.

My mother was one of two children born to my grandmother, Ethel Lee Allen. My grandmother was not married to either of her children's fathers at the time she gave birth to them. After her two children were born she subsequently left home to go north to start her life without them. Why did she leave her two babies behind? I'll probably never know the answer to that. I am unsure of when she left, but her marriage certificate says she was married in Waterbury, CT in 1948 to Cephus Allen.

My mother and her brother were raised by my great grandfather and great grandmother, Andrew Abney and Missie Lou Abney. Given that they raised them as their own, my mother was named after my great grandmother's mother, Sallie Mason and her brother was named after my great grandfather's father, Fred Abney.

Although my mother wasn't born an Abney my great grandparents just used their last name to keep everyone's name in the household unified. Back in those days record keeping was scarce and nobody really kept track of paperwork that closely.

My great grandmother use to tell me stories of when my mother and uncle were growing up and how mischievous my mother was. She once told me a story about how my mother was always hardheaded and constantly ignored her when she told her not to jump into the laundry basket after school. According to my great grandmother my mother would always blindly jump into the laundry basket to hide after school. My great grandmother said that in order to stop her from doing that she had killed a big black snake in the yard and put it in the basket for when my mother got home from school. According to my great grandmother my mother came home from school as usual took the lid off the basket and blindly jumped in it. The next thing you know my great grandmother said she heard my mother scream; she knew exactly what had happened. From that day on my mother never jumped into that laundry basket again.

In 1958 my mother graduated from high school in Saluda, SC. Her brother had graduated two years earlier from the same high school and was now married and living at home with his wife. Also, in 1958 my great grandfather, Andrew, passed away. By this time my grandmother, as well as several other family members, had found employment and were settled in Waterbury, CT.

Later that year my great grandmother, mother, uncle and his wife, along with their baby girl, all moved to Waterbury, CT to be with their family. This is where things become tricky. My biological father, William Lee Felton, was already living in Waterbury, CT at the time my mother and her family had arrived there. He was two years younger than my mother and graduated from high school in Waterbury, CT in 1960. Upon going to California and visiting my brother I looked in my biological father's high school yearbook that my brother had. Inside I found two of my mother's close cousins that played football and graduated with my biological father. I can't prove it, but I believe my mother knew William way before he got married in 1963. I also found out later that my mother was friends with William's younger sister and worked with his older sister at Uniroyal. My mother seemed to be well connected with his family.

My mother's penchant for keeping secrets was notoriously known. Growing up I would catch my mother lying about some of the most ridiculous things that she didn't need to lie about. Sometimes I think she would just say things without thinking and when she got caught up in them she just refused to acknowledge that what she said was not the truth. Later me and my stepfather and I would talk about this. Some of the things he told me about my mother and how she had lied to him about things throughout the years was ridiculous. Some of the lies were just absurd and uncalled for.

Another trait of my mother was talking about other people and being a busy body. This especially bothered me because I am not that kind of a person. Although my mother liked sticking her nose in other people's business you better stick your nose in hers. She was known for her fiery temper and vicious attitude which made people keep their distance. Although my mother didn't drink, smoke nor curse she still had her share of issues. Make no mistake there were and are far worse mothers than mine, I'm just saying that on the surface she presented herself as something much different than what she really was. She was always very stylish and conscious about how she presented herself to the world and would turn on that southern belle accent when needed.

In 2020 my mother had a near death episode from Covid 19. You would think having a near death episode from Covid might make her softened her stance on things, but not my mother. There's an old saying that goes "Whatever doesn't kill you makes you stronger." If that saying is true then my mother must be Wonder Woman by now.

I'm not one to believe in Karma or divine intervention but maybe my mother survived Covid so that she could be confronted by her past. Maybe that was the closure that I needed. My mother is old now, but she still hasn't lost her fiery temper. Why would she still have so much contempt for a man who has since been long gone, I don't know. Maybe it isn't contempt, maybe it's embarrassment or rejection. Either way it's unhealthy and uncalled for. Many people in our family have tried to talk to her and explain to her that I had the right to know these things, but my mother is just self-centered and all she cares about is what is best for her. My mother is a broken person, just like many of us are, but she first needs to forgive herself so that she can move on with her own life and fix whatever is left of her life.

I often wondered where my mother got her anger from. Did she grow up that way or did she become this way after meeting William? As I got to talk to my other newfound siblings I found out that my mother wasn't the only angry woman that William was involved with. Several of my siblings gave similar accounts of their mothers growing up. For me forgiveness was not necessary in order for me to move on as long as I didn't let my anger destroy me from inside. I used that anger to move forward and not look back. I made the decision to be the captain of my ship.

I sometimes wish there were something that I could do to help my mother, but I know there isn't. I take no joy in knowing she is like this, full of anger and resentment, but I also know there's nothing that I can do about it. I truly do wish her the best and hope that one day she will forgive herself and make amends.

My Childhood

was brought into this world in February of 1964, three months after President Kennedy was assassinated in Texas and during the height of the civil rights movement. Technically I was born without civil rights seeing that the act didn't become effective until July 2, 1964. I don't know if I was welcomed into this world, but I arrived here none the less. No child makes the decision to be brought into this world, that decision was made for us. Being born is like playing cards, you are dealt a hand and hopefully you get a good enough hand to play with to win. But getting a good hand doesn't mean you will always win. I have seen many people in my lifetime that had everything and then lost it all.

I grew up in a poor to middle class household. What that means is we didn't go hungry but there was very little money left over for extras. I remember things like putting plastic over the windows in the winter to keep the draft out to stay warm because the only source of heat we had was from the stove. There was a heater built into the wall in our apartment, but it rarely ever worked. I spent many cold days and nights in that house. As a child I promised myself that when I grow up I was never going to live in a cold house again. That's a promise I have kept to this day. When it came time for breakfast on school days there was no such thing as a hot breakfast. Hot breakfast was reserved for the weekends and special occasions. This also applied to any meal. There were no choices when it came to what you ate. The few times I asked my grandmother what was for dinner the answer was always the same, food. Eventually I stopped asking. My family was a bunch of hardworking people who did their best to get by on what they had.

As a child I remember hearing the word no an awful lot. If it wasn't a necessity the answer was always no. I think my childhood theme song was NO!. Can I have this, NO! Can I go there, NO! Can I get that, NO! Can I have some money, HELL NO! Coming from the south that was the way it was for them. My great grandmother told me a story one time of how she got a slice of pie and a pair of shoes for

Christmas. I just looked at her and said quietly to myself don't try that shit with me.

Christmas was my favorite time of the year. I loved Christmas so much that for a number of years I always ended up in the hospital for asthma attacks on Christmas Day. I would get so excited the night before until I would trigger an asthma attack that required a trip to the hospital on Christmas Eve. I really loved Christmas. I guess being the only child in the house had its perks. There was one time I was in the hospital's children's ward for Christmas, and they had Santa Claus come to our room and give us presents to cheer all the children up.

When I was a child I was a huge fan of Elvis Presley. I watched all his movies and knew his songs. I remember asking the nurse if they could give me a face lift so that I could look like Elvis Presley while I was there. That nurse must have thought I was crazy. An African American child wanting to look like Elvis Presley. I'm just going to go with maybe I had a fever.

I had no cell phone nor television with all the premium channels or video games. I spent most of my time growing up outside. I would be told to go outside to play and to be back before the sun went down. I remember the one time I pushed it a little too far and came back when the sun was down and all you could see was the orange glow over the horizon. My grandfather was standing at the gate waiting for me. I knew it wasn't going to be good, so I came up with something quick to say before I approached him. Out of nowhere I said, "The sun isn't completely down." He just looked at me and said, "You're pushing it. Next time I better be able to see the sun when you come home." I dodged any consequences that day, but I made sure that it never happen again. Other kids in my neighborhood were on the street light method. When the street lights came on you had better make your way into the house.

I remember standing on the street corner with friends playing a game called "That's my car." This was a game that if you saw a nice car drive by you claimed it by saying "That's my car." Being poor we knew the chances of owning any of these cars was probably not in our future, but you can't stop a kid from dreaming. When I became an adult I owned many of those cars that I thought were just a dream as a kid. Always encourage your kids to dream big, if they miss the moon they will still be amongst the stars.

We often went to the Goodwill store to shop for clothing. I remember my great grandmother sewing patches over holes in my clothes to make them last longer. There were also those cheap iron on patches that never really seemed to go on right. When it came to sneakers I could get whatever sneakers I wanted as long as they were the Uniroyal rejects that they sold in the basement of the Uniroyal factory for two or three dollars a pair. Trust me it beat wearing skips. I remember that old song, "Skips, they make your feet feel fine, Skips, they cost a dollar ninety-nine." The last thing you wanted was a bunch of kids doing a chorus around you with that song. As a child I was taught the value of a dollar and to only spend on what was necessary. I can't speak for all my siblings but I'm sure some of them may have shared similar experiences growing up.

We did, however, do annual trips to South Carolina to visit family and friends. This was a family ritual. Sometimes they would do two trips, one before the summer and one after it ended before school started. Sometimes they would leave me in South Carolina in the beginning of the summer so I could hang out with my family and pick me back up at the end of summer so I could to go back to school. Before each trip there was always the ghetto NASCAR inspection to make sure that the family car was up for the trip. Later when my family had more money they would rent a car for the trip rather than trust or put the mileage on the family car. They always saved room in the car to bring back meats, peanuts and other items that they liked which weren't available to them in the north. Those were their treats for that feeling of being back home. I used to think how sad it was that people had to leave the place that they loved and grew up at just because of the way some people treated them because of their skin color. There was also the issue of lack of job opportunities available for them. The north provided greater opportunities.

It's amazing how many jobs they had for Black people when they didn't have to pay them and the audacity of White people to blame the slave economy on their lack of employment opportunities. Did they ever think to blame the greedy business owners for their lack of employment in the south? Then to add insult to injury, when the civil war was over and slavery was abolished, White immigrants came to this country and felt they deserved employment over the Black people who had worked in this country for hundreds of years without pay and under inhumane conditions. This explains a lot of what we see going on today in this country. I believe the term they use is White Privilege.

My great grandmother was our family cook and everything she made was made from scratch. I know because I was her assistant in the kitchen doing whatever prep work she thought I was capable of doing. As I got older I became her garden assistant, turning over the soil and picking fruits and vegetable when they became ripe.

I was born on a street named Newell Place in the north end of town in Waterbury, Connecticut but by the time I became a one-year-old my family bought a three-family house and we moved to Putnam Street in Waterbury, Connecticut. Putnam Street was a predominately White neighborhood when we moved there, but by the time I became a teen it was just the hood. I experienced the same thing when I became an adult and bought my first one family house in the east end of town. I don't know if it was the minorities following the minorities or if it was the White people making an escape. Either way that's just the way it went, minorities in, Whites out.

There were a few White families that did stay in the hood. Those were the ones whose families were too poor to keep up with the other Whites. But even those Whites as they grew older seemed to do better economically than their minority counterparts from the same area. This is usually a sour subject for some White people because they think that just because they started out with us they weren't thrown a few bones along the way to help them along with their progress. They fail to recognize, or don't want to recognize, just how badly African Americans in this country were treated and abused for hundreds of years and that we are still fighting the effects and injustices of those times today. This also holds true for anyone who appears to be of African descent. They have to suffer the same racial injustices that society dishes out to us daily.

As integration started to increase segregation still continued, just in different forms. Separate but equal was just a slogan. There are those who want to keep us separate and will die before there is ever any real sense of equality in the USA. Separation of the less fortunate creates money and power for the wealthy.

Fortunately for me I was able to make a good thing out of some bad news. There were many times that I wondered if my mother ever thought or wished that she had not brought me into this world. I never heard her say it, unlike other stories where people said they did hear their mothers say that about them. I know that is a terrible thing to say, but if I'm going to be honest with myself then why pretend that it never crossed my mind? My mother never was and still isn't a loving, nurturing type of person. There were many times growing up when my mother proved this to be true, but there were three times that this really stood out.

The first was when I was in the eighth grade. When I told my mother about the eight-grade graduation her response was, "you're that old?" I don't know if she was joking but it sure didn't feel like it. The second time was when I was seventeen years old and got into a motorcycle accident. She never wanted me to ride a motorcycle and her reaction to my accident showed it. I spent a few days in the hospital after the accident and not once did my mother call or come by to see how I was doing.

The third time was when I was twenty-one years old, and I got shot as a victim of an attempted robbery. I was in the hospital for a week, and she came by to see me one time. Not to ask how I was doing but to scold me as to what was I doing to get shot. I was the victim of a random robbery attempt. Wrong place at the wrong time. I didn't even know the person. There were plenty of other times that my mother showed her coldness, but these three times always stand out to me.

My mother was living with my great grandmother when she got pregnant with me. If she did get the thought to terminate the pregnancy it would have been short-lived because my great grandmother wouldn't have gone for her not having the baby. Family was important to my great grandmother and terminating her great grandson would not have been an option. I believe it was my great grandmother's idea to name me after her late husband. Some mothers have no idea how much they can make or break their child with their life decisions.

As I found out later in life, my mother had a lot of animosity towards my biological father. After finding out who my biological father was and seeing photos of him I could see why. We shared many similar physical features. I was probably just a constant reminder to her of the man that she despised so much.

I have always been very ambitious. Since as long as I can remember I always believed I could be or do whatever I wanted to do if I put my mind to it. Life was nothing more than time and opportunity, but I wasn't totally oblivious. I knew I was an African American male in America and that meant ambitions with limitations. Equality is something we hear about, but does it truly exist? From the beginning points had already been deducted from me. I was labeled and stereotyped just because of who I was and what I represented. I was from a broken home. This isn't to say that you can't succeed in life just because you weren't dealt a perfect hand, it just meant you would have to work twice as hard to get half as much. A lot of young Black children were told growing up that they would have to work twice as hard to get half of what White people get. I truly don't believe we got half. It was more like less than half.

As Africans our identities were stripped from us as soon as we landed in this country. African people in America didn't create the environment that they lived in; it was forced upon them. They lost everything. They lost their ethnicity, their names, their culture, their religion and their freedoms. These were just a few of the things they lost.

Africans didn't create biracial children; they were created through them. I personally don't believe there is any such thing as biracial for Black people. Everyone knows if you have one ounce of Black blood in you aren't White. White Americans will not accept you as one of them.

Our problems in life were created for us a very long time ago and we still pay for them today. I say these things not to blame White people for all of the problems Black people endure, we create enough of our own problems, but without knowing this how can you honestly judge someone? This is the education they don't want children to learn in school. They don't want woke people, they want people who are walking in their sleep, obeying what they are told and never questioning anything. They want people who are able to function but not able to comprehend, the walking dead.

When I started first grade I was labeled a disruptive child in school by my teachers. I guess that was the label back then that they gave to kids who were hyperactive. Fortunately for me someone recognized what was going on with me and scheduled a meeting in school with my mother. During that meeting which I attended, they told my mother they wanted to give me a series of aptitude tests to determine my learning level. Whoever came up with this idea may have saved my life and didn't even know it. Lots of kids during that time were just punished and pumped full of drugs that made them sluggish and incoherent. I guess it was just the easiest thing to do back then.

After I took the aptitude tests my mother was called back into school for another meeting. What the school found out from the tests was that although I was in the first grade I was reading and doing schoolwork on a third-grade level. I attribute a lot of this to the fact that I loved to read and was curious about everything. Before I started school I could read and do math. My great grandmother was great. She constantly worked with me when I was small, teaching me things and reading to me. She had a dictionary, which I still have to this day, that I would constantly read and learn from. I also read old encyclopedias and magazines when I could get my hands on them.

I started out as a left hander, but when my great grandmother realized it she quickly made me start using my right hand to do things. Left-handed people were looked upon as odd back then. She wanted me to be right-handed because just about everything in life was set up for right-handed people. It sort of worked out because I ended up being ambidextrous.

When my mother returned to the school I remember the principal telling her that they needed to move me up to the third grade in order for me to be at my learning level. This would have put me with kids much older than me and made me look out of place. That's when they told my mother that there was a program that just started that would be ideal for me. They wanted to send me to a school in Litchfield County where their learning level was higher, and their first-grade learning level matched the learning level where I was. This program, however, required me to be bused there daily. This required me to take a forty-five-minute bus ride there and back every day. I don't know why my mother agreed to this, but I'm sure glad she did. Maybe she felt it kept me out of her hair longer every day.

For five years I took that ride and soaked up all the knowledge and cultural differences that came along with going to a rural school. It wasn't until I went to school there that I realized exactly how poor we were. When you're living around a bunch of people that are just like you everything seems normal because everyone is poor.

I did very well in school, but I carried a secret that haunted me for my entire life. My mother had never told me the identity of my biological father. From the time I was old enough to ask she always avoided the question. When I was around the kids in my neighborhood in Waterbury it was never an issue because most of the kids from my area came from broken homes with absentee fathers. It was more of the norm rather than the exception. My life growing up in my neighborhood was like a television game show called "Who's Your Daddy." This became even more obvious when I became an adult and started reading the obituaries. You would be surprised at who was whose father, sibling or relative when they died.

When I started attending school in Litchfield the family dynamics were very much different. Mostly all of the children in my classes came from traditional two parent, one family homes. This was very different than what I was accustomed to back in Waterbury and I started becoming ashamed of how I was living and being raised.

Shame had always made it difficult for me to talk about this subject and I didn't realize the effects it had on me throughout my life until now. I would avoid conversations about my family to everyone, not because they were mean or I was ashamed of them, but because I didn't think others from Litchfield would understand my situation. I didn't want to explain why my parents had a different last name than me or why I didn't look like my father. I never expressed this to my family in fear that they would take me out of this school and make me attend local public schools in Waterbury. I really liked the new environment and was willing to adapt to it. Once you are introduced to something better there is no turning back.

Around this time my mother met my future stepfather, Leroy. I say future because I don't know when they actually got married because my mother never told me. For all I know they were married when he moved in with us. For a while we all lived together in my great grandmother's apartment until they found an apartment to move into. I don't know if my mother left me behind with my great grandmother because she knew I wanted to stay there or if it was an easy way for her not to have to deal with me. Either way I'm glad I stayed.

I really enjoyed living with my great grandmother. Although you wouldn't think it to look at her, my great grandmother was sixty years old when I was born. We lived in a three-family home occupied with all family members. Me and my great grandmother were on the first floor, my grandmother and grandfather lived on the second floor and my uncle Fred lived on the third floor. Being the only child in the house I pretty much had full range of the entire building. Growing up around the older generation taught me a lot about our family history, at least on my mother's side of the family. I learned things about my ancestry that I would have never learned in school. It's amazing because now they want to ban books in school but not assault weapons. It just goes to show how frightened some people are of others learning the truth. They want their children and everyone else's to believe the same old racist, homophobic, antiquated beliefs that most of them grew up believing.

Although my great grandmother only had one child she raised several children in our family throughout the years. Before moving to Connecticut from South Carolina my great grandmother and great grandfather were the matriarch and patriarch of our family. Everyone called them mama and daddy because that's who they were to them.

To say my mother treated me badly would be an overstatement. She didn't treat me badly in a physical way, but she was never a loving type of mother. She didn't shower me with hugs and kisses and tell me how much she loved me. Till this day I can say my mother has never told me or said to me that she loves me. Maybe that's why some people say I don't smile and have an uninviting demeanor. Like I say, you can't make someone give you something they don't have.

I never had a birthday party or any kind of celebration growing up. Part of this was due to my grandmother being a Jehovah's Witness. When I did go on trips or family outings it wasn't because my mother arranged it, she just joined in with me and my grandparents.

I'm not faulting her; it was just who she was. My mother didn't grow up with her birth parents so to her it might have been normal for me not to have grown up with her. I know I wasn't the only kid who didn't grow up with their biological father, but it sure felt like I was. The sins of our parents are not our sins to carry but are sins we can learn from..

Revelation

November 2019 was the start of the Covid pandemic. This pandemic would eventually take the lives of millions of people all over the world. During the early part of the pandemic, I lost several family members due to its effects.

In March of 2020, my mother decided to go to the funeral of my stepfather's twin brother in South Carolina. I asked my mother not to go to the funeral due to the pandemic and the dangers it posed. Many people were wearing masks and the number of deaths from the pandemic was just starting to rise. One thing to know about my mother is that if she wants to do something there is no way of talking her out of it. When I told her it wasn't safe nor a good idea to travel during this time, especially not in a place where many people would be congregating, she said "Those news people don't know what they are talking about." There was no need in saying anymore to her.

Within the first week of my mother returning home from the funeral she became very ill from the virus. Her illness required her to be hospitalized for several weeks.

During this time most people who were hospitalized with the virus were usually dead within two weeks of their admission or they never returned home. During that time visitors weren't allowed to visit patients due to the risk of further infections from the virus. People who did want to visit their loved ones had to do so by video chat where the hospital had a monitor in a room so you could see your loved one as you spoke to them. I worried the entire time that my mother wasn't going to make it out. She had two things that didn't work in her favor. The first thing was that she was elderly, and the second thing was that she was African American. The virus seemed to have a harder impact on the African American population that it did on others. Those were the longest two weeks of my life waiting to see if my mother was going to make it. I don't take the death of close relatives and friends very well. Thankfully, my mother made a full recovery and was able to return home after a short stay in a rehabilitation center. Maybe God was sparing her for what was to come next.

As I got older my family history became more important to me. Unfortunately, I had to learn this the hard way. I constantly question myself as to why I never pursued the truth sooner. When I became an adult I should have asked my mother flat out, "who is my biological father and where is he today?" Deep down inside I wanted to, but something just kept stopping me from doing it. I guess because I thought I had gotten the truth from my great grandmother I figured there was no need in starting a fight with my mother over something that she made clear she didn't want to talk about. Besides, by this point I had already formed an opinion of my biological father as someone who didn't care about me so why should I care about him? The few times I did ask my mother about my biological father was when I was a child. She always pushed the narrative to me that he didn't do anything for me, and he didn't care about me. When you're a child that's a hard pill to swallow.

The bad part about exposing lies and finding new relatives that you never knew existed is that not everyone will be happy that you found them. Some will welcome you with open arms while others will push you away as if you were some kind stray animal looking for a warm home and a free meal. This can be both hurtful and disappointing, especially when you are just someone that wants to find their family.

I already knew this, so I came into this with an open mind. I made it clear to myself that whatever reaction I got from these family members I was willing to take, even if that meant rejection. I learned that from the time you are born the clock starts ticking and no one knows just how much time you have on it until it's gone. I would advise everyone if you have any unresolved issues to resolve them before your time is up or the answers that you are looking for disappear. The truth can be both hurtful and invigorating but the truth is always the truth. The truth is always better than the alternative.

My whole life changed in August of 2020 when a female approached my stepfather, Leroy, at his job with some unexpected news. This was not just any female; she was someone who me and my stepfather knew very well. Darlene was a local woman with a colorful past. Very loud and brash. The kind of person who spoke whatever was on her mind regardless of the fallout. Not the kind of person that would lie about anything. Her life was like an open book to everyone. When Darlene came into my stepfather's place of business she initially asked him if he had a number that she could contact me at.

Knowing how I am about my privacy, my stepfather told Darlene that she could give him her phone number and he would pass it along for me to contact her. He advised her that I probably wouldn't call if he didn't give me some information about what she wanted. Hesitant to say what it was about, Darlene just blurted it out to him, "I just found out that he's my brother." Leroy said he couldn't believe what he was hearing. Not only did my mother not tell me who my biological father was, she also never told him either. I couldn't imagine how someone could be married to a person for so many years and never tell them the truth about who their stepchild's biological father is. Leroy had been with me since I was a little boy and always treated me as his own.

Later that day when Leroy contacted me he said, "are you sitting down." When I answered yes he said a woman named Darlene had come to his office today and told him that she was my sister. I could hear the shock and surprise in his voice as I remained silent on the other end of the phone. Sensing that I didn't seem surprised by this news he asked, "did you know this?" My mother may not have told Leroy who my biological father was, but he knew who Darlene's father was.

As I took a deep breath I started to lay the story down to him. I told Leroy that I had been ready and waiting for this day for most of my life. I then told him the story of how my great grandmother had told me who she thought was my biological father and how I have been keeping this secret for more than fifty years. I told him that I vowed to myself that I would not go searching for anyone on my biological father's side of the family, but if I ever got approached by anyone I was going to want to know the whole truth. The reason it didn't shock me was because Darlene's father was the same man that my great grandmother had told me many years ago was my biological father.